Kindred Lives

Wendy Hurley Smith

To my dear friend Kathy,
whose smile always
brightens my day.

Wendy Hurley Smith

ISBN 978-1-61434-224-3

Printed in the United States of America.

BookLocker.com, Inc.
2011

First Edition

Dedication

This book is for my Grandmother Laura Jane, whose memory lives on.

Chapter One

The fact that her grandmother may have been euthanized always bothered Naomi. Not the act of euthanasia itself, she just wished she knew for sure. Her mother had only alluded to it once and when pressed for details had shut off the conversation in a hurry. It was so like her mother to give you a small glimpse into what was on her mind and then retreat. There was a side to her mother that she never revealed, not even to her daughter.

Though the discussion took place a long time ago, Naomi remembered it clearly. They'd been discussing the Vietnam War. Knowing her grandmother died in 1964, when Naomi was four, she had asked if Gran had been aware that the war had taken place.

"Not really. She'd had a series of strokes," her mother explained. "She really didn't know what was going on."

"Could she talk?"

"No, it just came out garbled. It didn't seem to make sense."

"What did the doctor say?"

"He didn't come by very often; it was rural British Columbia, don't forget. The district nurse used to call though. She said it was to be expected at Gran's age."

"How old was Gran?"

"Seventy four or seventy five, I can never remember which." Her mother paused. " She had been ill for so long."

"Was she paralyzed by the strokes?"

"Only partially at first. Toward the end, she seemed to lose all muscle control."

"I remember her not being able to move. What did she eventually die of?"

Her mother didn't answer right away. She seemed rooted in the past. The words, when they came, were spoken in a trance like way, as though she was still in that faraway place.

"Well, there was talk that they helped her go."

Naomi was stunned at the confession. "Who?"

"The girls, they were watching her while Kath and I went bowling. It was their idea for me to get away for a while. When I came home she was gone."

"You mean dead?" Naomi asked.

"Yes, just lying there in bed, looking for all the world like she was sleeping." Her mother paused, reliving the memory of that night. "I couldn't believe she would die without me there. I had cared for her for so long."

Naomi couldn't see her mother's face. Characteristically, she had turned away to hide her emotions. There was a prolonged silence between them as Naomi fought to recover from the shock of what she was hearing. All she'd known to this point was that her mother nursed Gran for a number of years. As the youngest daughter, and the last one left at home, the duty naturally fell to her mother. Some help came from a sister, Kath, and the other women in the family stopped by occasionally. But Naomi knew her mother bore the weight of the responsibility.

Pressing for other details, Naomi learned the "girls" were two of her aunts: Edna and Violet. Also implicated was Aunt Gwen, married to her mother's brother Bill. All three had been sitting with Gran the night she died.

"Mum, who said they thought Gran was euthanized?" Naomi asked.

"Euthanized?" There was slight astonishment in her mother's voice, as though the word had jolted her. There was a long pause; she was measuring her response. When it came, Naomi found it unconvincingly vague.

"Oh, I can't quite remember. It may have been the district nurse or Mrs. Dukes next door. Perhaps it was another friend of Mum's. I really can't remember, Naomi."

The tone of her voice signaled her mother's reluctant to continue. There was so much more Naomi wanted to know: how had they done it, if they did do it, and why? She never found out. Over the years, she'd tried a few times to ferret out the information. Each time her mother refused to talk about it, and now she was dead.

The cat broke into Naomi's thoughts. He jumped up between her and the computer screen, where she'd been sitting for an hour, unable to begin work. This was her second novel. The first was published to a modest success two years before.

"Oh, poor Spike, naughty old Mummy forgot to feed you," she hugged the cat and carried him to the kitchen. "Brrr, it's cold in here," she said aloud, pouring food into Spike's bowl. The house was cold. Naomi turned up the heat before putting on the teakettle.

With the kettle whistling, she almost missed the phone's ring. It was her sister, Louise.

"Hi, sis, how you doing?" Louise was concerned about her. Their mother's death had been hard on Naomi, coming as it did so soon after her divorce.

"Hi, Lou, I'm doing okay, but I just realized my house is damn cold. Kevin used to take care of things like that, so I tend to ignore them. Spike let me know he was cold and hungry. I'll just have to establish a new routine for myself."

"What were you doing not to feel the cold? Writing I hope?"

"I was at the computer but hadn't written a word. Mum keeps coming into my thoughts. I guess that's natural when you've just lost a loved one."

"I guess so, sis. Were you remembering when we were girls?"

"Yes, then I got to thinking about Mum and Grandma. You remember how Mum told me she thought Gran had died."

"Oh, not that again, Naomi, please," Louise sounded frustrated, "why can't you leave it alone. Mum was just trying to get rid of the guilt she felt for not being there. Let's not go down that path again, please Naomi."

"I can't help it Lou, something keeps bringing it back to me. Maybe it's because they say I was Gran's favorite. I don't know. It's strange really, I hardly remember her. I was only four when she died. You were older; it's funny Mum never mentioned it to you."

"Only two years older. I don't think there was anything odd about it. You were the one who lived close to Mum. You spent much more time with her," Louise explained. "I wish you'd drop it. *I*t's not like you're ever going to prove it. They're all dead now."

"Well, we don't know about Aunt Edna. She could still be kicking up her heels somewhere."

Louise laughed. "They'd be pretty old heels by now. It would be nice to find out what happened to the old girl. Wouldn't it?"

"See, you're curious just like I am about Gran," Naomi stuck her ground.

"It's not the same, sis. I'm curious to find out how Aunt Edna lived, not how she died. You really need to stop thinking about death and get on with your life. How's the book coming? Do you think you'll have it ready for Spring '97? That's when they planned to publish, isn't it? That's less than a year away."

Louise had succeeded in steering the conversation in a different direction; she'd always been good at that. As the older sister, Louise in many ways seemed less mature than Naomi. But on occasion, she acted her role. There were only the two of them and they had a deep love for each other. Louise had an appetite for life that showed in everything she did. Naomi knew she'd never quite had Louise's flamboyance. Though there had been a time when she'd glowed with happiness. That was before Kevin left her, before the pressure of publishing deadlines, and before watching her mother die of cancer. Alone now, Naomi was trying to remember what it felt like to be happy.

Louise was doing her best to help. Before hanging up, she got Naomi to commit to visit soon, to take better care of herself now that she lived alone, and to get out more. Presumably, so she could find someone to replace Kevin. Happily married, Louise couldn't accept that Naomi was, for the time being, content to be on her own.

It felt so different. She'd married Kevin right out of college, going from home, to the dorm to Kevin. Now, for the first time in her life she was living alone. Partly it excited her. It was all the small details that sapped her confidence. First her mother, then Kevin had seen to the multiple chores that make a house a home. Naomi wished she'd paid more attention.

Catching sight of herself in the hall mirror, she spoke to her reflection; "It's just you and me now, baby. Don't mess it up."

Naomi studied her face. The years had been kind: her 36 birthdays didn't show. She'd inherited her mother's youthful skin and her father's blue, blue eyes. A guy in college had told her he felt he could swim in her eyes; they were so blue. They were, without a doubt, her best feature. She'd once toyed with the idea of darkening her hair to show her eyes off more. Her hairdresser talked her out of it. 'Dark blond hair is to die for,' she'd said. So, Naomi left it and it fell about her face, not quite curly, more tousled. It was an attractive face and she was happy with it. Now if only she could get rid of the worried expression she'd worn of late.

Late on a Thursday night, Naomi sat in the library parking lot frustrated beyond belief. Her car wouldn't start. It was Louise's fault. If she hadn't made me promise to get out more, I'd have done my research on the web, thought Naomi. Now here I am in a dead car, with the library closed.

The staff had ushered her out at closing time. By the time she'd organized her paperwork the parking lot was deserted. What to do now? In the old days she'd have called Kevin to come and rescue her. Well, scratch that, she thought, I'll have to fend for myself.

First things first, I'll call for a tow, Naomi decided. Even as the thought entered her head, she gave a wry smile. The telephone was in the library lobby, now safely under lock and key. The cell phone was one of the few things Kevin had taken with him, saying he needed it for work and she didn't. Naomi hadn't bothered to replace it, just another luxury she could ill afford until she finished the book. There was a payphone a quarter mile away. The distance wouldn't bother her, but it was dark and rainy. She hadn't brought raingear and had to admit she was somewhat afraid. When the library was built in this out-of-the-way spot, surrounded by trees, plans were to build a community center adjacent. But funds had never been available, leaving the library in isolation.

A new thought occurred to her; did she have towing on her insurance? Rummaging through the glove compartment, Naomi came up empty. Kevin had given her the paperwork, saying, "Now put this one in the car." But she obviously hadn't. Who was her agent? Naomi didn't know, but she'd have to find out. One more thing she'd have to do for herself now. There were so many things to get used to. Louise said being married to Kevin was like having a wife; he took care of all the details, freeing Naomi to write. They made that agreement after the success of her first novel.

That success was largely responsible for their breakup. Writing her first novel had been fun. They'd scrimped and saved so she could work part time, then eventually quit to write full time. There was really no pressure then, just her desire to be finished and feel she was contributing. The elation they both felt when the novel was accepted for publication was something Naomi would never forget. The money didn't matter; they were both on top of the world.

All that changed with the second book. This time there was an advance and a deadline. Her time became more valuable. The rift growing between them was apparent, but Naomi was too busy to do anything about it. When the book was finished, she'd deal with it. But the book still wasn't finished. One day Kevin had told her quietly, "Naomi, I'm sorry; there's someone else."

It still hadn't hit her as she watched him pack. He did so with tears in his eyes, and had actually broken down and sobbed a couple of times. Naomi didn't cry. She just felt numb. Kevin didn't take much: the old mantel clock that had been his grandmother's, a woodcarving they bought in Montana, the Minolta camera and his telescope. As he went to leave, Naomi slipped the wedding band off her finger; the one he'd given her, promising to love her forever. Not a word passed her lips as she handed it to him. It had been his grandmothers. Why keep it? Kevin looked as though he was about to hug her, but she turned and walked away.

Still trying to make up her mind whether to be devastated by the breakup or angrier than hell, Naomi was sidetracked when her mother fell ill. There was no leading up to it: one day her mother was fine, enjoying life in her new condo. The next day she was dealt a death sentence. Naomi had talked to her the day before she went to the doctor. It was a happy call, her mother having just returned from a trip to Hawaii with some girlfriends. They'd all acted like silly teenagers, she'd told Naomi.

"That's great, Mum, but I hope you didn't get thrown out of anywhere."

Her mother giggled. "We probably came close a few times, but they would have looked at all the gray heads and decided we were harmless. By the way, hon, I can't come up tomorrow, I'm going to Dr. Wiseman. Jan noticed a place on my back she didn't like the look of. It's probably another skin cancer."

Dr. Wiseman was her mother's dermatologist. He'd already removed a few basal cell cancers from her mother's face and shoulders. Naomi saw no reason to worry. But the next day her mother's friend Jan called with the bad news: melanoma, growing rapidly. They would do what they could, but it didn't look good.

Louise and Naomi held hands in the hospital waiting room and prayed for a miracle. Dr. Wiseman couldn't deliver; it had grown too quickly. They hadn't been able to get it all. The doctor gave her mother two to four months at the most. Naomi was in turmoil, but her mother was surprisingly calm.

Four months later, almost to the day, her mother died. Seeing their mother in pain, the sisters had wished for the day to arrive. When it did, they were devastated. Their last parent was gone. A work accident had claimed their father many years before. Louise had her husband, Sam, and two sons. Naomi had only Louise.

The ensuing months were something of a blur for Naomi. Divorce from Kevin became a reality. Somehow, the property got divided. Naomi got the house and the mortgage, no alimony and the cat. Kevin got most of their savings, the cell phone and the newer car.

Now here she was in the older car, broken down in the dark. It was all too much. Naomi laid her head on the steering wheel and let the tears flow: tears of anger, frustration and sorrow. Her mother was dead, her marriage over, the book wasn't finished and her car wouldn't start. Sobs racked her body as she let out the emotions she'd been holding in.

Her sobbing grew so loud; at first she didn't hear the tapping on the window. When she did, it startled her.

A man was calling out to her, "Are you all right?" Naomi nodded, at which he yelled, "Can I help?"

The rain and her tears prevented her from seeing well, but she noted he was riding a bicycle. A rain parka shielded most of his hair, which appeared to be gray. He didn't look threatening, but this was a secluded spot. Naomi rolled the window down a crack.

"My car won't start," she said with a catch in her voice.

"That's what I figured." His voice was gentle. "Will the engine turn over at all?"

She shook her head, "Completely dead. I don't know if I'm covered for towing." The tears started to well up again.

"Okay, not to worry. I can ride up to the store and call my sister. She lives close by and can come and give you a jump. If that doesn't work, she has a cell phone, so you can go from there. Sorry I can't do it. Not much help on a bike, I'm afraid. I'm late for an appointment or I'd come back. Don't worry though, Diana will get here soon."

Naomi sniffed a thank you, "Will she know what to do?"

The stranger broke into a big smile. "You haven't met Diana. Trust me, she knows how to do everything. You'll be in good hands, don't worry."

Naomi gave a watery smile, at which he mounted up, called out good luck and was gone.

It seemed an eternity before an old pickup pulled into the lot. In reality, it was no more than 20 minutes. A very large woman got out; not fat, just large framed, tall. She introduced herself as Diana, and soon had everything under control. They jumped the car, but it wouldn't start. Diana suggested she take Naomi home to check her insurance before calling for a tow. Naomi reluctantly accepted a ride home, when Diana assured her it wasn't far out of her way.

Her rescuer proved to be a funny, big-hearted woman. When she smiled, her face lit up and had sincerity written all over it. If her brother told her he found Naomi crying, Diana didn't let on. She ranted about the unreliability of cars, the terrible lighting in the parking lot and her stupid brother for not using his car.

"Imagine living in rainy Oregon and riding a bike everywhere," she snorted, "It's not like he can't afford to drive. He says he doesn't need to add to the pollution." She shook her head. "Writers, they're a funny lot!"

"Your brother's a writer," Naomi perked up at this news.

"Yes, Ben Ferguson, you've probably never heard of him. He writes environmental stuff for academic journals and the like. It's all way above my head." She laughed heartily. "He's a good guy though. He'll probably call tonight to see if you made it home okay."

"I'm really very grateful to you both. I was in such a mess." Naomi swallowed hard to stop the tears from coming. She tried to explain herself, "I just went through a divorce, and I'm trying to adjust to taking care of myself. Not doing a very good job, am I?"

"Hey, who knows about cars? Well, I suppose I do, but I don't know much about anything else, except horses. So, if my car won't start, I ride a horse."

Naomi laughed; the tension was broken. They talked more and, before she realized what was happening, she poured her heart out to Diana: the divorce, her mother, and the book she was stalled on. By the time she finished, they were pulling into Naomi's driveway. She looked at Diana and said; "I think I hit the bottom tonight."

Diana switched off the engine and laid her hand over Naomi's. "Let me tell you something, Naomi. I'm a good bit older than you, so don't be offended or think I'm interfering. You're a long way from the bottom. You're looking at an empty cup, but it's not really empty. I'm sorry you lost your mother when she was still so young. It's a fact of life that we all lose our parents at some time. Now what you do is turn to your memories; that's how we keep them alive and with us. You'll learn, wait and see. It works for me."

She paused for a minute before continuing. "I was so close to the folks. Ben and my sister loved them too, but I lived with them. It was so hard at first. It gets better, trust me. Do you have siblings?"

Naomi nodded, " Just one sister – Louise."

"Are you close?"

"Very."

"That's good. I take it she doesn't live here, since you didn't want Ben to call her?"

"No, she lives in Redmond."

"Redmond, Washington or Redmond, Oregon?"

"Redmond, Oregon. Just outside of town on the Deschutes River."

"Great horse country."

"She rides."

"I like her already. Now about the divorce: I may not be a lot of help there, never having married. It's something you may never get over, but at least it wasn't messy. I mean no children, right?"

Naomi shook her head.

"They say that helps," Diana said. "Okay, Naomi, what are you left with? Your talent, that's what. You take that cup you think is empty and fill it with your writing talent. Throw yourself into the book, and everything else will fall into place."

She reached into the glove compartment for a notebook and pen. "Here," she instructed Naomi, "write out your phone number and I'll give you mine. We'll keep in touch. I want you to be able to tell me I was right."

She makes it sound so easy, Naomi thought, switching on the hall light and calling to Spike. Diana seemed to have an answer for everything. She could see what Ben meant when he described his sister. Naomi had to admit she did feel better.

She picked up her cat and gave him a hug. "Sorry old buddy, I came up against an obstacle. Don't worry, I'll find a way around it. Now let's get you some dinner."

Chapter Two

The package arrived on a Saturday. Naomi would always remember, because she was loading plastics in her car when the mailman arrived. Plastics recycling day was the last Saturday of the month.

It had been three weeks since the library incident. Her car, a whopping $297 later, was now running perfectly. She now knew her insurance agent, having established contact with him. She did have towing. Kevin added it when he signed the car over to her. How could she hate him?

She had spoken to Diana again and really liked the woman. It occurred to Naomi that Diana had the same gift as Louise: talking to them always made you feel better, more confident.

"It's a good thing you're here; it's a bit fat for the box," said the mailman, handing her a well-stuffed manila envelope. Uttering thanks, she turned the package over and noted the New Zealand postmark. She leaned against her car studying the name of the sender, Robert Hillman, but couldn't place him. Her mother had a friend in New Zealand. She'd recently written to tell her of her mother's death, but this name wasn't right. She mulled it over and over before the obvious occurred to her and she said aloud, "Open the darned thing, Naomi!"

Naomi sat on the living room floor, the contents of the package surrounding her. She had identified the sender: the son of her mother's friend, but from a first marriage. He had enclosed a short note, thanking her for passing on the news of her mother's death. His own mother was now in the middle stages of Alzheimer's, so wouldn't be responding. In clearing up her estate, he found a number of items of interest to Naomi—including photographs of her mother—and was including them. There was also a letter in her mother's handwriting. Part of it was missing, he explained, but he thought Naomi would like to have it.

This is too much fun, Naomi thought as she surveyed the pile. She needed time to enjoy this—the plastics would have to wait. She made a cup of tea and sat down to slowly go through it all. This is going to bring back some memories, she thought. Diana would be happy about that. Naomi vowed not to let it make her sad.

The five photographs beckoned first, and she savored each one. One showed her mother with her friend Mamie. They looked to be around twenty, arms entwined, mugging for the camera. It was their clothes that Naomi enjoyed, typical forties suit with enormous shoulder pads and lapels. And the hair! They both sported pageboys with big rolls on top. Along with the high heels, the hair made her mother, a tiny woman, look tall. The picture would have been taken around 1947, shortly before her mother's friend married and left British Columbia for New Zealand. The ever-present pile of logs was visible in the background. Both girls' families were loggers. A notation on the back read, "May and Mamie, ain't we cute."

In another photo, the two girls were much younger—around ten or twelve. Their mothers could just be made out in the background. There was no doubt where this one was taken; the Spruce Creek Logging Company sign was clearly visible. Almost everyone living in the small hamlet of Spruce Creek worked for the company in those days. The company owned the town. Scrawled on the back of the photo, Naomi could just make out: "Mamie with May Cavenish, Mum and Mrs. Cavenish in back."

The telephone interrupted Naomi. She barely recognized her sister's voice, "Louise, you sound dreadful!"

"I know, I've got the flu and I'm feeling really sorry for myself," Louise sniffed, "Sam has taken the boys to the river to get them out of my hair."

Louise had two sons, Craig and Brian, eight and ten respectively. They were the only children in Naomi's life and she adored them.

"How are my nephews? I take it they aren't sick?" Naomi asked.

"No, they're healthy little tykes, just a bit of a runny nose, but not enough to keep them down. Sam doesn't feel too hot though. I expect he'll be next. How's the book coming?"

"You'll be happy to hear I'm making some headway. In fact, I'm doing so well I was taking the afternoon off. Thought I'd take the plastics to recycle, but I was just leaving when I got an exciting package."

Louise asked excitedly, "What, what? Don't tell me it's just something you ordered on the web."

"No, Lou, do you remember mum's old friend Mamie? The one who lived in New Zealand?"

Louise did remember.

"I wrote to tell her about Mum, but she's got Alzheimer's and is in a home," Naomi explained. "I got a package of stuff from her son."

"How nice. What kind of stuff?" Louise asked.

Naomi started telling her about the photos. "I haven't looked closely at the others yet, but it looks like they were all taken in Spruce Creek or Powell River. There's also some high school stuff, I can see a dance program and something about the hockey team. There's a letter or part of a letter mum wrote to Mamie. That should be interesting."

"Is there a date on it?"

"I can't see one."

"Let me know what it says."

"I will when I get to it. I'm enjoying the photos first."

They chatted on for a few more minutes, before Louise declared she was dying and needed to soak in a hot tub. Naomi promised to call back later if she discovered anything exciting.

Two more of the photos were similar to the others. Another one showed May and Mamie with Naomi's Aunt Kath. The youngest of her mother's sisters, Kath was the only one Naomi and Louise had remained in contact with.

The last photo sent her rummaging for a magnifier. It was a group shot of her mother's family. All the children were there along with Gran. Her mother and Kath stood on one side of Gran. On the other side, she realized, were the three her mother suspected of taking Gran's life: Edna, Violet and Gwen. It gave Naomi a jolt to think about it. Edna had her arm around Gran. Uncle Bill stood behind Aunt Gwen. The only one missing was Violet's husband, Ralph. Naomi knew it was taken after World War II, because that's when Uncle Bill brought his Welsh bride home. Perhaps it was a homecoming photo. She would have to scan it, and try to enhance the image. Right now, she was anxious to get to the letter.

Naomi read the letter three times trying to make sense of it. Not only was there a page missing; one page had a chunk torn out of it. Most of it was chatty stuff about May setting up house in Oregon. Her mother's death had finally freed her to join her husband. That dated the letter to after 1964, Naomi realized. May related to her friend how wonderful it was for Louise and Naomi to see their daddy every day, not just once a month. The paragraph that held Naomi's interest was the one with the tear.

" Thank you for the flowers you sent for Mum's
funeral. They were lovely, especially the carnations.
No, I haven't gotten over losing Mum yet. I feel so

guilty for leaving her that night. She had seemed quite well for a few days. I quite thought she was going to lly. So you agree with me that it all seems a bit icious. I was glad to get away from there, I could ly look at the girls. Edna showed up in fancy new She said she's going to leave soon and London again.
ow about the money. I never did hear member you telling me about it. I d's accident, but it obviously wasn't. e others about it. Edna's the oldest one getting the papers now. Of course if oes to London, Violet will probably take over. I wonder how much it was supposed to be, what sizeablc means? You…"

The following page was missing.

Naomi was perplexed. What on earth were they talking about? She didn't have a clue. Perhaps Louise would know.

Louise sounded very groggy. She had contemplated not picking up the phone, but guessed it would be Naomi.

"Well, did you pick up any family gossip from Mum's letter?"

"Not exactly gossip," Naomi said, "but listen to this." She read the letter out to Louise, trying to explain the missing part. "Lou, did you ever hear about any money? I thought our grandparents were poor."

"They were: dirt poor. I don't know what on earth Mum was talking about. It wouldn't have been an insurance policy on Granddad, he'd been dead quite a few years." Louise paused, "It's funny, Aunt Kath and I were close but she never mentioned it. Why would Mum be writing to her friend about it? It almost sounds like the friend told Mum about it. I don't know; it's a mystery, sis."

"It sure is. I'll e-mail you a copy. See if you can fill in the blanks. I've been trying. Boy, I wish that last page hadn't been missing."

"So do I. There's no one left who could tell us about it."

"Except maybe Aunt Edna. We really should try to find out if the old girl is still alive. Oh, Lou," Naomi sounded distressed, "I just had a horrible thought. If there was money involved, could it have been," Naomi's voice dropped to a whisper, "murder? Is that why Mum was so distressed?"

There was silence on the other end of the line. Naomi finally said, "Lou?'

"I'm trying to think here, sis, just give me a minute." Louise sounded somber. "I am curious about the money, but you're reading something into Gran's death that wasn't there. She was dying, Naomi, don't forget that."

"But you heard what mum said in the letter, she appeared to be getting better. I'm sure the word that's half missing is "suspicious." Think about it, Lou."

"I am thinking, but you know what, my brain's not working with this flu. E-mail me the letter and let me get back to you. Okay?"

Naomi agreed, hung up the phone and put the letter in the scanner. Her stomach felt queasy. She couldn't get the word murder off her mind. Could this be why something kept gnawing away at her? Why she couldn't put to rest the death of a grandmother she'd known so briefly?

Chapter 3

Naomi was surprised her sister hadn't called back yet. The package arrived two weeks ago. She was tempted to call Louise, but remembered how perturbed her sister had seemed. She decided to give her a little more time. Naomi was mystified by her sister's reaction. Why wasn't she curious to learn the truth about their gran's death, about a possible inheritance? What harm would it do? She would wait a little longer, but Naomi knew, with or without Louise, she would have to find the answer to this family mystery. The writer in her just wouldn't leave it alone.

The writing part of her life was going well right now. She had completed the chapters her editor was waiting for and was about to mail them. As she packaged them up, she thought about Diana telling her to throw herself into writing. It was certainly paying off.

Diana had called once since rescuing her at the library. They'd had a good chat, and Naomi got off the phone feeling she'd made a friend. Friends were something she lacked right now. It hadn't occurred to her before, but just about everyone she knew in this town was either part of Kevin's family or one of Kevin's friends. He had grown up here in Walkersville, so it was logical to move here after they married. Since the divorce, the only time she saw any of his family was at the grocery store. They were pleasant enough, but she knew they blamed her for the breakup. If the truth be told, so did she.

She'd thought more than once about selling up and moving over to Central Oregon to be near Louise. Naomi knew leaving her little frame house with its picket fence and flower garden would be hard. It was a bit out of the way—four miles into Walkersville—but she loved being surrounded by fields and trees. They had chosen the house thinking it a good spot to raise children. Somehow, that seemed an eternity ago, and driving into Walkersville leant credence to that thought. The town was growing by leaps and bounds: inevitable with the interstate so close. Naomi knew she'd be trading a lot of conveniences by moving to the high desert. For the time being she'd stay put, friends or no friends. When the book was finished, she'd take another look at the situation.

Naomi called Spike in from the garden. He was an outdoor cat in the good weather, but she liked him in when she wasn't home. It was late spring now, and rain was never out of the question in Oregon. She settled Spike in her bay window seat, and told him, "Mummy will be back soon."

It was a little cooler out than she expected. She was vacillating on whether to go back inside for a warmer jacket, when someone hailed her from the road. A cyclist pulled up and leaned his bicycle against her fence. He waved a package at her and fumbled with the gate.

"It looks like I just caught you. Just wanted to drop this off," he held out the package while struggling to remove his helmet.

Naomi hadn't a clue who he was, but he obviously thought he knew her. She studied him, trying to place him. He was a good-looking man, with a wonderful smile, warm hazel eyes and a shock of white hair. Naomi guessed he'd be in his forties. He was tall and lean, and had an air of relaxed confidence that always attracted her. She reached out to accept the package, her expression giving her away.

He laughed heartily. "You have no idea who I am, do you?"

"I'm sorry, I'm trying to place you. Is it the library or the post office?"

"Well, the library is close." He was teasing her. "Would it help if I told you Diana sent the package? It's her famous banana bread."

Naomi's cheeks flushed. She couldn't hide her embarrassment, "Oh, you're Diana's brother; my knight in shining armor. I'm sorry I didn't recognize you. I couldn't see you very well with all the rain. It's Ben, isn't it?" Naomi stuck out her hand, "I'm Naomi, thanks so much for helping me."

He shook her hand. "To be truthful, all I could see of you was the color of your hair. I knew I had the right house because of the fence. Diana would have dropped this off herself but she's waiting for the vet. Her horse tangled with some barbed wire."

"Do thank her for me. No, I'll call her later." Naomi felt flustered. Why did she always get this way around an attractive man? "Your sister's a lovely woman," she assured him.

"Yes, she is. I don't know what I would have done without her."

"She seems so capable. Has she always been that way?"

"Always. If she'd been with Napoleon, history would have been rewritten."

They both laughed and she noticed how his eyes sparkled with humor. There was an awkward pause, before she asked, " Would you like to come in for coffee? It's the least I can do."

"No, but thanks. I really do want to talk to you more. Diana tells me you're a writer."

Naomi nodded.

"A friend and I are working on a piece of fiction. We could use some input, if you wouldn't mind."

"I'd be glad to help," Naomi assured him.

"Good. Then we'll have to talk shop some time soon." He gestured to his bike. " Believe it or not, this is part of my exercise program. It looks as though you're headed for the post office. Tell you what, next time you're in town in the morning, stop by the coffee shop across from the post office. I'm there most mornings. The owner's a friend and he let's me hole up there and write. Would that work out with you?"

"Sure, and this time I will recognize you."

He laughed and held out his hand. "I'm unforgettable." His eyes held hers briefly. Then he hopped on his bicycle and was gone.

Naomi felt a flush of pleasure as she walked the banana bread through to the kitchen. Wow, she didn't realize Diana's brother was so attractive. Did she detect some interest when he looked at her? Had he liked what he saw too? She paused in front of a mirror. And why not, she thought, I'm trim and Kevin always said I was pretty. At the thought of Kevin, Naomi came back to earth. What was she doing even thinking about another man? That's the last thing she needed right now. Still, she made a mental note to stop at the coffee shop one day soon.

Louise called the next day. "Sorry, sis, I've been up to my eyes in it. Just as I was feeling better, Sam came down with the flu. You know what that's like: my head hurts, I'm sore, I can't breathe. Will you rub my chest? And they call us the weaker sex."

Naomi laughed. "Poor Sam, I can see he doesn't get much sympathy from you."

"Oh, he does all right. How are you doing? Having much luck with the book?"

"As a matter of fact I mailed off some chapters yesterday. Now I have a little breathing space. How are my favorite nephews?"

"They're your only nephews and they're fine. School, sports and 4-H keeps them busy. They want to know when Aunt Naomi's coming to see them. What about it, sis, we're germ-free now, and it sounds as though you can spare the time. Why don't you come for the weekend?"

Naomi thought out loud, "I could use a break. If the neighbors can feed Spike for me, I don't see why not."

"Great. Can you drive out Friday? We've got a new place we go to eat. The food is fabulous."

"Sure. I'll try to get there about threeish. I think I'll drive the Santiam Pass, it should be pretty with all the spring growth."

"The boys will be excited. Oh, and sis, I haven't forgotten about Gran. I've been looking into it. I'll fill you in when you get here," Louise explained. "Don't forget to bring the photos with you."

They were sitting in Louise's kitchen—Naomi at the table and Louise, as usual, perched on the counter. Naomi marveled at what an agile woman her sister was. Louise didn't look anywhere near her age: 38 in a few weeks. She looked beautiful framed by the snow-capped peaks of the Cascade Range, visible through the kitchen window. Louise had her father's dark hair and blue eyes—not as blue as Naomi's, but still lovely. Her skin was tanned from long hours in the saddle. She looked every bit the horsewoman.

This was Sam and Louise's dream home, built on a ledge of lava overlooking the Deschutes River. It was quite a hike down to the river, but the view from the house was fantastic. Naomi had to admit she did love this country. The air was so fresh and pungent. Maybe moving to Redmond wouldn't be such a bad idea. It would put her close to those she loved.

Sam had taken the boys to baseball practice. Naomi and Louise had the place to themselves, and had just finished looking at the photos from New Zealand.

Louise shook her head. "I know the photos are all black and white, but it's like you're looking through a gray veil. It must be the poverty. Oh, Naomi, it makes you realize how lucky we are. Thank goodness Mum and Dad had the good sense to move here." She took a sip of coffee. "I found the letter fascinating. It sounded as though Mum thought for a long while that Mamie had given her false information. Something changed her mind, I wish we knew what. I wish the darned letter hadn't been torn. I have to admit the money intrigues me. But murder, come on, sis, people do that for scads of money. We've never seen evidence of that."

Naomi wrinkled her brow. "What if it was Aunt Edna? She just disappeared; maybe she took the money with her. Oh, I don't know, Lou. Maybe murder is too strong a word, but something's fishy. I'm itching to find out what it is."

"I'm with you there, and I've already started the ball rolling. Curiosity got the better of me. I don't expect to find a fortune hidden away somewhere. But there's no smoke without fire. There must be some money involved. What intrigues me is that Mum and Aunt Kath never mentioned it. Funny, isn't it?"

"Yeah, not so funny with Mum," Naomi agreed. "She always did treat us like kids. Maybe mothers always do. You'd think Aunt Kath would have said something though. She was more of a friend to us—maybe because she didn't have children. I'm inclined to think Mum and Aunt Kath didn't know about it. In fact, I wouldn't be surprised if Gran didn't know either. It's like a jigsaw with pieces missing. How are we going to put it all together?"

"Well, I've made a start. It might not pay off, but we'll see." Louise jumped down from the counter and leaned her elbows on the table. "You know Sam's sister has been doing a lot of genealogy on the web?"

Naomi nodded.

"She's given me a bunch of leads." Louise continued. "It seems she has a few contacts in England. We've e-mailed one, a lawyer, to see how to look up any paperwork there might be. We're also researching the Cavenish name. Maybe something will turn up there. One of her English contacts is a real whiz at this kind of thing. It's actually loads of fun."

"I'll bet it is. The ultimate mystery—one that involves you personally."

"Just call me Magnum PI," Louise spoofed.

They both laughed at the thought, then Louise turned serious.

"Sis, promise me you'll stop thinking about Gran's death. I find it so macabre. Let her rest in peace. No matter how it happened, it was long overdue. I remember Aunt Kath saying Aunt Gwen, who was a nurse, couldn't believe anyone would last that long in Gran's condition. It was a blessing she died, and we should just accept it as that."

Before Naomi had time to respond, Louise had another thought.

"Speaking of Aunt Gwen, what about trying to contact her children? We haven't seen them since Uncle Bill's funeral. I used to send Christmas cards, but they stopped years ago. You never know, they might have heard something about the money." Louise grimaced. "I never much liked Michael, but Susan was all right."

"It's funny you should say that, I thought about them the other day. My book's at a point where I need to do research on Vancouver. I've got one chapter set at the Capilano Suspension Bridge. Do you remember it?"

"Yes, that thing scared me to death."

"Me too. Anyway, I need to refresh my memory about the area. I thought of going up to Vancouver and getting in touch with Michael and Susan. That's if I can find them. Michael was in Vancouver, wasn't he?"

"Yes, but I'm not sure about Susan. She married a doctor and they did talk about doing mission work somewhere. Still, Michael would be a start. I think it's an excellent idea. When would you go?"

"That depends on how quickly my editor gets back to me, but probably in a couple of weeks. If I find Michael, how will I find out what he knows without letting on, Lou? His mother was one of the three Mum suspected, after all."

"He doesn't know that. I would just get the conversation around to the Cavenish family," Louise suggested. "Ask him what he knows about family history. Say we're working on it, which is the truth. He was old enough when Gran died to know what was going on." Louise looked pensive. "Only thing is: he was never too friendly. I'm rather hoping you can find Susan."

"Me too," Naomi agreed.

"Come and look at my latest painting," Louise said, changing the subject. "Sam thinks it's pretty good."

The walked to the studio, attached to the garage. Louise was trying to establish herself as an artist. Naomi agreed with Sam, the new piece showed promise.

"It's good, Lou, you're definitely getting better. You should show it to that woman from the gallery in Bend."

"I did. She said if I do a series, they'd give me a show. They seem to like the way I use color."

Naomi was happy her sister was achieving success.

The weekend passed too quickly. Her nephews, Craig and Brian, monopolized most of her time. Naomi didn't mind. She'd hiked down to the river with them that morning. They'd hunted for frogs and she'd been privileged to see the boys' secret tree fort. Now on the drive home, her calf muscles were letting her know they didn't appreciate the sudden burst of activity.

She hadn't mentioned Ben Ferguson until she was ready to leave.

"By the way, sis, I met a really nice guy the other day."

Louise feigned horror, "And you waited 'til now to tell me!"

Naomi turned to Sam. "See why I didn't tell her before, Sam?"

"Yep, she'd have dragged you out shopping for a wedding dress yesterday," Sam said with a smile.

"Okay, okay, you guys," Louise said chastened, "but I have to know more. Come on, Naomi, out with it. Who is he, and on a scale of one to ten just how hunky is he?"

Naomi laughed, and then told them about meeting Ben. By the time she was finished, Louise was practically jumping up and down.

"You are going to have coffee with him, aren't you?" It was more a command than a question.

"Maybe," Naomi didn't sound fully convinced.

Louise grabbed Sam by the arm and marched him off to the house, "Go away, Sam," she said playfully, "My sis needs some girl talk."

"Why wouldn't you go, Naomi, he's a writer. You'll have a lot in common. You don't have to jump in bed with the guy…yet," she gave an impish grin.

"That's precisely why," Naomi shook her head, "I don't want to start anything. Besides, he may not be interested. Anyway, I don't need complications in my life right now. I'm putting all my energy into the book. Distractions are the last thing I need."

"Which means you are *really* attracted to him. Oh, come on, sis, you've got to be horny. How long's it been?" She saw the look of irritation on Naomi's face. " Okay, but just meet the guy for coffee, please. What harm would it do? You could use a friend."

Naomi thought that was the end of it, but as she drove off Louise called out, "And don't forget to fill me in on all the sordid details."

That Louise, Naomi thought, as she drove alongside the Santiam River, she should have been the writer, not me. But she knew that wasn't true. Louise did have a vivid imagination, but she was far more comfortable on the back of a horse than hunched over a computer. Still, she did make you laugh. On a scale of one to ten, indeed!

How would she rate Ben? Well, based on looks—that's all she had to go on right now—he'd be about an eight, Naomi thought. She'd give it 'til Tuesday before going to the coffee shop. She didn't want to look too obvious.

Tuesday morning Naomi got cold feet. She tried to tell herself to just think of Ben as another writer, but it didn't work. She was attracted to him, and that was that. If she just happened to run into him in town, it would be another matter. She vacillated back and forth all morning. When her cuckoo clock announced the noon hour, she was still no closer to solving her dilemma.

"Oh, Spike," she said to her cat in frustration, "just look at me, I'm acting like a silly teenager."

Spike wasn't sure how to respond, but was saved by the telephone. It was Diana. She passed a few pleasantries before turning the conversation around to her brother. Ben had enjoyed meeting Naomi, she said, and was looking forward to talking about writing. Diana thought the idea of meeting at the coffee shop was great. Ben didn't know any other local authors. It would be good for him and his writing partner to talk fiction with Naomi. They had a good start on their book, Diana said, but fiction was new to both of them. She believed Naomi would enjoy the camaraderie, and asked if she planned to meet them soon.

Naomi acknowledged that she did enjoy meeting Ben, and intended to meet with them sometime.

"Can you make it soon?" Diana responded. "I know they're anxious to get your opinion on a couple of points."

Naomi felt trapped. "Maybe I'll stop in the coffee shop tomorrow," she said weakly.

"Great, I'll tell him to look for you."

Well, that took care of the jitters, Naomi thought, hanging up the phone. Now I'll have to go. Ben apparently wasn't attracted to her, or he would have said so to his sister. Diana would have told her if he was. Wouldn't she? You'd better cut out this silly schoolgirl stuff, Naomi, she admonished herself. The man just wants to talk books.

As Naomi pulled up to the coffee shop, it occurred to her the last time she was here was with Kevin. They'd taken Spike to have his nails trimmed at the vet's, two doors down. Sipping coffee while they waited, Naomi was acutely aware of the wall they were building between them. Conversation was stilted. Not like the old days, when they were brimming over with plans and ideas. Would things have been different if she'd said something then? Or had they already lost the spark that ignited their love in the first place. Water under the bridge, she thought, but maybe I learned something from it.

Ben wasn't surprised to see her; Diana had told him she was coming. He was encamped at a table in the back, his laptop surrounded by reference materials. A table for four had essentially become his office. He saw the bewilderment on her face.

"Wondering how I get away with this," he said playfully. "Gus, the owner, has become a good friend. He's the one who talked me into the fiction. He used to teach, and saw a need for what we're working on. My condo is so small; I was hanging out here a lot. Odd for a writer, but I actually prefer having people around me. It's probably a throwback to my academic days. Anyway, we have this deal: he's running the place on a shoestring, so he hires help sparingly. He's here alone most of the time. If he has an errand to do, I take over."

"You know how to do all that espresso stuff?"

"Sure, Diana's not the only capable one in this family. Gus is busy in the back, so I'll show you what I can do. What'll you have?"

"I hate to burst your bubble, but I've switched to tea lately. It sits better on my stomach."

"Well, I'm not nearly as impressive with the tea, " he joked, "but I'll get it to you good and hot."

"That's just the way I like it. I'll have Darjeeling, just black, thank you."

He disappeared behind the counter and she realized with relief that she felt very comfortable talking to him. How odd that he chose to write in such a public setting. What kind of writer would do that? She answered her own question—a lonely one.

They talked about writing for the best part of an hour. Ben's friend, Gus, joined them as business allowed.

Their project, Naomi learned, was a book on the environment, aimed at seventh-graders. She was able to help them somewhat, and promised to return. They never did get around to talking about their private lives. Naomi guessed Diana had told Ben some of what she told her. Perhaps he steered clear of personal matters not wanting to upset her, Naomi thought. Talking about writing was inspiring to her, and she looked forward to their next meeting.

Naomi's trip to Vancouver was put on hold at her editor's request. They needed her available to answer questions for a few weeks. This meant she was able to meet with the two men a few more times. She was still very attracted to Ben, in fact, even more so. It was hard trying to hide it. She found it very hard to read him. Their conversation was almost entirely about writing. But on occasion, she'd swear she saw something more in his eyes. She knew he watched her as she talked to Gus. Maybe he was shy and needed more time.

The Vancouver trip was finally arranged, and she was able to stop by the coffee shop the day before she left. Gus was dealing with malfunctioning equipment, and left Naomi and Ben alone most of the time. She felt a certain tension in the air and it made her nervous. To cover it, she asked Ben how he went about research in the field.

He was able to give her a few timesaving hints she could use in her research. She hadn't planned on discussing her new novel, but he seemed genuinely interested. They talked plot and background, and he confided in her that one day he wanted to try his hand at adult fiction. And then he surprised her.

"I have your novel at home. I checked it out at the library," he laughed when he saw the astonishment on her face. "Relax, I haven't read it yet. Maybe I'll get to it this weekend."

Naomi was uncomfortable with the thought. "It appeals to women more. I don't know how you'll like it."

Ben wasn't to be put off. "I'll give it a try, and don't worry, I won't critique it. It'll probably give me an insight into who you are though. Does that scare you?"

"Yes, you bet it does. You might not like what you see."

"Aha, so there's a skeleton in your closet, is there?"

"Don't we all have one?"

Ben was serious for the moment. "Indeed we do." Then he gave her a long, penetrating gaze. His eyes, she noticed, were a very greenish hazel. When they weren't smiling, they looked sad.

"So you're off to Vancouver. When?" he asked.

"I'm leaving tomorrow."

"Driving up?'

"Yes."

"Naomi, I've really enjoyed this." His words were businesslike, but his eyes told her he felt something else. She felt it too.

She stood to leave. "I enjoyed it, too," she said, somewhat shaken. "Next Wednesday then. I'll be back before then."

She held out her hand and he took it in both of his, holding it tightly.

"Drive carefully," he said earnestly.

Naomi hadn't heard someone enter the coffee shop. As she turned to leave, a man was nearing their table. She noticed a dog collar and gray hair, but very little else about him. He appeared to be heading straight for Ben. Naomi had her hand on the door handle when the clergyman spoke, rather loudly.

"Ben, how's your wife coming along.

Chapter 4

Naomi didn't notice the miles speeding by and was approaching Seattle before she knew it. Her mind had been elsewhere: trying to deal with her disappointment and bewilderment over Ben. What was she to make of it all? He is married! 'How is your wife coming along' is what the clergyman said. He'd said it loudly, obviously intending Naomi to hear it. She hadn't turned around, so didn't see Ben's reaction.

What was a married man doing having coffee with a single woman? She could have accepted he was only interested in her in a professional capacity, but he had flirted with her. She wasn't stupid, she knew when a man was attracted to her, and Ben definitely was. He hadn't said so in as many words, but his eyes spoke for him. And the way he'd taken her hand in both of his, that must have been what the clergyman saw.

Then there was Diana. She'd seemed so eager for Naomi to get to know her brother. Had she misread Diana's intentions too? Neither one of them had mentioned a wife. That in itself was odd. When Ben had talked about his condo, he said 'my condo', not our condo. So where was his wife? Was she ill? It almost sounded like it.

Seattle traffic was horrible as usual. Naomi decided she must put Ben out of her mind and concentrate on the road. She hoped to make it to Vancouver before dark. The going was slow until she got well north of the city. Fortunately, she knew how to get to her motel on the north side of Vancouver. She'd chosen that area to be close to the Capilano Suspension Bridge, featured in her novel. The web had been useful to get a lot of statistical information about the bridge, but she needed to feel what it was like to move around in the area. It had been years since Naomi was there, and she wanted to refresh her memory. Also, according to the web, her cousin Michael lived on that side of town. She hadn't found a listing for Susan, but that didn't surprise her. Susan was probably away doing mission work somewhere. Michael would know her whereabouts, Naomi thought. She could always write to Susan if Michael was no help.

She hadn't let Michael know she was coming. She'd do that tomorrow, but first she needed to figure out what she was going to ask him. She sat on her bed in the motel trying to figure out her approach. Maybe he knew if Aunt Edna was still alive and where she was. She'd start with that. The stuff about the money, Naomi decided, she'd keep to herself. She'd find a way to get him to disclose what he did know. Perhaps if she concentrated on Aunt Edna it would be easier. Michael was that much older than Naomi, he was bound to have noticed how Aunt Edna behaved after Gran died. He was really their best hope of unraveling the mystery. Although in her mind Naomi regarded Aunt Edna as the prime suspect, she reminded herself that Michael's mother was also implicated. That could make things tricky.

Naomi spent the morning in downtown Vancouver, picking the brains of government employees as she worked down a long list of questions. Research, she decided, was not her favorite pastime. In the afternoon, she made her way to the bridge. It was every bit as awesome as she'd remembered. Tourists were everywhere as she approached the swaying structure. As a girl, she'd been terrified to go on it, afraid the ropes would break.

This time she got almost halfway across before panic set in. That's enough realism for one day, she decided.

That evening, Naomi called Michael. She was pleasantly surprised he sounded quite congenial. Not at all like the Michael she remembered. She and Louise had always thought Michael was the living image of his father. Uncle Bill, although not unkind, didn't smile much. He didn't go out of his way to befriend his little nieces. In truth, they were a little afraid of him.

"Hi, Michael, it's your cousin Naomi."

"Naomi, what a surprise. Jean and I were just talking about you girls the other day, wondering how you were doing. So how's the weather in Oregon?"

"As a matter of fact I'm in Vancouver. I had to come up to do some research. I was wondering if we could get together while I'm here."

"That would be great. Where are you staying? Are you by yourself, or did Kevin come with you?"

Naomi's stomach did a little flop. "I guess you hadn't heard, Kevin and I are divorced. It happened just before Mum died."

"Gee, I'm sorry, I didn't know." Michael sounded awkward. "Naomi, we're also sorry we couldn't make it to your mum's funeral. I'd just had the back surgery and wasn't mobile. Hang on a mo, Jean's trying to say something." There was a pause while he put his hand over the receiver. "Jean says can you come for lunch tomorrow. She'd like you to see the garden while it's still light."

"I'd love to, thank you."

They made the arrangements and Naomi got directions: only three miles from the motel. She thought of calling Louise to report their cousin's new friendliness, but decided to wait until she'd made the visit tomorrow. With any luck, she'd have a lot more to report to her sister.

Michael appeared to live in a very affluent neighborhood, Naomi thought as she searched for his house number. When she pulled into his driveway, her mouth dropped open. The house was beautiful: a new faux-Tudor that must have cost a fortune. Wow, you can do this on an engineer's salary, she thought.

They had been watching for her. Michael had put on a considerable amount of weight since she last saw him. He always had favored his mother's side, in looks and now weight. Any resemblance to Uncle Bill, who had been slim his whole life, had gone. He moved with difficulty, she saw, probably because of his back. It couldn't be age related; Michael was still in his forties. He surprised her again by giving her a big bear hug.

"How are doing, cousin? Gosh, it's good to see you. My only other cousins are in Wales." Michael turned to his wife. "Jean, doesn't she look good?"

Jean moved forward to welcome Naomi. She too was looking a little thick around the middle. But she had retained the scrubbed, well-groomed look that Naomi had always admired.

"Welcome, Naomi, it's so good to see you again. You do look so well, so much like your mother," she said. "So you're writing another novel? We read the first one and thought you did a good job, didn't we Michael?"

Michael nodded vigorously. "We were very impressed, Naomi."

With the pleasantries out of the way, Jean commandeered Naomi for a tour of the garden. She was very proud of it and Naomi could see why. It really was beautiful: a combination of English and Chinese features, complete with koi ponds. Naomi thought they surely must have help with it. They said no, they did it all themselves, with occasional help from the children. Naomi inquired about their two children.

"Sarah finished university and got a government job over in Victoria. She hasn't married yet, but it looks promising with the young man she's dating now," Jean explained. "Andrew is still studying. He hopes to get a civil engineering degree. He lives with us, but he's at a friend's this weekend. I'm sorry you're going to miss him."

They made their way inside, where Jean had laid on a nice lunch. They were anxious for Naomi to see their new home, so gave her a tour before sitting down to eat. It was every bit as lovely on the inside and large by local standards. In the main living area, they had opted for the open look or greatroom that was gaining favor. They had done a good job of blending the openness with an English country cottage feel. It appeared there was no expense spared with the furnishings: wonderful, overstuffed, brocaded sofas and chairs, heavy velvet drapes and some of the plushest carpets Naomi had ever walked on. She wondered again how they managed this on one salary. To her knowledge, Jean had never worked outside the home. They were both very proud of their home and told Naomi over and over, "God has been good to us."

Naomi was fascinated by the joy radiating from both of them. She wondered what earthshaking event had set them on this course. Over lunch, she was finally made privy to the change in them. They were born-again Christians, they explained, and had never before felt such joy and contentment. This gave Naomi the lead she'd been waiting for to discuss the family.

"Michael, I thought you'd always gone to church. Didn't your mother sing in the choir? I remember my mum saying what a beautiful voice Aunt Gwen had."

"Yes, I did when Mum was alive, but I'd strayed for awhile afterwards," her cousin explained. "Susan stayed true to her faith, but not me, sorry to say."

"I hardly knew your mum, but I do remember a lovely Welsh accent. My mum and Aunt Kath were both fond of her," Naomi paused. "I can't say the same for Aunt Edna."

Michael took the bait. "Oh, Aunt Edna, she was quite a girl, wasn't she? I remember the last time we saw her. It was a couple years after Gran died. She showed up in Spruce Creek dripping in furs and fancy jewelry. The folks waited until she was gone, then we all had a good laugh. She'd dyed her hair red, but she'd overdone it. It almost throbbed. Then there was the accent. She'd affected a BBC voice. You can imagine how well that went over in Spruce Creek."

They all had a good laugh at Aunt Edna's expense.

"And you never saw her again?" Naomi asked. "Do you know if she's still alive?"

"I have no idea," Michael sounded surprised, "I just assumed she'd be dead. Let's see, how old would she be? Dad was born in 1920, Aunt Vi came between Dad and Edna, and so she must have been born around 1915. That would put her at least 80. I suppose she could still be alive, although the others all died much younger."

"Do you have any idea where she was going when she left Spruce Creek? She was working in Vancouver wasn't she?"

"She had been, but had lost her job. She didn't tell the folks anything about it, but we heard she'd been caught embezzling from the firm."

Naomi was shocked, "You're kidding!"

"No, that's what we heard. She worked for a car dealership, and did all the paperwork for the rental cars. The old fellows who owned the place were too trusting. Edna managed to get away with it for quite some time apparently," Michael explained.

"Wow! I never heard that story before," Naomi shook her head in disbelief, "Mum and Aunt Kath never mentioned it."

"It was typical of that generation, Naomi," Michael explained. " They died with many a skeleton in their closets. They were probably embarrassed that it happened in their family. Aunt Kath and your mum were already in the states, but they must have heard about it. As for where Aunt Edna was going, my guess is back to England. She told the folks she was going to travel. You know, she didn't get along with my dad, so it's not surprising she didn't disclose much to him."

Naomi was deep in thought. The embezzling would explain Aunt Edna's sudden show of wealth. Or would it? Surely they would have prosecuted and got it back. Did she leave the country before they had a chance to? If that were where the money came from, it would eliminate Aunt Edna as a suspect. There must be a paper trail, Naomi thought. She could trace it if Michael knew which car dealer it was.

"Oh, let me see, you've got me there," Michael wrinkled his brow. "I should know it. Aunt Edna gave me a pen once with the name on it, had that pen for years. It was on the south side. Burnaby, I think." He thought some more, and had a sudden inspiration. "I'll tell you what, they're the ones with the commercial where a guy gets lost on the lot." He turned to his wife, "You know it, Jean, what's the name of that place?"

"I know I've seen it, but I couldn't tell you, hon. I've never paid attention."

So much for that idea, Naomi thought. She could always check the court records, but that would take a lot of time.

Michael broke into her thoughts. "How come the sudden interest in the family, Naomi? Is it because you just lost your mum? Trying to hold on to something?"

"Partly that," Naomi admitted, hoping to quell any suspicion, "but mostly it's for Louise. She's getting into genealogy, trying to work out a family tree for her boys." Naomi felt a little guilt, but it was almost the truth. Perhaps it was time to steer the conversation away from Aunt Edna. She asked Michael about his parents.

"They met in England during the war, you know. Mum was a nurse. She was from the Welsh mining country. To tell you the truth, I'm not sure what she saw in Dad. He could be a miserable bugger. All work and no play, that describes him to a tee."

Jean chipped in, "But to be fair to your dad, hon, he wanted a better life for you kids than Spruce Creek could offer. He did see to it that you both went to university."

"Yes he did, I'll grant him that," Michael agreed. " He was a good man, I'm not saying he wasn't. It's just that I never really got to know him."

"He did quite well at Spruce Creek Logging, didn't he?" Naomi asked.

Michael nodded. "He worked his way up to management, then quit to start his own business. He sold insurance out of Powell River, and did quite well at it. They had enough money that he didn't need to keep working, but you know he worked until the day he died. Not me though. I'll quit at 55 and we'll do volunteer work through the church, won't we hon?" Michael glanced at his wife.

Jean nodded her assent, adding, "God willing."

"What about Aunt Violet?" Naomi asked. "She died overseas didn't she?"

"Yes, somewhere in the south of France. She was a lovely woman," Michael said fondly. "Always so quiet, but so good to Susan and I when we were kids. It's a shame she didn't have kids of her own. Perhaps she didn't want any with that husband of hers."

"Michael!" Jean jumped in with a reprimand.

"Sorry, hon. Judge not, that ye be judged. You're right, but no one was sorry to see him go."

"What happened to him?" Naomi asked.

"He died in a fire soon after Gran died. It gave Aunt Vi a new lease on life. She must have been stashing away her salary, because she took off on a cruise right away. She spent years traveling around. We'd get postcards from all over, before she settled in France. I'm surprised she never came back to Spruce Creek. Susan thought maybe she ran out of money. We were planning to go over and see her when we got word of her death. It was heart failure."

Naomi saw an opening. "Is that what Gran died of?"

Michael pursed his lips, thinking, "That could have been part of it, I expect. Dad and I were off on a fishing trip when it happened. I think Mum was there. Poor old Gran had so many things wrong with her. She must have been bedridden for three years or more. She got so big. I remember seeing your poor mother trying to lift her up in bed. It was all she could do, even with me lifting her feet. It was a blessing when she went, it really was."

"That's what Louise thinks," Naomi said.

"How is Louise? And the boys; they must be getting big?" Jean asked.

"They're all fine. Craig's eight and Brian ten now. They're as healthy as horses—involved in 4-H, baseball and terrorizing the local frogs. Sam keeps them busy, and they're doing all right in school."

"Does Sam still work for the city?" asked Michael.

"He's with the water bureau. We all tease him that he's got a cushy job, but he's actually got a lot of responsibility."

"And Louise, is she still riding horses and painting?"

"Oh, yes. She's getting pretty good. I keep telling her she needs to approach some galleries. You should see their house, it's lovely and the view is incredible."

Michael leaned forward in his chair. "You know, we really should come down there. Jean and I were just saying that. Perhaps when Susan and Paul get home this summer we can have a family reunion. If not in Oregon, then here, but we'd love to see that country, wouldn't we, hon?"

Jean agreed, saying they'd definitely have to plan something.

"Is Susan still doing mission work?" Naomi asked.

"Yes, they're still in Guatemala. They built a lovely clinic down there. We've got photos somewhere. I'll find them in a minute. They're coming back for three weeks. I think they're still trying to decide whether the clinic can run without them now. "

They spent the next hour or so looking at family photos, before Naomi announced she should leave and get back to her research. Michael promised to keep in touch. He wanted to keep the family reunion idea alive. Naomi took her leave in a happy frame of mind. Though Michael's information hadn't helped much, she was glad she came and knew she would visit her cousin again. As she pulled out the driveway, she glanced in her rearview mirror. How they could afford such an elegant home mystified her.

It was early evening before she was able to reach Louise. She'd tried, without success, several times before dinner. Now she was showered, lying on the motel bed with the TV on, not really watching.

Louise was astounded at the change in Michael.

"You mean he was friendly!"

"Absolutely," Naomi assured her, " in fact, he wants a family reunion this summer, when Susan gets home. At his place if you like, but they'd rather come to Oregon."

"Wow, that's sure not the Michael I remember. Let's keep him to it, sis. It would be fun and we might learn something. Speaking of that, what did you find out?"

Naomi filled her in on Aunt Edna and the embezzlement. Louise was as perplexed as Naomi that their mother and Aunt Kath had never mentioned it. They were trying to decide what to do about it when something on the TV caught Naomi's attention.

"Oh Lou, hang on a minute." She reached for the control and turned up the sound. A car commercial was airing. Did they say what she thought she heard? Sure enough, they were going through a bunch of silly antics looking for a customer lost on the lot. This had to be the one Michael referred to. She listened intently until the name came up: McFarland Motors.

Naomi got back on the line with Louise. "Bingo!" she sang out triumphantly.

Chapter 5

Louise

Exhaling sharply, Louise hung up the phone. She absent-mindedly began tapping the kitchen counter, drawing Sam's attention away from the television.

"Naomi was calling from Vancouver?" he asked, sounding surprised.

"Yep." Louise nodded. She walked back to the living room. "She thinks she's hot on the trail of Aunt Edna," she said, plopping down next to him.

"Oh, good," he replied, eyes still on the TV screen.

Louise curled her legs up under her and hugged a pillow to her chest. She sat deep in thought until the next commercial.

Sam glanced over at her. "Oh, oh, I know that look. What's wrong? Did I say the wrong thing?"

"No, it's not you," she said. "It's Naomi."

"What did she say?"

"It's not what she said. I'm just worried about her delving into the family history."

"It's unlikely she'll find out anything, hon. Why worry?"

"But what if she did? I told Mum I would take care of her." Louise felt her neck muscles tightening. "It wouldn't be bad if she was just curious about the money. She's fixated on this euthanasia business. I don't know how to get her to drop it. No good can come of it."

Sam's program was returning. He reached for the remote. "I'll turn this off."

"No, no," Louise insisted, "you like this show." She rubbed her neck. "My neck's seizing up. I think I'll get in the shower, run some hot water on it."

"You sure? I don't want you calling me a big, insensitive clod."

She threw the pillow at him. "When have I ever said that?"

"All the time," he called after her retreating figure.

The hot water felt good. When her neck seized up, she always worried another migraine was about to rear its ugly head. She let the water pound her head and visualized herself on horseback, galloping her horse, King Lear, through the sagebrush. It always helped to picture herself this way. Louise knew she didn't handle tension well, especially when it involved those she loved. Her first inclination was to run away, to ride away. Her high school teacher had noted on a report card, "Louise won't be able to control others, until she learns to control herself."

Well, she had a lot of self-control now. Marriage and children had taken care of that. The tomboy Louise was reined in most of the time. And most of the time, she could bear it. But there were times when her responsibilities threatened to overwhelm her. Times when her Gemini twin, as she called her alter ego, urged her to cut loose, to put herself first. Louise resisted. Her love for Sam and the boys was absolute; she would never do anything to hurt them.

She wished her mother hadn't added the responsibility of Naomi. It happened shortly before her mother died, in fact, the day before she was hospitalized. Naomi had gone to the pharmacy, leaving Louise alone with their mother.

"Louise, I want you to promise me something," her mother's voice sounded so feeble.

Louise trembled. The words carried the tone of finality. She swallowed hard. "What is it, Mum?"

"Take care of Naomi. She's had a rough time with the divorce, and now me. I worry so much about her. She doesn't take good care of herself."

Her mother paused, tired, and let Louise wipe her brow. You could hear a pin drop in the room as Louise waited for her mother to continue.

"I've never worried about you, sweetheart, you've got your father's bold spirit. When life throws you a curve, you're ready for it. But Naomi doesn't see the curves coming. I could see what was happening with Kevin long before she did." She turned soulful eyes to Louise. "Perhaps I should have said something."

Louise shook her head. "It wouldn't have helped, Mum. They'd grown too far apart. Don't worry so much about Naomi, she's strong and smart."

"Yes, but she doubts herself. She'll need you now, Lou." Tears filled her eyes. "My sweet, Louise, tell me you'll watch out for your little sister."

Louise didn't falter. "Of course I will, Mum. You know I love her. Naomi and I will always be close." She hugged her mother gently. "I'll see that she's happy, Mum. I'll see that she's happy."

Two days later, her mother died. Died without hearing what was really in Louise's heart. What she couldn't say, had never said to anyone, was that she resented Naomi getting all the attention. That she, Louise, had been like a boat without a rudder when her father died, and her mother hadn't noticed. No one thought to ask how "Daddy's girl" was feeling. Her mother, wrapped in grief, had clung to Naomi. Louise had never fully forgiven her mother. She'd never quite understood her mother's actions. Did she truly not notice my nine-year-old heart was broken, or did she feel too overwhelmed to deal with it? Louise pondered the answer. Was there a little jealousy? Did she resent the close relationship Louise had with her father? It was difficult to fathom. All Louise was left with was the memory of those lonely days.

She was in high school before she really confronted her feelings. The assignment was to analyze the effect both parents had on your behavior. Louise wrote of growing up in a totally female environment: no father, no grandfather, no uncles or male cousins living close, and a mother who didn't date. Her essay was picked out for class discussion. They wanted to know if she had an unusually close relationship with her mother and sister. She said yes, but it gave her food for thought. She knew it wasn't as close as she'd portrayed. The class agreed the female environment had made Louise the strong, confident person they saw. One guy she'd turned down for a date drew a chuckle when he observed, "That explains it."

Louise went home with mixed emotions. Why did everyone assume she was this totally confident person? Did she hide her fears, her frailties so well? Did she hide them from her mother too? Didn't anyone realize the self-doubts she dealt with?

That night she paid particular attention to the way Naomi and her mother related. Her sister, Louise noted, verbalized all the high and low points of her day. Their mother responded by trying to solve all Naomi's dilemmas, superficial though some of them were. It got mother and daughter talking, and although it was all about Naomi, the atmosphere was relaxed and loving. Their mother seemed to enjoy being the problem solver. Louise, thinking she'd give it a try, blurted out a niggling problem she'd been having in school.

Her mother thought about it for a minute, before responding. "Oh, Louise, you'll figure it out, sweetheart, you always do." Then she went back to Naomi's problems.

Louise left the room, but not before seeing Naomi's look of concern. Later, in the bathroom they shared, Naomi brought it up.

"Lou, she doesn't mean to cut you off, you know."

"Well, what does she mean?"

"She just thinks you're smart enough to solve it yourself."

Louise gave her sister a patronizing look. "And you're not?"

Naomi gave a lukewarm smile. "She likes to think that."

"Well, why do you do it? Why get her involved? It's not like she doesn't have enough on her plate with work."

"I figured something out about Mum. She has to have something to take care of. Maybe it's because she was Gran's caregiver for years." Naomi gave her sister an impassioned look. "I'm the baby, Lou; she's still babying me."

Louise smiled. "Some baby! But why doesn't she want to baby me? I'm only two years older than you."

"Oh, Louise, get real. Who could ever baby you? You'd tell them where to get off." Naomi laughed.

Louise busied herself trimming her bangs. She wondered if there was any truth in what Naomi said. Was it her manner that kept her mother at bay? Maybe now, but not when she was nine-years-old, and needed her mother so desperately. No matter what Naomi said, she couldn't overlook that. She glanced at her sister.

"Couldn't we get her a cat?"

Naomi shook her head. "I suggested that. She said she'll think about it when we're both in college."

"She'll be lonely then. I wish she'd date. Does she ever talk about it?"

"No, she won't talk about herself. She always brushes me off if she thinks I'm getting too personal."

Louise toweled off from her shower. She could hear Sam in the kitchen; his program must have finished. He was moving quietly, so as not to wake the boys. She threw on some sweats and went to join him.

"Feeling better?" he asked.

Louise nodded. "I think I'll get some warm milk before bed."

He walked over and began massaging her neck. "Have you taken anything for it?"

"Yes, I took Advil. But your magic hands will do the trick."

"Anything for a free massage," he teased her.

"Shades of when we met," Louise responded.

Sam smiled at her lovingly. "I'd had my eye on you long before that. You were the prettiest filly on campus, and spirited too."

Louise smiled at the memory. She knew he'd been attracted to her; she'd caught him watching her. Truth was, she found him attractive too. They met in 1982, on the campus of the University of Oregon in Eugene. Louise had long finished her studies and had taken a job in the college admission's department. Sam was there on the G.I. bill.

She'd first seen him a few days before school started that fall. Her roommate had called her to the living room window.

"Louise, get over here. The Marlborough Man just moved in across the street."

"What's he like?" She called back.

"I can't tell from here, but you like cowboys. Come and get him."

Louise giggled and ran to the window. Sam was unloading a pickup truck. She noticed with pleasure his long, lean body, clad from head to toe in Western gear. “Um, that’s nice,” she purred. “I’ll watch out for him on campus.”

Her roommate shrieked. “ Are you crazy? You want to let all those young coeds at him? Get over there and ask if he wants to borrow a cup of sugar.”

Louise, laughing, went back to what she was doing. “I want a closer look before I commit myself, Sharon.”

She got her closer look a few days later. Sam’s schedule must have coincided with her own. He was approaching his truck as Louise was pulling away from the curb. Their eyes met briefly, but it was enough to spark an interest, at least where Louise was concerned. She saw him a few times more, but always from a distance. On a weekend, she’d taken to washing her car at curbside or cleaning out the inside, slowly, deliberately. Although he’d watched her through the window, he never came outside. All the extra care she’d taken with her appearance appeared wasted on him. She was thinking of taking drastic measures, like backing into his truck maybe, when fate stepped in a leant a hand.

Louise, at her roommate’s insistence, took part in a run for charity. The run finished on the campus, where participants were promised snacks, foot analysis and a free ten-minute massage. Despite a less than stellar performance, Louise still made it to the finish before her roommate. She was killing time in the snack tent when she saw him. Sam was one of a handful of people giving free massage.

‘Oh great,’ Louise thought, ‘I finally get a chance to meet him, and I’m all covered in sweat.’ She grabbed a few napkins and tried wiping her face and neck. There were tendrils of moist hair framing her face, and her cheeks were flushed. She wore no makeup, but was thankful she did have a color-coordinated running outfit. ‘Well, here goes,’ she thought. ‘Now how can I make sure I get the massage from him?’

She didn't need to. Sam spotted her the moment she walked into the tent. Before anyone else could react, he yelled, "This one's mine, she's my neighbor."

The ten-minute massage soon became twenty minutes. Somewhere during that space of time, Louise made up her mind this was the man for her. Fortunately for her, the feeling was mutual. Sam told her later he'd been watching her for weeks, trying to pluck up courage to approach her. His shyness attracted her. He finished up the massage and stood tongue-tied looking at her.

Louise gave him her most flirtatious look. "If you ever need a cup of sugar, you know where I live."

He looked relieved. Later that day, he was on her doorstep with an empty cup.

Louise ushered her sons out the door, where Sam was waiting to drop them at the school-bus stop. She smiled lovingly at her two boys. It pleased her that she had sons. She related well to males, starting with her father. Perhaps she should have been a boy; the family always accused her of being a tomboy. Her relationships with women were a little more strained, she thought. She and Naomi were close, it's true, and Aunt Kath had been a good friend. But Louise felt she kept women at a distance.

Maybe it started with her grandmother. No, it wasn't fair to blame Gran. It's true they had played together before Naomi came on the scene. But as Gran became less and less mobile, it was natural she found comfort in baby Naomi. Four-year-old Louise didn't want to hang around indoors; she wanted to swing, climb trees and dig in the dirt. It's no wonder Naomi became Gran's favorite, and it wasn't Naomi's fault. That's why I've never blamed her. Or have I? Louise wondered.

Naomi was Mum's favorite too. Is that what this is all about; why I resent feeling responsible for Naomi?

Louise pushed open the door to her studio, and stood looking at her latest canvas. It was good; she knew it was good. Now, if she could only stay focused long enough to do a series, she'd really feel like an artist. Staying focused had always been a problem for Louise. She joked that her tombstone should read, 'Here lies Louise. Her forces were scattered.' Sam said that's what he loved about her; every day was a new experience. She did approach life with enthusiasm. Responsibilities, though frustrating, couldn't keep her down for long.

She began to paint, and soon put the problem of Naomi out of her mind. Painting absorbed her. That's what she liked about it. A ringing phone broke into her trance. It was her neighbor, Carol.

"Louise, did you forget you're helping me pick out my bedroom colors this morning?"

"Oh, bugger, is it ten already? Sorry, Carol. I'll be right over."

"Coffee's on, and I've got some strudel."

"You've said the magic word. I'll be right there."

Louise sat facing her neighbor across the kitchen table. The colors had been decided, now Carol turned her attention to Louise.

"Okay, Louise, I've known you long enough. What's eating you?"

Louise laughed. Her neighbor worked for years as a psychologist. Nothing got by her. "Of course you'd notice," Louise said, before explaining. "I think I may have figured out a basic truth about myself. I'm jealous of my sister."

"Jealous of Naomi? How so?"

"She's a published author, and what am I? She's a much nicer person than me," Louise explained.

Carol studied her for a minute before speaking. "But that's not it, is it?"

Louise hesitated. It was hard to hide anything from Carol. "No, although that's the truth. Naomi's so basically nice, she was everyone's favorite."

"Define everyone?"

"My mother and my grandma."

"How about your father?" Carol asked.

"Not my father. He and I were very close, but he died when I was nine," Louise explained.

"And you felt abandoned?"

"Yes, very much so," Louise emphasized. She told Carol how her mother reacted at that time.

Carol nodded in understanding, but didn't comment. Louise continued. She explained how her mother always showered attention on Naomi. How Naomi had become Gran's favorite, and, finally, how her mother had made Louise responsible for her sister.

Carol broke in. "Now we're getting somewhere. You really resent that, don't you?"

Louise looked a little uncomfortable. "Yes."

"That's all right, it's natural." Carol explained. "Now, tell me a little about Naomi. I've only met her briefly."

They spent the next half hour exploring the differing personalities of Naomi and Louise, before Carol announced she had some conclusions.

"Tell me," she asked Louise "is there anything about me you're jealous of?"

"Yes, Dave," Louise said without hesitation, naming Carol's husband.

Carol laughed. "And that's what I envy in you."

"What?" Louise was puzzled.

"Your instant sense of humor. I'd love to be so witty. But notice I said envy. I'm not jealous of you, just envious. You're confusing the two, Louise. Oh, you may have had feelings of jealousy when you were a child; wishing to deny Naomi some of the attention she was getting and divert it to you. But would you, for instance, want to see her not able to write?"

"No, but I wish I could."

"Yes, and she probably wishes she could paint like you. It's a form of admiration really; admiring a talent someone else has. We all do it, but it doesn't always mean we want to have that same talent. For instance, I really envy someone with the courage to parachute from an airplane. Would I want to do it? Not in a million years."

"So, you're saying I don't have a problem?" Louise asked.

"Not in the way you were looking at it. You're envious Naomi has published a book, and you're still trying to get established as an artist. But, from what you've said, Naomi envies you the boys and Sam. She sees you with a happy marriage and two wonderful boys—and I should know, I live next door to them. I think what you're dealing with, Louise, is a little self-doubt." Carol smiled at her. "I'm glad we talked about it. That's what you lacked as a child."

"They didn't seem to notice."

"Your zest for life makes it hard to spot. Try to forgive your mother; her grief was profound. Naomi was cuddly and you were the tomboy. The important thing is she loved you and had faith in you." Carol stood up. "Now go and paint for the sheer joy of it."

Louise smiled and hugged Carol. "Will you send me the bill?"

"When I get yours for the color consultation."

Talking to Carol had really helped, Louise decided. She felt empowered as she stood before the canvas. Soon, paint was flying. There were red flecks in her black hair and a yellow smudge on her nose. She was just cleaning up for the day when Carol called.

"I forgot one thing, Louise; the promise you made to your mother. You cannot *make* someone else happy. All you can do is love them, offer them advice, and be there when they need you. That's really what your mother was asking of you. Naomi has to be allowed to make her own mistakes."

Louise hesitated. She hadn't told Carol about the family mystery, and was reluctant to do so over the phone. She thanked Carol, and told her it had all helped. The boys would be home soon. She hurried with her cleanup, her mind on Naomi the whole time. 'Naomi must be allowed to make her own mistakes.' Digging up Gran's death would be a mistake, Louise was certain. What good could possibly come from it? Am I wrong in feeling this way? Louise thought not. Stopping Naomi might be impossible, but I certainly won't help her, she decided. A new thought entered her head. Perhaps the new man in Naomi's life would take her attention off Gran. Louise hoped so. It was time she gave some attention to the 'little men' in her life. Craig and Brian would need help with homework, and they were bound to be starving.

Chapter 6

McFarland Motors was on a busy street in Burnaby. Naomi, pulling onto the lot, guessed that it wasn't nearly this busy when Aunt Edna worked here. The younger McFarland's were obviously doing a good job with the place. She'd called that morning and found out the old brothers who founded the place had retired. Two sons and a daughter ran it now. They wouldn't remember Aunt Edna, but surely would know something about the embezzlement.

Naomi was a bit embarrassed to have to discuss it with them, since one of her family had stolen from them. She tried to figure out how she would approach it. Perhaps the genealogy story would work best. She'd appeal to their sense of mystery. That's what she did in her writing every day. It was a loose end that had to be tied. A lot would depend on what kind of people they were. Her apprehension had tied knots in Naomi's stomach; she'd be so glad to get this over with and head on home.

She needn't have worried. The McFarland's were obviously fun loving people, and were amused at Naomi's query. They teased her and asked if she'd come to pay them back. Naomi was soon at ease, and asked if any of them remembered her aunt. They didn't, which wasn't surprising since Edna had only worked there for two years at the most. The younger McFarland's were away at college during that time. They did remember some of the details of the embezzlement though. The business did a brisk trade renting cars to visitors from Hong Kong. One person was in charge of the rental office. Since foreign currency was involved, it was easy to hide the embezzlement.

"It's funny," Alice McFarland said, "my understanding was it had been going on for years, but you say your aunt only worked here for a couple years."

"Well, I could have that wrong, " Naomi admitted, "I'm not entirely sure when she came back from living in England. Maybe it was earlier than I supposed."

Bill McFarland had left the room, and now came back carrying an old photograph.

"It just occurred to me we had this company photo from around that time. It's an anniversary of some sort, and it looks like most employees are in it." He handed it to Naomi. "Can you see your aunt there anywhere?"

It was a black and white photograph, but Naomi didn't need color to spot the redheaded Aunt Edna. Characteristically, she'd anchored a spot in the front row, next to one of the owners.

"That's her there," Naomi explained, "she was a redhead, if that helps."

It didn't, but Bill had an idea.

"I'll tell you what; our accountant, Percy Wing may remember her. He's been here for years." He turned to his sister. "Do you know where he is, Alice?"

"Yes, he's having cataract surgery today. He'll be back in a couple days." Alice leaned toward Naomi. "Assuming he remembers her, what exactly do you want to know, Naomi?"

Naomi wasn't sure how to answer, but after a moment's thought said, "I suppose verification that she had done it; whether or not she was prosecuted, and if she paid it back. We're really just trying to drag another skeleton out of the family closet."

They all laughed, and after a brief discussion of family skeletons, the meeting came to an end. Alice promised to have the accountant e-mail Naomi in a few days with any information he may have. After trying to sell her a new car, they said their goodbyes. Naomi left in a much calmer state than she arrived.

It wasn't until she crossed the Canadian border and was on home soil again that her thoughts turned to Ben. What would she do when Wednesday came around? She was supposed to meet him again at the coffee shop, but she didn't think she could. Even if they kept the conversation on a professional level, it wouldn't work. The sexual attraction between the two of them would get in the way. She felt a profound sense of disappointment. For the first time in a very long while, she'd felt her body awakening.

Naomi knew Louise would be full of advice, but she hadn't told her sister when she called from Vancouver. She'd e-mail her tonight and let her know about her meeting with the McFarlands. She wouldn't call her just yet.

She did think about calling Diana. But what would she say: How come you didn't tell me your brother was married? Boy, did that sound juvenile! She didn't want to lose Diana's friendship either. Perhaps the best thing to do, Naomi thought, is nothing. When and if Diana called her she'd be nonchalant; better than looking the fool. She wouldn't meet Ben again and the book could be her excuse. She'd tell Diana she was swamped with rewrites at the moment. Ben should understand that. Perhaps, if enough time went by, she could meet him again without her heart fluttering. Fat chance, Naomi, she thought, oh, damn, damn, damn, why does he have to be married.

The miles went by and she was able to put Ben out of her mind by focusing on the family mystery. Her cousin Michael had been away on a fishing trip when Gran died, so he wouldn't have known the circumstances of her death. Her mother had suspected all three girls, Edna, Violet and Gwen, of euthanizing Gran. Did she mean together, or just that any one of them could have done it?

Naomi had been so ready to put the blame on Aunt Edna; mainly because she was a difficult woman, and had flaunted her sudden wealth. Now it looked as though her money came from the embezzlement.

That left Violet and Gwen. Michael seemed to think that Aunt Violet used her life's savings for her many trips, and died poor. Naomi hadn't known her well, but like Michael, she thought her a kind woman—too kind, surely, to kill her mother. (There's that word again, kill, Naomi thought. So much better to think euthanize.)

If it wasn't Aunt Violet, that left Aunt Gwen, Michael's mother. She was a nurse and would know what to do, that's for sure. As far as she knew, Aunt Gwen and Uncle Bill had always lived simply. They'd sent both children to very good colleges. But Michael said his dad was fairly successful in his insurance business. Still, Naomi wondered, where did Michael's money come from? How could he afford such an extravagant home?

Then there was the money itself. How big an estate was it? When did it come through, if it came through? She hoped Louise was able to find out something from her web buddy in England.

As she drove along the details kept swimming around in Naomi's head. It was all so fascinating. In a sudden burst of enlightenment, one thing became clear to her. A self-satisfied grin spread from ear to ear and she said aloud, "Well, I guess I know what my next book will be about!"

Chapter 7

Gran

Bertha Cavenish willed her hand to move. With every fiber in her being she willed it, but it lay motionless on the cover. All she wanted was to give this little child an indication that she heard her. Before the last stroke, she'd been able to reach out to Naomi, bringing a smile to the girl's face. Now the little one seemed confused. She was after all, only four-years-old. As though privy to her thoughts, Naomi spoke.

"It's okay, Gran, I 'spect you want to sleep. I'm going to make cookies with Mummy and Louise." She patted the old woman's hand. "I'll come back later."

Bertha watched the tiny figure disappear from view. Her eyes were the only part of her she felt able to control these days. How cruel a fate: not to be able to hold that precious child or her sister. She'd been ailing most of their lives. Perhaps Louise, being the elder, remembered her Gran able to talk and walk. Naomi's memories wouldn't go back that far. She will remember me, Bertha thought, as being part and parcel of this accursed bed.

She remembered the minister's wife saying to her when Frank died, "God never gives us more to bear than we are able to."

Well, He was certainly testing her. Taking her husband in mid-life, leaving her with all those children. And then the pain of losing her firstborn son to war. Finally, He preserved my mind, while destroying my body, Bertha thought. Finally? Would this be the end of it? Would God have mercy on her now and call her to Him? In spite of her anger, she still prayed to Him. Every day the same prayer: "End my life today, please Lord."

She sometimes wondered if her children were uttering the same prayer for her. Her role as a mother had ended. What use was she to the children now? She had given them her best years. Motherhood had been overwhelming at times, but she'd endured. She didn't have a lot to offer them, but she figured they turned out all right. Life wouldn't have been much different if their father had lived. They'd have stayed in Spruce Creek either way. Logging was all her Charlie knew—he'd made that clear when he proposed to her.

On occasion, she mulled how life would have turned out if she hadn't met him. No doubt she'd have stayed in Alberta, close to her family. It was a harsh life, but then so was this. She couldn't think who she would have found to marry in Alberta. Local farmers wouldn't have their sons marry a tenant farmer's daughter. Besides, she'd seen them at church and wasn't interested.

Maybe she'd have stayed single. Perhaps moved into town and worked in a shop. There had been many times during her life when she'd pictured herself doing just that. Oh, the freedom to be master of your own destiny again!

But Charlie Cavenish had knocked on their door one day. He was working his way west to log in British Columbia. What he wanted was an odd job or two, in exchange for a meal and a place to put his bedroll. He left with a wife.

He was a charmer all right, her Charlie. If she closed her eyes tight, she could see those laughing eyes of his so clearly. Frank had those same eyes.

She'd never given a thought to being a mother. Her pregnancy didn't prepare her. Being a wife was a lesson in progress when the baby came along. She was Bertha Cavenish, silly young girl; right up to the minute the midwife put Frank in her arms. There were a few minutes of panic as the truth took hold: she was responsible for this new life. This helpless child was totally dependent on her. Fear of failure had swept over her.

A laugh gurgled in Bertha's throat at the memory of that day. She'd never again questioned her abilities as a mother. The children came along so fast, six in all. There was never time to wonder if she was doing it right. Still, it was a wonderful memory, those first moments with little Frank.

Looking over at Charlie, she'd seen such pride and love in his eyes. Together they'd manage. Together they'd learn to be parents, as they were learning to be husband and wife. The war in Europe threatened that sense of security shortly after Frank was born. Charlie narrowly missed being sent overseas. Bertha remembered how anxious they'd been. But she was pregnant with Edna before his number came up. By war's end, they had three children.

Frank was her favorite. She made no excuses for that. He was probably Charlie's favorite too, although they'd never talked about it. Everyone loved little Frank. He had a way of lighting up a room, just by entering. A bit of a rascal, to be sure, especially when he reached the drinking age. She could never stay mad at him. Even when she'd caught him, drunk, peeing up the back door. No, Frank could charm his way out of everything.

He'd straightened up in a hurry, though, when his father died. He would have been how old? Bertha struggled to remember. He must have been around twenty, because he'd already been logging with his dad for some time. You'd have thought seeing his dad die on the job would have put Frank off logging, she thought. It didn't. He worked at it with a vengeance for four more years. When World War II erupted, she had a feeling it would be Frank's ticket out of Spruce Creek. Oh, how tight he held her when he told her he was enlisting. What could she say? Only that she loved him, and to come back safely. But, of course, he didn't.

Tears welled up in her eyes and tumbled down her cheeks. They disappeared in the folds of her neck. She closed her eyes and tried to find sleep. The smell of fresh-baked cookies drifted up the stairwell. May was a good little mother. Imagine, she thought, of the four girls I had, May is the only one with children. It didn't surprise her that Edna never had any. Violet and Kath would have made good mothers, but not Edna. She was something else, that Edna.

She was difficult right from the start. Such a demanding baby: cry, cry, cry, Bertha shuddered at the memory. It had been a surprise to have a redheaded baby. Her friends had joked that she'd have difficulty with a redhead. They'd laughed together, but it proved prophetic. Edna was a bit contrary, but not too bad until she got to high school. That's when I stopped loving her, Bertha thought. God forgive me.

One incident stood out in her mind. Edna was convinced she didn't belong to the family. Her red hair proved it, she reasoned. The truth was, she was ashamed of their humble circumstances. Ashamed of us, Bertha thought. She had been understanding to a point, but when the girl started demeaning her siblings, she'd had enough. "If you don't like it, my girl," she remembered saying, "there's the door. Close it on your way out."

She'd called Edna's bluff that time. Once the girl was out of high school, though, Bertha knew she'd be on her way. And she didn't care. Edna had managed to antagonize them all. May, being the youngest, escaped some of it and Edna seemed fond of her. Perhaps that's why she kept some contact with them. She hadn't written often while she was in London. Lord knows what happened over there, Bertha mused. Edna acted more than ever like she wasn't one of them now. She did come up from Vancouver occasionally. It was May's birthday soon. She'd probably come then. Bertha could tell Edna felt sorry for May.

At the thought, her tears started flowing again. No one, she thought, feels sorrier for May than I do.

As her daughter adjusted her position in bed, Bertha winced in pain. She tried to hide it, but saw the look of concern on May's face. If only she could comfort her daughter, tell her she understood. Tell her…oh tell her so many things.

May had just finished straightening the covers when the phone rang. Bertha could tell from the conversation it was her daughter Kath. She could hear most of what May was saying, but knew when her voice dropped they were probably talking about her. Kath would be supportive, helpful. They were both such good girls, the best two, really.

It's funny, Bertha thought, when my girls were growing up, I assumed Violet would be the closest to me. She was such a sweet-natured girl, always trying to please me. Her problem was she was too shy and too pretty. The boys wouldn't leave her alone, and she didn't know how to handle it. It was all right with Frank around. If anything, he was overprotective. If only he hadn't died.

Bertha gave a heavy sigh. Here she was brooding over Frank again. Most widows brood over their lost husbands. But with her, it had always been Frank. Perhaps she should feel guilt over that, but she didn't. It was hard for her to analyze. She *had* loved Charlie, but in a detached sort of way. He was this other being she felt love for; he was not a part of her. On the other hand, Frank carried with him a part of her soul.

Naomi and Louise broke her train of thought. They came tumbling into the bedroom, each trying to get to her bedside first.

"Look, Gran, look, I made a cookie with a face on it," Naomi pushed the misshapen cookie under her nose.

Bertha attempted a smile.

"Mum said we could show you, Gran," Louise explained. "Can you see mine?" Louise peered into her eyes. "It's a flower."

A groan escaped from Bertha.

Naomi's eyes widened. She turned to Louise excitedly. "Gran is trying to talk."

"Silly," her sister admonished, "Gran can't talk. You know that."

Bertha felt Naomi stroke her arm.

"But she wants to, Louise. Why can't she?"

"Mum already told you, Naomi. Gran's too old."

Naomi turned sorrowful eyes to Bertha.

"I don't think she's too old." She leaned in so close; Bertha could feel the child's breath caress her cheek. "You're not too old, Gran, you're just right."

Close to tears, Bertha was saved when May appeared in the doorway.

"Okay, girls, you've got some clean-up in the kitchen. I'll be right down."

The sound of clattering dishes had died down, Bertha realized. The girls must have finished their cleaning. Now the distant drone of television drifted up to her. May would be up soon to switch hers on. She liked to watch the news, but the rest of it was a load of drivel. It did take her mind of things, though. Bill had bought the little TV for her. He was a good boy, her Bill, but not loving like his brother.

She heard the doorbell, then the soft sound of Violet. Funny, I was just thinking about her, she thought. She must be on her way home from work. May would like seeing her. They all loved Violet; they just felt helpless seeing her live like she did. If only she would pluck up the courage to leave that husband of hers. She was afraid of him and it was no wonder. I knew he'd turn out to be trouble; I should have stopped her marrying him, Bertha reproached herself.

Violet came softly into the room, approached the bed and kissed Bertha on the forehead.

"How are you, Mum? I've just stopped for a minute. Ralph will be waiting for his supper. I didn't want to leave without looking in on you, though."

Violet's lovely face was wrought with anxiety. She stroked Bertha's cheek. She's much too thin, Bertha thought. Her whole life is one big worry. Poor Violet, she should have got some of Edna's courage.

May walked in and switched on the television.

"She likes to watch the news," she explained to Violet.

"Do you think she can take it in?" asked Violet.

May shrugged. "I'm not sure, but just in case, I'll keep doing it."

Bertha chuckled to herself. It was almost laughable sometimes the way they thought she'd lost her marbles. One minute they were talking to her quite normally, and then they'd begin debating whether or not her brain was addled. It was almost laughable, but so frustrating that she couldn't set them straight.

Violet kissed her goodbye and followed May down the stairs. Bertha tried to keep her mind on the TV news. They were still full of the American president's assassination: what a terrible thing, and his young wife there beside him. Oh, it didn't bear thinking about. I expect we'll be hearing about it for weeks, she thought.

She must have dozed off. May was tapping her arm.

"I've got some dinner for you, Mum."

Her daughter spread a towel across Bertha's chest, pulled up a chair and began spoon-feeding her mother. Swallowing was difficult, although May puréed everything. Next to toileting, this was where Bertha most felt the loss of her dignity. That she should be spoon-fed like a baby was so hard to bear.

May was keeping up a steady chatter. It's meant to soothe me, I know, Bertha thought. Occasionally, May was distracted by the television and almost missed her mother's mouth. Bertha didn't want the food. After a while she'd stop swallowing; the only way she had of indicating when she'd had enough.

"Kath called earlier," May said, "she can't get home this weekend. She said she'd try for next month."

Bertha knew how much May looked forward to her sister's visits. No wonder she seemed sad tonight. Her husband wouldn't be here for a few weeks, either.

"I expect Bill and Gwen will be over tomorrow, though, Mum." May smiled at her. "You'll like that."

Yes, I will like it, Bertha thought. She liked her son; he reminded her of her own father. Very serious most of the time, but with a soft core he kept hidden. Bill worked too much. He didn't take enough time out to enjoy his family. If only she could express that thought to him. He had a lovely wife in Gwen, and their two children were so well behaved. They didn't seem happy children, though, not like May's two.

Bill was always after more money. Bertha remembered before she had the last stroke, Bill telling her his business was doing well. Yet, he never took a vacation. Perhaps it's because he grew up so poor, she surmised. Still, she was glad he was around to give May advice. Not that May needed much; she was smart, her May. Bill and May were the smartest two, all right, much smarter than their mother. That thought didn't irk her. Quite the contrary, she was delighted to have produced children with brains. Bill was using his, but May, poor May…

Bertha watched her daughter mopping up the remains of her meal. It was all so mechanical. May was so engrossed in attending to all the details; she didn't meet her mother's eyes often. Just as well, Bertha thought, I can't stand to see the sadness.

May picked up the tray and paused at the foot of the bed. "I'll be back with a bedpan in a little while, Mum." She smiled weakly. "I'd better see what the girls are up to."

Bertha, watching the retreating figure, anguished over her daughter's fate. She could only imagine what it would be like to care for an old, bedridden person. Her sister had spared her that responsibility. When she thought about it, she hadn't seen much of her parents in old age. The distance was too great, and the money too scarce. Her Charlie had died in his forties; she hadn't seen him grow old. Old age was a mystery to her. She would be seventy-five next birthday, if she had a next birthday. She didn't want a next birthday.

Bill and Gwen didn't stay with her long. What was there to say? It's not like they could hold a conversation. Bertha was sorry they hadn't brought the children with them this time. They'd gone on a school outing, Gwen had explained. Maybe they had, maybe they hadn't, Bertha thought. As they'd got older, visiting Gran had lost some of its luster. She couldn't blame them.

Now she could hear Bill and May talking downstairs. They didn't realize how much of their conversation she could hear. Without the TV on, it was so quiet in her bedroom. Snatches of their conversation were drifting up to her. She'd heard it all before. Bill was trying again to convince May to put her, Bertha, in a home.

"It's too much for you, May, with the girls and all," Bill sounded persuasive.

May was quiet, as she usually was.

"The girls need to be in Oregon with their dad," Bill continued.

"He's right, pet," Gwen added.

Bertha strained to hear what came next, but household noises drowned out May's response. Oh, God, please let them persuade her, she prayed. They must have walked back in the kitchen, because she couldn't hear them now. Perhaps Bill will be successful this time. Perhaps May will put her husband and children first.

Bertha hadn't approved May's choice of husband at first. He spoke broken English, which she didn't hold against him. It seemed he was quite well educated, and he did have good manners. He was thoughtful and generous to a fault. His only crime, in her eyes: he was a logger. She thought May, smart as she was, could have done better. She could have found a man in a less dangerous profession, a man who could buy her a house in a real town, with sidewalks.

Oh, Spruce Creek wasn't all that bad, Bertha supposed. The houses were warm, and she and Charlie, with their big family had qualified for a larger, two story home. It was just the way the town looked, carved out of the forest, ringed by a perimeter of stumps. The only paved road was the one into town.

Town, Bertha thought, that's a contradiction for you. It's one big logging company really. Settlement probably described it better, but Spruce Creek Logging called it a town. It was their town so they could call it what they liked. All that's here, she thought, is a bunch of company buildings; one holding the company store, post office, barbershop and café. Then there's the volunteer fire department, the school, the church and the bowling alley—where most of Spruce Creek's social life took place. A single men's bunkhouse sat a discreet distance from the family homes. She'd never been inside it, but she had been in their cookhouse. It was connected to the bunkhouse by a raised boardwalk, softened by years of caulked boots stomping along it. Her children liked to run along it when she had them out for walks. She kept them well away from the shower building out back. Not that there was any harm there. Spruce Creek was a dry town, as were most logging communities. Violet's Ralph managed to find plenty to drink though. So did Frank and his buddies, she thought wryly.

No, Spruce Creek wasn't all that bad. It was just that she wanted May to raise the girls in a prettier, quieter place. All the tree stumps, and the incessant thumping of diesel generators—used to provide power—robbed the place of ever meeting those goals.

It had always been May's goal to move away, Bertha knew that.

Thinking about it now, Bertha smiled to herself. May was her baby and she wanted so much for her. Only now could she see how much May loved her husband. The separation was so hard on them. Bertha had to hand it to him; he had more ambition than most men in Spruce Creek. The move to Oregon proved it. Maybe one day May will have that house, she thought. Then the reality of the situation hit her. The only thing preventing it, she thought angrily, is my miserable life.

The trio downstairs moved back where she could hear them.

"I'm so worried about you, pet," she heard Gwen say.

Bill's tone was pleading. "May, just let me make some inquiries, see what's available."

May's reply filled Bertha with despair.

"Have you seen those places, Bill? There's no way I could put Mum in one of them. I just can't do it. She deserves better than that."

"So do you, May," Bill stressed.

There was a pause, before May responded. "My time will come soon enough."

Bertha felt rage welling up in her. Not at May, at herself, her condition. How she longed to be able to cry out, "May, for God's sake put me in a home. Get on with your life."

Frustration gave way to tears. She closed her eyes and tasted salt from the tears sliding into her mouth. Her muffled sobs prevented her from hearing Naomi enter. She jumped in surprise when the small hand touched her arm.

"Don't cry, Gran. I can sing to you."

Chapter 8

The Thursday morning after Naomi returned from Vancouver, the phone rang. Naomi knew who it would be. She didn't want to talk to him, so she let the machine answer it.

"Hi Naomi, it's Ben. Just wanted to say the Walkersville Authors' Club missed you yesterday. I guess you are still out of town. Anyway, hope to see you next time. By the way, I enjoyed your book. Maybe it appealed to my feminine side, but I thought it was good. Take care."

He sounded so relaxed, not at all like a married man pursuing another woman. Perhaps his motives were innocent, and it was all in her head, Naomi thought. Maybe Louise had hit the nail on the head when she guessed Naomi must be horny. Well, it didn't really matter. For the sake of her career, she must push Ben out of her thoughts and concentrate on her manuscript.

She'd had a good workday yesterday. The trip to Vancouver had really helped. She was able to finish off her Capilano Bridge chapter, rich in detail she had just gathered. Now she concentrated on making notes of downtown Vancouver, while it was still fresh in her mind.

This time when the phone rang Naomi answered it. She knew it wouldn't be Ben. If it was Diana, she had already rehearsed what she was going to say. It wasn't Diana.

"Hello, this is Percy Wing," a high-pitched male voice came over the line. "Are you Naomi?"

"Yes, this is Naomi, what can I do for you?"

"Alice McFarland asked me to get in touch with you."

Of course, the accountant, Naomi had expected him to e-mail her.

"Mr. Wing, thank you for calling, how nice of you. I was expecting an e-mail."

"Well, yes, but when I told Miss Alice about your aunt, she said I should call you right away."

"You do remember my aunt then, Mr. Wing?"

"Oh yes, she was quite a character, your aunt. I used to call her Red."

Naomi swallowed hard. "And I believe she stole from the company. Did she ever pay it back?"

"Well, here's the thing, miss, she never did."

"She never did pay it back?" Naomi felt a tightening in her chest.

"No, no, miss, I mean she never stole from the company. That's why Miss Alice asked me to call; she wanted me to tell you in person."

"She didn't do it?" Naomi was caught off-guard. "But the McFarland's remembered the embezzlement."

"That they did, but it wasn't your aunt. You see we had two Edna's working here: it was Edna Blake who did the embezzling. She'd been at it for years when we caught up with her."

"Oh, I see," Naomi felt a rush of relief.

Percy Wing continued, " No, Miss, your aunt wasn't that kind of person. She wasn't what I'd call a model employee either, but she was always good for a laugh." He chuckled. "She came out with some stories all right. We all missed her when she left. Is she still living?"

"Well, that's the thing," Naomi explained, "we lost touch with her and don't really know. Do you have any idea why she left the company and where she was going?"

"She always talked about going back to England." He laughed, " She'd got the accent down pat; proper BBC. She left the company of her own accord. She'd come into some money, she said, and was going to travel. I don't remember her giving any more details. My memory's not what it used to be. I'll bet England was her destination though."

"Perhaps you're right," Naomi said, "I should look there first."

"If you find her, tell her Percy Wing sends his regards."

"I will, and thank you so much Mr. Wing. You've been a big help."

Naomi stood looking at the phone, digesting what the accountant had just told her. So, Aunt Edna wasn't an embezzler. That was good news, but it made her a suspect again. Especially since she'd admitted coming in to some money. If she had gone back to England, it was probably to London; that's where she lived before. Naomi still felt that if any one were guilty of euthanizing Gran, it would be Aunt Edna. They needed to trace her, and London would be a good place to start.

She caught sight of herself in the mirror above the desk, and asked her reflection, "Why am I doing this." What if she and Louise were able to track down Edna, found her still living, and learned she had bumped off Gran for her money? What then? What would you do to a woman in her eighties? She wondered now if it might be better not to know. Perhaps Louise was right. What was it compelling her to seek answers? It wasn't just that she was Gran's favorite, there had to be more to it than that. Whatever it was, she knew she wouldn't rest until she had some answers. Time to call Louise, she thought.

"Lou, hi, it's me."

"Hi, sis, I was just going to call you. What's up?"

"Guess who just called me?"

"Oow, your hot man?" Louise said excitedly.

Naomi knew she'd have to give Louise the lowdown on Ben, but not right now.

"No, Lou, the accountant from McFarland Motors. He remembered Aunt Edna."

"Great. What did he tell you?"

"Are you ready for this: she didn't do it."

"You have to be kidding, I thought the owners remembered the embezzlement."

"They did and there was one. But apparently they had two Edna's working there; the other Edna was the one who did it."

"Well, I'll be damned. I wonder how word got back to Spruce Creek that it was our Edna."

"Someone must have heard it was an Edna and just put two and two together. They knew our Edna worked there, and then she turned up in her fancy clothes and jewels. What more proof did they need?"

"Wow!" Louise let out a long breath. "What did he tell you about our Edna?"

"He seemed to really like her. She made him laugh, oh, and he called her Red."

Louise chuckled. "Did he say why she left?"

"That's the interesting part. He said she left by her own accord because she'd come into some money and wanted to travel."

"Hmm," Louise was silent for a minute. Naomi could imagine the wheels turning in her sister's head. When she spoke, it was with a new air of confidence. " Well, it looks like there was some money involved, and Edna's our girl. I still don't believe she was involved in Gran's death, though. What we need to find out is where she went. That's where we should start."

"She told the accountant she wanted to go back to England. I figure we should look in London first. Do you think your web buddy would help us?"

"I know she would," Louise affirmed. "That's why I was going to call you, sis: she's already found something. It's not Aunt Edna, but remember I told you she was going to research the Cavenish name? She's traced it back to Scotland. We're not entirely sure it's our branch of the family yet, but listen to this: they owned extensive landholdings back there, and there was even a castle!"

"A castle! Cavenish Castle?"

"Yep, I told Sam he'd better start treating his blue-blooded wife with more respect," she joked.

"Well, who owns it all now? " Naomi wondered.

"Don't know yet, she's still working on it. Exciting, isn't it? Hey, you could write a book."

"Funny you should say that," Naomi countered, and proceeded to tell Louise her thoughts on the subject. They chatted on about the book and family issues for some time. Naomi thought she'd dodged the issue of Ben, but she should have known better.

"So, how's your love life?" Louise inquired.

"Louise, he's married."

"You have to be kidding," Louise was shocked. "How did you find out?"

Naomi gave her sister all the details of her last meeting with Ben. She ended with the message he'd left that morning.

Louise was obviously disappointed. "How odd. You're sure the clergyman was speaking to him?"

"Lou, there were no other customers, and he said it louder than necessary, so I would hear."

"He could have been kidding."

"A clergyman kidding like that; I don't think so. Besides, his tone was anything but light."

"Still it doesn't add up, sis. Why wouldn't his sister have said something? What are you going to do now?"

"Nothing. I doubt he'll call again. When I don't show up next week, he'll get the message loud and clear. It's his sister that's the hard part."

"How so?'

"I really like her, Lou. I thought I'd made a good friend."

"I think she owes you an explanation. Before you give up on him, why don't you call his sister?"

"And say what: why didn't you tell me your brother was married? I thought about it, but it sounds ridiculous. What if they were both looking on it as a professional friendship?"

"I don't think so, not by what you've told me. Sexual attraction is sexual attraction; you can tell when it's there. Give his sister a try, Naomi. You could begin by asking if his wife is ill. Promise me you'll call her soon?"

Naomi said she'd give it some thought.

Chapter 9

Ben

As he went about the mechanics of making breakfast, Ben tried to analyze his feelings about the upcoming meeting with Naomi. He'd missed her so much last Wednesday and had been thinking about her on and off all week. He knew it was wrong, but he couldn't help himself. Now here it was Wednesday again. How he hoped she would be there. He had left a message when she didn't show last week, but hadn't heard from her. She would surely be there today.

He poured granola in a bowl, spooned on vanilla yogurt and finished up with a fresh fruit topping. The coffee maker was gurgling on the counter. His movements were those of a man used to a routine. His tight living quarters made it necessary to have a place for everything, and everything in its place. After his spacious home, this condo was almost claustrophobic. Still it was only temporary. The question was how temporary?

When he'd moved here he thought it would all be over one way or another in a matter of months. That was almost two years ago. Diana had found the place for him and got him all set up. She had been a tower of strength to him. Maybe he should talk to her about Naomi, she'd help him sort out his feelings. The trouble was, he wasn't supposed to have those feelings. The woman he was supposed to have those feelings for was lying in a hospital bed not a mile away from here.

When he thought of Elaine, sadness engulfed him. His lovely Elaine: friend, lover and wife, now in a world of her own. The only comfort he could derive from the situation was that Elaine wasn't feeling his pain, wasn't feeling her own pain.

Their world had been torn apart suddenly that dreadful night close to two years ago. He was still teaching at the time, and was just finishing up a seminar at the community college in Bend. They had recently finished building their dream home in Central Oregon, on twenty acres between Bend and Sisters. They both loved the high desert country, and had chosen a spot nestled into the foothills of the Cascade Mountains. There, Ben taught and wrote books, while Elaine worked tirelessly for underprivileged children. Her work took her away from home more than either of them liked, but she was dedicated to her cause. She was on her way to Portland to seek funding for a new venture when the accident occurred.

According to the sheriff, a horse trailer rig lost control on the winding approach to Warm Springs. A car swerving to miss it hit Elaine head on. They said she was lucky to survive. Or was she? The wounds had healed long ago, but she still lay in a coma these many months later. The doctors were perplexed, and couldn't offer Ben any hope.

At first, he had hoped. His life was in limbo as he waited for Elaine to wake up. They moved her to a long-term care center close to the hospital, and Ben set up housekeeping close by. But as the months went by, he realized he'd have to create some sort of life for himself. He still needed to earn a living. Although they had wanted children, he now felt relief that they hadn't been able to have them. He had only himself and the ranch to care for. There was nothing more he could do for Elaine, but wait.

His sister Peggy, freshly divorced, was living in the ranch house and taking care of the animals. Oh, how he missed the place—the smell of sagebrush and juniper, the gentle rustling of Ponderosa Pine in the wind, the soft breathing of the llamas as they nuzzled his face, and the companionship of his two dogs, Gertie and Bart. If he thought about it too much, depression could overwhelm him.

He tried to get over there as often as he could, but he was always afraid Elaine would come out of the coma when he wasn't there. The doctors had warned him Elaine might have sustained brain damage. He feared her waking up as much as he hoped for it.

The sexual side of his life had been dormant, until he met Naomi. He wondered if Diana had a motive in having him meet Naomi again. He knew his sister wanted him to begin living again. Had she guessed he would be attracted to Naomi? He wasn't sure what Naomi hoped to get out of it; Diana would have told her about Elaine. Perhaps she just wanted a friend, but he thought he'd detected more than that. He could be her friend, but try as he might, he couldn't get sexual thoughts of her out of his head.

On the way to the coffee shop, Ben decided what he needed to do. They had always talked about their professions, nothing personal. This time he would try to get Naomi talking about personal matters. If she wanted more than friendship, it would probably show. Then he could discuss Elaine with her. He wanted Naomi to know, up front, that he loved his wife. It sounded like a reasonable approach, but a little voice kept telling him, slow down, slow down. He pulled up to the coffee shop with as much confusion as he'd started the day.

Naomi didn't show up. He waited until noon before trying to call her. He got the message machine, but didn't leave a message. His next call was to Diana.

"Hi, it's Ben, I'm here at the coffee shop. Naomi didn't show up this morning. I was wondering if you had heard from her?"

"No, I haven't spoken to her since before her trip. I tried calling the other day, but just got the machine. I should have left a message, but I figured she might still be in Vancouver. How long was she going for?"

"Just a few days, and it's been two weeks or more. Perhaps she didn't like the idea of the authors' club," Ben said apprehensively.

"No, I'm sure that's not it."

"Diana, I'm in a real dilemma here. I know it's not right, but my interest in Naomi is more than professional. I'm so attracted to her; I can't get her out of my mind. She was giving off vibes too, so I don't know what to think."

"This may surprise you, but I don't doubt my intuitions, Ben. You two are made for each other."

"God, I hope you didn't say anything like that to her."

"Of course not. Nature will take its course. Maybe she's struggling with her feelings because of Elaine; feeling wrong about taking it any further."

"What did she say when you told her about Elaine?"

There was a pause on the line before Diana responded. "I didn't tell her, I assumed you would."

"And I thought you had."

"Well, she doesn't know then, so it can't be that. I'll tell you what, I'll call again and leave a message if I have to." Diana said, and then thought better of it. "No, I'll stop by this afternoon. I have to go out anyway. Do you want me to mention Elaine?"

Ben was about to say no, he would handle it, when a customer entering the shop caught his attention. He had a sudden flashback to the last time he saw Naomi: Pastor Hillier had entered the coffee shop as Naomi was leaving. The minister's words rang in his head: "Hello Ben, how's your wife doing?" Naomi had to have heard.

"Oh God, Diana, she already knows," Ben said with concern.

Chapter 10

If Naomi had wanted to hide from Ben, she wouldn't have been able to. She was on her knees in the garden, with edging shears going, and didn't hear him approach. He was already inside the front gate before she caught sight of him. Her stomach was flip-flopping as she struggled to stand up. Ben held out a hand to help her, but she ignored it.

She wasn't sure how to act, but determined not to show any emotion.

"Hello, Ben, what brings you here?"

She noticed his hazel eyes were etched with concern. He seemed to be struggling for words.

"Naomi, I feel I owe you an explanation. I thought Diana had told you about Elaine. I don't want you to have the wrong impression of me." He gestured to the garden bench. "May we sit down?"

She nodded, unsure where this was going and uncomfortable in the extreme, but she would hear him out.

His shoulders sagged with relief as they sat. "Thank you. I feel so bad about this." He held her gaze as he spoke. "I naturally assumed Diana had filled you in on my circumstances. She figured I'd do it myself. I honestly wasn't trying to hide anything. My wife, Elaine, was involved in a car accident almost two years ago. She's still in a coma."

"Oh, I'm so sorry," Naomi, said with sincerity.

His features softened. "It's been hell, waiting and wondering."

"Do the doctor's give you much hope?"

"They really don't know. There was some brain activity initially. The worst part is, if she comes around, they don't rule out brain damage." His eyes filled with tears. "That scares me so."

She nodded her head and reached out to touch his hand. He grasped her hands and held on as he continued.

"I've been living the life of a hermit, as you can imagine. Most of the people I knew growing up here have either moved away, or have their own families."

"You have no children?"

"No, it never happened, I'm not sure why. Anyway, Diana has been concerned about me; that's why she got us together. Meeting you was so… so…" His words trailed off and he was quiet for a minute, dropping his eyes to gaze at their hands. "God, this is so difficult."

Naomi wanted to help him but didn't know how. She sat quietly waiting.

Ben looked at her intently as he continued. "Maybe this conversation is premature, Naomi. Maybe you just want a friend. I want to be your friend, but I can't hide from you how much I'm attracted to you. I know it's not right, but I can't help myself." His grip tightened. "Just say the word and I'll leave you alone, I promise."

She looked deep into his eyes and knew she was about to enter uncharted territory. If she accepted him, the future could hold immense heartache—there was no way of knowing. But if she rejected him, she may regret it for the rest of her life. She was struggling for words, but he needed none. Ben read in her eyes all he wanted to know. He cupped her face in his hands, intending to say more, but passion overwhelmed them. Their lips met, at first tentatively, then with an urgency that left them breathless. They repeated the kiss several times, and then sat holding each other for what seemed like an eternity.

Ben broke the silence. "Naomi, I have nothing to offer you."

"I know," she countered. "I'm not sure what we're doing either, but I'm willing to take it one day at a time. No commitments, I understand that. I just know that we both need each other at this moment." She pulled back from him. "I haven't felt this way in a long time. Can we take it slowly?"

He nodded. "We both need time to think. Perhaps we'd better meet in public places until our hormones settle down."

She laughed. "My sister Louise would love that."

"You have a sister? See I hardly know a thing about you. Let's talk about you—it's better than lifting car bumpers."

They both laughed, and then sat holding hands as she told him about her family, starting with Louise, Sam and the boys.

"I can tell you're very fond of them. Where do they live?"

"That's the bad part; they're over in Redmond. I don't get to see them nearly enough."

"Redmond, that's great!" Ben was excited. "My real home is just outside Sisters; the condo is just to keep me near the hospital. Gosh, my ranch is only 20 minutes away from your sister's. You'll love it. I have horses and llamas, and my two dogs, Gertie and Bart." He stopped himself, his expression clouding. "How can we talk about the future?"

"We can't, Ben. We just have to take it day by day."

"We'll become friends first."

"We'll become friends first," Naomi repeated and then at his urging, told him about Kevin and the divorce. She blamed herself, she said, for letting her work come between them. He was a good man, and she found it hard to be angry towards him. She admitted though, that with her mother's illness coming so soon after the divorce, she'd hardly had time to deal with her emotions. What she mostly felt for him now was tenderness.

"That may seem funny since he cheated on me, but he was probably craving everything I wasn't giving him. I haven't seen him since the divorce," she explained.

"How long were you married?"

"Eleven years."

"Elaine and I are coming up on fourteen. Did you choose not to have children?"

"No, I would love to have a baby. It just didn't happen for us either. I was planning to go to a fertility clinic when I finished the book."

At some point in their conversation, Spike came sniffing around their feet. He jumped onto Naomi's lap, then gingerly made his way onto Ben's. Naomi was pleased to see Ben liked cats. She already knew he loved his dogs.

He asked about her mother and how she died. Naomi told him the events of the past year, and about Spruce Creek and the rest of the family. It was a grim picture she painted of her hometown. Ben hadn't been there, but he did know and like Powell River.

"Yes, Powell River is nice," she agreed. "I was actually born in the hospital there. We left Spruce Creek when I was four. My grandmother died, so we were able to join my dad in Oregon."

"Is your dad American?"

"No, he was born in Czechoslovakia and emigrated to Canada. My real surname is so hard to pronounce, that I took my mother's maiden name, Cavenish, for a pen name. Dad was a logger," she continued. "Friends from the old country talked him into coming here to log; wages were higher. They needed to be. Both he and my granddad were killed in logging accidents."

"That's tough. It's a shame you didn't spend more time living with your dad. It must have been hard for your folks separated like that. Was your mum the only one who could look after your grandma?"

"She was the last one left at home. Everyone else had married or moved away. Gran was already disabled when my parents met, so Mum couldn't leave her."

"It was a little like that for Diana," he explained. "My other sister, Peggy, was married with a child, and Elaine and I were teaching in Seattle. When the folks got sick, Diana took over their care. She never did marry. I think she likes horses more than men. That's why the folks left her the farm."

"Were your parents farmers?"

"No, my grandparents were. Dad was a gentleman farmer—actually an engineer, and mother was a school teacher; middle school."

"So you grew up in Walkersville?"

"Yes, it was a different place then. When the freeway went through town, it changed things forever. The population was under a thousand when I was a boy. The down side was everybody in town knew you, so you had better behave. It was a real challenge trying to pull off teenage pranks without getting caught."

Naomi smiled and tried to imagine him a teenager.

Ben turned the subject back to Naomi's youth. "How old were you when your dad died?"

"Seven."

"Did you visit Spruce Creek much after moving here?"

"No, it seemed like Gran was the only thing holding the family together." Then she told him about the family mystery, Gran's death, the supposed inheritance and her aunt's disappearance. He listened with interest, interrupting only once—to ask if she believed someone hastened her grandmother's death for the money.

"I'd like to think not, but everything points to it."

"Were they a dysfunctional family? I mean was there animosity between siblings?"

"Not particularly. Aunt Edna couldn't get along with anyone for long. My mother was the only one to tolerate her. They weren't a close family. I think being so poor took a lot of the joy out of their lives. My mother and Aunt Kath couldn't wait to get away from there, which was the goal of every young person growing up there. Working for the logging company was their only option if they stayed. Aunt Edna and Aunt Violet made their escape soon after Gran died," Naomi explained.

"And your mother never did tell you who she suspected?"

"No. She seemed to carry a tremendous amount of guilt for not being there when Gran died, as if she could have prevented it somehow." Naomi sighed, "Louise thinks I should just leave it alone. Although she is curious about the inheritance."

"She may have something there. It's not like you're going to accomplish anything at this late date. You may uncover something you're better off not knowing."

"I know."

She didn't sound very convinced. Ben studied her face. He smiled in understanding. "It's an unfinished story, isn't it? I can see why you won't let go of it. You want to write the ending."

"This may sound funny, but I feel compelled to solve it. Almost like I was being guided by a force somewhere." A worried expression crossed her face. "Do you think I'm nuts?"

"Not at all." He looked into her deep blue eyes and stroked the side of her face. " If I can help, just let me know. Although it sounds as though Louise has made a start."

"Yes, she's trying to track down Aunt Edna now. We think she went back to England, and there's a chance she's still living. Louise will go at it with her usual gusto."

He gave a warm smile. "I'd like to meet Louise, but under the circumstances I suppose it's not possible?'

"She knows about your being married. Now I'll have to let her know you're not the cad I thought you were," Naomi joked. "I'd like you to meet her too. She's the only family I have. If dad hadn't died so young, they may have had other children."

"I'm surprised your mother didn't marry again. She was still young."

"She just devoted herself to getting us away from anything to do with lumber. She'd lost a husband and father to the industry. Along with the sorrow, it gave her the strength to make changes."

"You said she ended up working for the government."

"Yes, we moved to Salem and she used the settlement she got from the logging company to do a crash course at a business school. Once we were older, she took night classes and eventually ended up managing a fish and wildlife office. She owned her own home and put us girls through college. Quite an accomplishment, but it didn't leave much room for a man in her life."

"Was she happy?"

"Hard to say really. I think she was, but there was an underlying sadness that she never let escape." Naomi's voice itself was sad and her eyes filled with tears. "She never shared what was going on inside her, not even at the end. I wish she had."

Ben took her in his arms again and cradled her. They stayed that way for some time. There was no need for words. What was happening between them took place in total silence. Naomi had never felt so protected, so at peace. I could, she thought, fall so much in love with this man. The thought made her tingle with fear. Ben felt her shudder and held her even more tightly.

Chapter 11

May

Watching her daughters tumble and play on the lawn caused May to laugh with delight. The girls were such a tonic to her: four-year-old Louise, so confident, and two-year-old Naomi, who mimicked her sister's every move. Sitting outside like this, May could almost forget the responsibilities that lay within. Who would have thought she'd still be here five years after her marriage? Certainly not Conrad. When he'd taken the job in Oregon, they assumed they'd only be apart for a short while. Her mother's health had seemed so fragile; the whole family had expected to lose her any day. She rallied that time, but had slowly declined over the past few years. Now she was bedridden. Caring for her had become a heavy burden.

At times, May was consumed with guilt knowing she was just waiting for her mother to die. She longed, ached to be with her husband. They loved each other so much. And the girls needed their Daddy, not just once a month, but every day. Conrad was such a good father; full of Old World ideals. He was especially attached to Louise, now she was old enough to take fishing or hike in the woods. It wasn't fair to deny him the experience of watching the girls grow up. But what was she to do? They had talked about it, and Conrad was very understanding. In Europe, he told her, we would never abandon our parents. He fully supported May taking care of her mother. It was just that no one expected it to be this long.

Her brother Bill wanted to put their mother in a home, but she couldn't do it. Her sisters, Kath and Violet, hadn't offered an opinion, but she suspected they felt the same way. They helped May when they could. Kath was only home for an occasional weekend, and Violet's freedom was at the whim of her husband. Still, the moral support helped. Bill helped out with money—mainly paying the district nurse to make extra visits. Her other sister, Edna, was still in London.

May was brought out of her reverie by her neighbor, Mrs. Dukes.

"Here's your mail, May. It looks like a letter from New Zealand; that will be Mamie, I expect."

May thanked her. With no mail delivery, it was helpful having someone pick it up for her, but she did find it rather like living in a fishbowl. Knowing Mrs. Dukes, May had a feeling most of Spruce Creek already knew she had a letter from Mamie.

The girls had rushed over to see Granny Dukes, as they called her. Louise had to show her how strong she was now by picking up a struggling Naomi. She was only persuaded to put her down at the mention of candy, which Granny Dukes pulled from her pocket.

"Here, Naomi, let Mummy open it for you," May instructed her child.

"I can do it, I can do it for her, Mummy," Louise insisted.

May acquiesced. No sense arguing with Louise, the child felt she knew everything. She was strong-willed, like her father.

Mrs. Dukes laughed. Nodding to the house, she asked, "How is she this morning, May?"

May shook her head. "She doesn't feel too well today. Her legs are playing her up. I've just finished massaging them, trying to get some circulation going."

Mrs. Dukes patted May's hand. "You're a good daughter, May."

May watched her neighbor hobble from view. Yes, I'm a good daughter, she thought, but I want to be a good wife and mother too. How am I going to do this?

May had seen to her mother's needs and put the girls down for a nap before she had time to read Mamie's letter. It always cheered her up to hear from her friend, though the letters were infrequent. This time her friend's news wasn't good. She was divorcing her husband, and most of the pages dealt with that situation. She didn't sound like the scatter-brained girl May remembered. The one who got her all excited about an inheritance. Life would certainly have been different if it had come to pass. It sounded feasible at the time. May stared out the window, remembering the excitement of that day.

They had been walking on the beach in Powell River when Mamie dropped the bombshell. It was one of those rare days in British Columbia when the sun actually felt hot. It was approaching sunset and they still felt warm enough not to need a jacket. They'd both kicked off their shoes and were wading around on the pebble beach, the waters of the Strait of Georgia lapping at their feet. They presented an amusing sight from the rear: penciled stocking seams on bare legs, ending at the shoe line. The war was over, but hosiery was still a luxury item these lumberjacks' daughters could ill afford.

They had ridden over to Powell River that morning on transportation provided by Spruce Creek Logging. Just to get away from Spruce Creek was a treat. The girls would be the first to tell you it was a very depressing place to live. The war years were especially bad, with so many of the young men away. Now they were back and, after the euphoria wore off, it was obvious life would return to the way it was: small town life where everyone knew his or her neighbor's business.

For years now May and Mamie had talked about leaving Spruce Creek. They weren't sure how it would happen, only that it had to. It was 1947; they were both 22 and felt that life was passing them by. They had been talking lately about getting jobs as nannies in Vancouver. May's oldest sister, Edna, had done that and the family had ended up taking her to London with them—in fact, she was still there. They didn't want to go anywhere like London; leaving their families would be too hard. But Vancouver wasn't far away. They both hated their jobs: May waiting tables in the café and Mamie a file clerk at Spruce Creek Logging. They had talked and talked about moving, but now Mamie was in love.

"Oh, May, he's so dreamy. He's walked me home from work twice now and he always sits with me in the cafe. He's definitely interested. Oh I hope he asks me out soon," her friend finished with a huge sigh.

"He" was Ray Hillman, a new employee at the logging company. Not exactly what May thought of as dreamy, but to satisfy her friend, she agreed.

"I expect he will ask you out, Mamie," May sounded wistful, "He doesn't want to appear too forward, what with your father and brothers working there."

May was secretly envious of her friend. No one was showing an interest in her, well, no one she'd be interested in. She wasn't sure why; she was more attractive than Mamie by a long shot. May had the boyish, pencil-slim build characteristic to all the Cavenish girls. She was fair-haired and fair-skinned, with fine features and blue eyes tinged with hazel. She thought when all the young men came back after the war there would surely be someone she liked. So far, she hadn't found him. That's why she was looking forward to moving to Vancouver, or maybe Victoria. Anywhere but Spruce Creek. Now with Ray Hillman on the scene, Mamie was losing interest in the idea. May didn't think she had the nerve to go alone. Besides, she would miss her friend.

Mamie was still babbling about Ray Hillman. "If he does ask me out, May, it would be great if we could double-date. Isn't there anyone you fancy? What about Frank McLeod, he's not all pimply since he got back from the war.

"Yuk, Mamie, he's got terrible teeth." May sighed, "There's no one in Spruce Creek for me. I suppose Vancouver is out now, if you're in love. I wish I could get a job here; Powell River has more men to choose from."

"I expect you could if you tried. There are more cafes here."

"Oh, there's no way I'd work in a café," May said with authority. "I'd get an office job like you did."

"It's not as nice as you think it is, May, I'm bored most of the time. They don't trust me to do much more than file papers."

May didn't say so, but she had a good idea why that was. As fond as she was of her friend, she also knew her limitations. What Mamie said next was a good example of why her employers shouldn't trust her.

By now the girls had made their way to the north end of Willingdon Beach and were sat leaning against a massive driftwood log. The bright colors and stark lines of their clothing—juxtaposed on the bleached and sculpted wood—projected an image of a canvas created by two artists of differing styles. Behind them, a grove of cedar spilled over onto the beach. They loved to walk along a trail in the trees, until it petered out in Townsite: the original site of Powell River. They rarely saw anyone on the trail. Even so, Mamie looked around carefully before she spoke.

"May, I saw something at work the other day. I've been thinking about whether I should tell you or not. I shouldn't really tell you, but it's about your mum." She leveled an intense look at her friend. " If I do tell you, will you promise not to say a word to anyone? Not even your mum, or I'd get fired."

May promised she's keep it to herself, though she couldn't imagine what "it" was going to be.

Mamie spoke in hushed tones, "Mrs. Stewart gave me a file to put away the other day, and then she needed it back, but I couldn't find it. Anyway, she was called to a meeting in the conference room. I suddenly thought, maybe I got it mixed in with some files Mrs. Stewart took in to the boss. I'm not supposed to go in his office, but the coast was clear so I went in to look."

She paused to look around again before continuing. "There was an envelope on his desk marked confidential. Someone had penciled Cavenish on it, and I couldn't resist looking."

"Mamie, you didn't?"

Mamie saw the look of horror on May's face and explained quickly, "It was open. All I did was look. There was a letter from some barrister in England—said he represented His Majesty's Government something-or-other department. He was asking if they knew the whereabouts of your dad. Then something about a lawsuit with a sizable estate involved."

She looked at May wide-eyed, waiting for a response.

May was all ears. "Didn't they know he's dead?"

"Apparently not. There was a letter there for Mr. Scott to sign; he was writing to tell them about your dad's accident. Then he gave them your mum's name and address." She stopped to catch her breath, and then asked excitedly, " What do you think sizeable estate means, May? It sounds like a lot of money to me. Ooh, wouldn't it be wonderful if your mum were rich. She'd be the next of kin, wouldn't she?"

May was speechless. She couldn't imagine what it was all about. As far as she knew, her dad's family had been poor. Both his parents had died fairly young—before she was born. Her dad was an only child, so that would make him the heir, that's for sure. She didn't know much about his family, only that his parents emigrated to Canada right after they married. They came from England, or maybe it was Scotland. May wasn't sure. What she was sure of was that it all sounded too good to be true, and she wanted to know more.

"The letter must have said something more; like what the lawsuit was about, who was suing who? That sort of thing, Mamie, can you remember?"

Mamie didn't know any more. "Honestly, May, I've told you everything I can remember. There wasn't anything else in the envelope."

May, deep in thought said, "I wonder if my mum knows about it?"

"Oh May, you promised you wouldn't say anything, not even to your mum. I would get fired if Mr. Scott found out, and then I wouldn't see Ray. I couldn't bear it," the lovesick Mamie moaned.

"I wouldn't tell her outright," May reassured her friend, "but if I hinted around maybe she would tell me. That's if she does know something."

"If she knew she would have said something before. You're close to your mum. They'll probably write to her from England as soon as they get Mr. Scott's letter. She'll tell you, you see. It's so exciting, I can hardly wait."

Then Mamie was back to speculating what wealth would feel like, and how she wished it were happening to her. Ray Hillman would show an interest then, you bet he would.

May wasn't listening to her friend's chatter. She was still undecided what to make of it. On the one hand, she wanted to believe it, but Mamie wasn't always credible. Still, she wouldn't have made the whole thing up. May decided she'd wait, watching the mail to see what turned up.

Thinking back on that day at the beach brought a wry smile to May's face. It had lent a little excitement to her life for a few weeks. She folded Mamie's letter and put it away. Louise and Naomi were still sleeping, so she went back outside to enjoy the pleasant day. She walked around her clapboard-sided house to the apple tree in the yard. May stood leaning against the truck. How many times had she hurried past the tree on her way to look for the inheritance letter? Her memory was so clear it seemed like only yesterday. Leaving Spruce Creek had been uppermost in her mind back then too.

Every day she had the same routine: in the back door, through the undressing room off the kitchen. All the homes had one. Here the men, returning from the forest dripping wet, would leave their rubber fishermen's outfits or other foul weather gear; their Swede saw and axe. The room was devoid of lumberjack's gear even then, with her father dead and no sons at home.

May couldn't be sure her mother would tell her if she got the letter; she was a bit funny that way. She'd look around the house for signs of a letter, closely if her mother wasn't there, subtly if she was. It was a small house with few hiding places. She was confident of finding the letter, if it existed.

She remembered the day she finally took her sister Kath into her confidence. Her mother was out, probably next door at Mrs. Dukes. May walked through the kitchen—smelling of last night's cabbage dinner—to the living room. A quick sweep of the living room convinced her there was still no letter.

Days had turned into weeks and weeks into months since her talk with Mamie. To be sure, May was sometimes at work when her mother picked up the mail. Knowing her mother, it wouldn't be left lying around. Sometimes the temptation to tell her mother would almost overwhelm her. What kept her from doing it was the knowledge that her mother couldn't keep a secret. She'd tell her friend, Mrs. Dukes, then word would spread around the small community faster than prairie grass afire. Mamie would lose her job, just as she and Ray Hillman were becoming an item.

It was Mamie's romance that occupied May's thoughts these days. Since her friend began dating, she'd seen so little of her. She saw now it was a mistake to devote herself exclusively to one friendship. There were no other girls Naomi really liked in high school. When she looked at them now, she saw why. Many of them, already married, would slouch into the café, dragging a neglected child. If you turned the clock back a few years, the mothers themselves were neglected children. Nothing changes; May thought sadly, even the war couldn't break the cycle of despair that was Spruce Creek. And she vowed again to find a way out of there.

One good thing to come out of her diminishing friendship with Mamie was May's getting closer to her sister Kath—Kathleen. Just two years apart in age, the two had been practically inseparable during their early years. Kath had always been May's favorite sister. They had drifted apart during the last years of the war, when Kath left for Vancouver and work in the shipyards. Now she was home again, and it felt good to have her there. The house was so quiet these days, compared to how it used to be.

The war had changed everything. They became a houseful of women almost overnight. Her father had been dead since May was ten. She well remembered the day it happened, and the steam donkey, off in the distance, gave a series of short, urgent blasts. This was the signal to stop work because of an accident. All the wives made their way to the company office, waiting to see which family would grieve. That was the first time the Cavenish family grieved, but not the last.

May's older brother, Frank, signed up for World War II at the earliest opportunity. She adored this brother, and remembered sobbing openly when he left. He was an early casualty: the only one from Spruce Creek. The logging company put up a small memorial to him. May still couldn't look at it without tearing up.

Bill, her younger brother, had left for the war soon after Frank. May hated to see him go, though she wasn't as close to him. Bill was so serious, sometimes to the point of being dour. He'd never bothered with girls, so the family was surprised when he came back from the war with a bride in tow. Kath and May liked their new sister-in-law Gwen, with her soft Welsh brogue. But Bill wasn't apt to spend much time with the family.

Violet had already left home to marry Ralph Braun. Poor Violet, so pretty, yet so shy, she hadn't stood a chance against Ralph's advances. He had her at the altar before she knew what hit her. She tried to hide it from the family, but they all knew she regretted it.

That left just Kath at home with May and her mother. Kath, at 24, was still unmarried. She'd had a romance or two while working at the shipyards but nothing serious. She was a sweet-natured girl, and knew what she wanted: something or someone to take her away from Spruce Creek. For the time being, she seemed content to live at home. May needed the company and their mother was still grieving for Frank.

Kath was home alone the day May took her into her confidence. Finishing her letter search downstairs, May heard sounds from above. She called up the stairwell in the corner of the living room.

"Is that you, Kath?"

"Yes, come on up May, I've got something to tell you."

May climbed the stairs. At the top was a pocket sized landing. Straight ahead was her mother's room, the largest of the three. May's room was accessed through her mother's, and was a little smaller. Off to the left, the room Kath occupied had been her brother's. Standing with arms outstretched, the boys had been able to touch both walls. May had offered to let Kath share her room, but her sister had refused, saying she might not be around for long. May hoped that wasn't true.

Kath looked uneasy. "May, I got some news today. I didn't tell you before, because I didn't think anything would come of it. I've got a new job."

"That's great. Where is it?"

"That's just it—it's in Campbell River."

"Campbell River! You're going to work on the island?"

"I'll be able to come home occasionally; they'll even pay the ferry for me."

"Who are they?"

"Their name's Barnett. I answered an ad. He has to travel around the island with his job and only gets home weekends. Mrs. Barnett is sick and needs help with their two children. It sounds as though they've got plenty of money. The pay was so good; I couldn't resist applying. I really didn't think I'd get it."

May gave her sister a crestfallen look. "I know I should be happy for you, Kath, but I'm going to miss you. I'd just got used to having you here again."

"I know, but you're at work most of the week. I'll try to get home as often as I can," she assured her sister.

May was crestfallen, but tried to hide it as they talked about Kath's job. They also talked a little about May's aspirations, before tackling the subject of their mother's declining health. With talk of their mother, May chose to confide in Kath. She didn't set out to divulge everything, just to find out more about her grandparents.

"Kath, do you know much about our granddad Cavenish; where he came from?"

"Somewhere in England. I'm not sure what part, but that's where he met Grandma."

"So you don't know where the Cavenish family originated?"

"Oh, it's a Scots name. I think that's where they originally came from."

"Do you know if they had any kind of business?"

"Something to do with coal, I thought," Kath looked up from the hose she was darning." Why, what's up?"

"Did they have much money, do you think?"

"Well if they did they sure could have spread it around. Grandma and Granddad had a real hard time of it when they first came to Canada. That's what Mum told me. Why don't you ask her?"

May realized she was on the spot and she wasn't sure how to respond. If she couldn't trust Kath, who could she trust? It looked as though Mamie and Ray would soon get married. Ray had been talking about moving to New Zealand, so what harm would it do. Besides, Kath could keep a secret. She extracted a promise from Kath that she wouldn't, for the time being, repeat what she was about to hear. Then Naomi plunged right into Mamie's story.

"Jeepers," Kath let out a long breath," that girl will get herself into trouble one of these days." She sat stabbing her darning needle into her work, pondering what she'd heard. "She said the letter was from the government in England, not Victoria?"

"Yes, England. Why?"

"Well, Mum did get something from the government awhile back. It came from Victoria, though. She said it was to do with Dad's death. It seems he was due some government money because he died of a work-related accident. It had been overlooked before."

"Do you suppose Mamie got it mixed up?"

"It's likely that it started out in England, then was funneled through Victoria. I don't know where she got sizeable estate from. That Mamie, there's not a lot she does get right."

"I'm going to wring her neck for getting me all excited about nothing," May said with disgust. She thought better of it. "Oh, no, I can't, then she'd know I told you. Did they say how much Mum was going to get? Was it sizeable?"

"Oh, yes, enormous. We spent all of five minutes discussing how she'd spend it. We came up with a new kettle, some blankets and a waffle iron."

"That's all?" May asked incredulously.

"That's about all you can get with 36 dollars and 49 cents."

Both girls dissolved in laughter.

The sun went behind a cloud, getting May's attention. She shifted her weight on the tree trunk. The girls would wake up soon, and her mother would need attention. Time to stop thinking about the past. It had always intrigued her though, this thing with Mamie. Her friend may have got the details wrong, but she couldn't see her making the whole thing up. After thinking about it, May decided the small check from Victoria was not connected with the inheritance. If the long-awaited letter materialized, May never saw it. She would think about it from time to time. If there was anything to it, maybe it was settled in England years ago, and they forgot to inform her mother. She knew her mother didn't know about it. May dropped a few hints once, and it was obvious her mother hadn't a clue what she was talking about.

She stood at the backdoor looking up at the clouds, with a dreamy look on her face. Those clouds would soon be in Oregon, passing over her Conrad. One day, perhaps soon, they would be living there as a family.

Chapter 12

Naomi was sleeping so deeply she didn't hear the radio when it switched on, but Spike did. He crawled up to her face, gave a purr and let his cold nose brush her cheek. With her eyes still closed, she reached for him and hugged him.

"What a good cat," she crooned to him. "Yes, you're right, it's time to get up."

But she still lay there, eyes closed. Suddenly, events of yesterday flooded her consciousness and she broke out in a Cheshire cat smile. Thoughts of Ben filled her with a warm glow. They had talked more yesterday, and found they had so much in common. They both loved the outdoors and were concerned about the environment; they both preferred cross-country skiing to downhill; they both loved running on wet sand; and they both had a weakness for rhubarb pie. Naomi basked in her contentment. It felt so good waking, knowing there was someone out there feeling this way about her. As if privy to her thoughts, the telephone rang and Ben's mellow voice came over the wire.

"Hi, I think I forgot to tell you how beautiful you are."

Naomi chuckled. "You wouldn't think so if you saw me now."

"I can see you now, all I have to do is close my eyes. I keep trying to get you out of my thoughts, but you won't go away. How am I supposed to get my work done?"

"How about me? I'll probably start writing *you* into my novel."

They continued talking in a light-hearted manner. Yesterday they'd agreed all they could do was to take one day at a time, enjoy what time they had together and not focus on the future. It was easier said than done. When she hung up the phone, Naomi began thinking about the possible scenarios. It scared her so much, she hopped out of bed and began her day in a routine fashion: let Spike out, make and eat her wheat farina, let Spike in and feed him, put the kettle on, bring in the newspaper and settle down with her tea and the day's news. Better to focus on the problems of the world for a while; it was still too early to call Louise.

She had tried to reach her sister yesterday, but wasn't able to. What would she think of the situation? Louise, for all her flightiness, had a good head on her shoulders. A talk with her sister was what Naomi needed right now. Then, perhaps, she should speak to Diana. Ben confirmed that his sister wanted them to like each other. Naomi hoped Louise would be able to give her support, and somehow calm her fears.

At eight, she could wait no longer. The boys and Sam would have left for school and work, respectively. Louise knew in an instant something was wrong. Naomi poured out the previous day's developments. She gave her sister a moment or two to absorb it before asking, "What do you think?"

"Wow! It sounds like a novel or soap opera, sis. I can hardly believe it's happening to you. What a tragedy for Ben. Imagine carrying that weight around for two years. How stable is his emotional state? That's what worries me."

"How do you mean, Louise?"

"Well, you probably don't want to hear this, Naomi, but you need to. What I mean is: Is he just reaching out for comfort, without taking your feelings into consideration. How can you be sure he isn't just using you, without realizing it himself?"

Naomi's response was swift. "I'm sure, Lou. You should have seen how troubled he was over it, how he struggled to explain it to me. I have to trust my instincts, and they're telling me he's a good man."

"Okay. Let's hope your instincts don't let you down. What a bugger that he wasn't single or divorced. I'd like to say don't fall for him too hard, but it's a bit late for that, I suppose."

"Yes, but we did agree to take it slowly, try to keep it more a close friendship at this point."

"That's good. I know I was the one telling you to hop into bed with him, but under the circumstances that wouldn't be wise. How are you going to handle it?"

Naomi laughed. "We agreed to meet in public places, to help keep the hormones in check."

"Do you think you can stick to it?"

"I hope so, though it won't be easy. God, he's attractive, Louise."

"I want to meet him. Do you think that will be okay?"

"He said he wants to meet you, so we'll have to arrange it."

They talked more about a possible meeting, before Louise turned serious again.

"Sis, have you given much thought to what would happen if his wife comes out of the coma?"

"Yes," Naomi said softly.

"It could break your heart."

"I know, Louise, but what else can I do?" Naomi asked plaintively.

"Putting myself in your place, I'd probably do just what you're doing. I'm a great believer in fate: you two were meant to meet each other. Whatever happens in the future, if he cares for you as much as you do for him, he'll treat you kindly," she assured her sister. " So, I guess, just grab as much happiness as you can now."

"Should I feel guilty because of his wife?"

"Not under the circumstances. Look, his sister was largely responsible for all this. If she hadn't felt right about it, she wouldn't have done it. You should call her, by the way. You can only put your life on hold for so long. She wants Ben to start living again, and I imagine most people who know him feel the same. Trust your instincts, sis, and bring him over soon."

Naomi felt better after talking to her sister. It was an odd situation she found herself in. After the past year, a little normalcy would have been nice. What would her mother have thought? At times like this, she missed her. Yet, strange as it seemed, she was glad her mother wouldn't be shouldering this worry—because worry she would.

Louise had said call Diana, and she knew she must. Ben's sister would appreciate hearing from her. Naomi picked up Spike and a portable phone, and headed for the living room window seat. The house was always cool in the mornings, but she'd noticed a patch of sun warming the cushions. Curled up with Spike on her lap, she put through the call to Diana.

"Diana, hi, it's Naomi."

"I was wondering if I'd hear from you. I was going to give you until tonight, and then call you."

She had a heart-warming conversation with Ben's sister. Diana wasn't surprised at the turn in her relationship with Ben. She claimed to have insight into such things. He had told her how he felt about Naomi, and she had given him her blessing. It was time he wrenched a little happiness out of life, she said. She asked Naomi to forgive her for getting her involved in a difficult situation. Diana agreed all they could do was take it one day at a time. She didn't have much hope that Elaine would recover, but she wanted to be sure Naomi knew one thing.

"I love my sister-in-law, Naomi. If—against all odds—she should recover, I would have to give her my support. I'm not sure where that leaves you, because I care a lot for you too." She paused, unsure how to continue.

"Diana," Naomi said earnestly, "I understand, really I do. We'll cross that bridge when and if we come to it. I just needed to know if you approved of what's happened, and you've satisfied me on that score. Thank you."

She sat for a long time after the call, trying to make sense of what was happening in her life. There were no easy answers. To hope for a future with Ben would be tantamount to wishing Elaine dead, and she couldn't think that way. Taking it one day at a time was going to be harder than she thought.

Louise called again later in the day.

"Naomi, I just checked my e-mail and Pat in England had found Aunt Edna, then lost her again."

"How could she do that?"

"She didn't give me all the details, but she's pretty sure it's our Edna. There were a few addresses, ending up in Kensington where she vanished without a trace."

"Kensington! That's a pretty ritzy neighborhood for our Edna. Your friend really thinks it's the right one?"

"She was sure up to that point, but the thing is, she vanished in 1961. That was before Gran died, and there's no trace of her since. She would have been eligible for a pension over there, but Pat says she's never claimed one. I'm beginning to think she didn't go back to England. Perhaps we should try Canada. Maybe she never left."

"Well there's a thought. We could see if she's ever had a Canadian pension. I suppose she could have moved over to Toronto or Montreal; she seemed to like the city."

"Of course, but if she ever married, we wouldn't know what name to look under."

"Oh, let's hope she didn't," Naomi said, "Shall I start looking in Canada? I had a good bit of luck with the government when I researched my book. I don't suppose they would give out her number or whereabouts, but they might tell me if she had claimed a pension."

"Okay, see what you can do. Pat in England is going to work more on the Cavenish estate now. I'll let you know if she finds anything. By the way, have you heard back from cousin Michael about a reunion?"

"No, nothing yet. I expect he's waiting to hear when Susan is coming back. It would be much more fun with both our cousins. If we find out anything about the Cavenish estate, do you think we should tell them?"

"It depends on what we hear. I tend to think if Gran did inherit something, Uncle Bill would have been privy to it, being the only son. If that were the case, why wouldn't Michael have said something? It's his father, after all."

"I suppose we should just wait until we know more. Well, I'll get busy on Aunt Edna, but first I've got to get some writing done. Hug my favorite nephews for me."

It was hard to concentrate on the book, what with Ben and all the family stuff running around in her head. The only consolation, she thought, was that her next book should be easier if she incorporated her family's mystery into it. She fidgeted in her small office chair and vowed to get a new one soon—one without a space between the seat and backrest. She'd been reading up on Feng Shui and that was apparently what she needed for success. Also, her desk really should be reversed. It faced a window, with the door behind her: bad karma. Not wanting to lose her view of the sky and clouds—the window was high—she'd hung a mirror in front of her. It gave a good reflection of the door, and Naomi hoped this would suffice. The desk was an old oak one that weighed a ton. It wasn't suited to computers, but she was so attracted to the lovely old grain of the wood and the solidness of it that she couldn't bear to part with it.

She loved her office. It had been the breakfast nook in the old home. Naomi had lined the walls with bookcases, leaving just enough room for her desk and chair. There was an opening to the kitchen on the left, and behind her, the doorway to the dining area and living room. They had knocked those two areas into one while Kevin still lived there, and built a small sunroom off the end. Naomi spent most of her time in her office or the sunroom—except in winter, when she and Spike took up residence in front of the living room fireplace.

The house had been built in the 1920s, and they'd uncovered the original wood siding and restored the brick chimney. Naomi had come up with a color scheme for the outside, but Kevin had left before getting to it. She'd get to it someday, but somehow her heart wasn't in it now.

Finally able to concentrate on her manuscript, she worked right through the dinner hour, pausing only when light began to fail her. Once away from her desk she realized how hungry she was. She was busy in the kitchen concocting a meal, when she was startled to hear the doorbell ring. Rarely did anyone call on her in the evening. She was far enough out of town to be off the canvasser's circuit. She wondered briefly if it would be Diana, and then hoped, though not without trepidation, that it would be Ben. Her heart was beating wildly as she looked through the peephole in her door. When she saw who stood there, her breathing almost stopped. It was Kevin.

He looked uncomfortable, as though he didn't know how to greet her. Was he supposed to hug her or just shake her hand? He did neither, perhaps waiting for a sign from her.

"Hi Naomi, sorry to just show up out of the blue. There's something I need to talk to you about. Can you spare me a few minutes?"

"Sure," she sounded so calm, but felt anything but. "Come on in, I was just fixing some dinner."

He followed her to the kitchen, noting the computer on. "How's the book coming?"

"I'm seeing a light at the end of the tunnel, and they like what they've seen so far. Mum's death really put me behind though."

"I'm sure it did. About the funeral Naomi, I really wanted to be there but we were away. I only found out when we got back."

She had always wondered why, and been hurt that he hadn't attended the funeral. Her mother had been his mother too for a number of years. This explained it she thought, but they could have had this conversation before now. She wondered why he'd chosen this time to bring it up. But that wasn't what brought him here.

He looked uncomfortable as he continued. "I wanted to be the one to tell you Star and I are getting married."

Star, her name was Star! "Well, it's not once bitten twice shy with you, is it? I suppose this is where I'm supposed to say I hope you'll be happy," Naomi said, sarcasm dripping from her voice.

"I'm sorry, Naomi, I didn't plan for any of this to happen you know."

"I know, I know," she composed herself, "neither did I, Kevin. I really do wish you happiness. God knows you tried to make me happy." She smiled at him. "So when's the wedding?"

"Well, that's the other thing I wanted to tell you, before someone else did. It's going to be soon, next week in fact." He paused, searching for words, then blurted out, "Star's pregnant."

Naomi felt as though a soccer ball had been kicked in her chest. She almost gasped for air, but felt his eyes on her. All those years of marriage and not once was she pregnant, although they'd hoped she would be. They'd even talked of going to a fertility clinic after she finished the book. Now here was Kevin telling her he'd fathered a child. Oh, my God, she thought frantically, that means I'm sterile.

Kevin must have read her thoughts. He reached out to her and she let him take her in his arms. He hugged her and stroked her hair. "I'm sorry Naomi, I'm really sorry. You see why I came. I couldn't bear for you to get the news at the store or on the street." He gave her a little time, and then asked, " Are you all right?"

She nodded and fighting back tears pulled away from him. "I need a cup of tea," she almost whispered.

"I'll make you one."

How quickly they slipped back into their old routine of Kevin taking care of her. They sat quietly while she drank her tea. Spike had come in and showed no surprise at finding Kevin there. Kevin fondled him as he waited for a sign that Naomi was ready to continue their conversation.

She sat deep in thought, sipping her tea and trying to come to grips with what she'd just heard. It had always been her belief that the infertility problem was Kevin's. She didn't know why, but it never occurred to her that it was hers. At 36, she knew the clock was ticking, but she felt all along that she would have a child one day. Now what he was telling her made her confront the truth: she was never going to have that child.

Her thoughts turned to Ben. If he were free to marry her, would he want a child? He was 42 now. And then she remembered he and Elaine hadn't been able to have any. Was he infertile or was it Elaine? Did it really matter?

And then she confronted her own truth. What kind of a mother would I be anyway? Look, I couldn't even make room for Kevin in my life, how could I raise a child? As much as I love my nephews, I never envied Louise the feedings and diapers. Young children delight me, but babies scare me. I can always adopt a young child. The thought comforted her and she looked over at Kevin with a tender smile.

"I'm okay now, Kevin. Thanks so much for coming to tell me, it would have been awful to hear it from one of your relatives. Congratulations to you both. I take it you're happy about the baby?"

"Oh yes, we didn't plan it mind you, but we're both excited."

"Boy or girl?"

"We don't know yet, too early."

"Tell me about your…Star, where did you meet her?"

Kevin smiled. "We went to school together. I've known Star since fifth grade."

"Was she a girlfriend in school?"

"No, she thought I was too nerdy. She married one of the jocks, but that ended in divorce. We actually met at the store, got reacquainted. At first it was just friendship, Naomi, I honestly didn't think it would go anywhere."

But you didn't tell me about it, Naomi thought, but didn't say.

"Speaking of school," Naomi said, "did you know Ben Ferguson in high school?"

"He was a few years ahead of me so I didn't really know him, but his mother, Mrs. Ferguson, was my fifth grade teacher. She was a lovely lady. Do you know Ben?"

"Yes, he's a writer, you know. I suppose you could say we're good friends."

Kevin was quick to notice a slight flush in Naomi's face as she made the last remark. He smiled. "Good friends, huh? Come on Naomi, it's me, Kevin, you have something more written all over your face."

She flushed even more. "It's not something I want broadcast around Kevin, but it may well be more than friendship."

"That's great, Naomi. He was always well liked in school, so it looks like you've got yourself a good guy there. I remember hearing about his wife. She must have died then?"

"No, Kev, that's why I don't want you to say anything. She's still in a coma. We're trying to keep it at a friendship level because of that. We may not have a future together. It's a toughie."

Kevin was understanding and promised to keep her secret. He seemed visibly relieved that she had found someone. Perhaps he didn't feel so guilt-ridden now. He pecked her on the cheek as he left.

"Let me know if I can help," he told her.

She knew that he meant it.

Chapter 13

Several weeks had passed since Kevin's visit. Naomi read a blurb in the local paper about the wedding, and had finally seen the face of the woman who replaced her. A nice face, she thought. She looked kind and would in all probability make Kevin a good wife. She bore them no ill will.

Ben was now a constant in her life. They saw each other two or three times a week and—despite a longing they both felt—had been able to keep their commitment not to take the relationship to the next stage. Diana aided them in this.

She had given her blessing to Ben and Naomi, and issued frequent invitations to join her on the farm. Out of the public's eye, they were able to hold and kiss each other or walk hand-in-hand beside the creek. Had they been younger, they might not have succeeded in keeping control of their emotions. As it was, they had only to think of Diana somewhere close by and their passions subsided.

As they walked along, stopping occasionally to look for crawdads and fish in the creek, they would talk about writing, history, geology or current events, but never about the future. It was as if they were holding their breath. Naomi wondered how long they would remain like this. Ben rarely mentioned Elaine; he knew it was too painful for them. Naomi knew Diana would pass on any news of Ben's wife, but day in and day out there was no news.

They were walking beside the creek one day when Ben came up with an idea for finding Aunt Edna. Naomi had tried every which way to get information out of the Canadian government, but was dealt one roadblock after another. She was voicing her frustration over the latest hurdle, when Ben came up with a possible solution.

"I've just thought of something," he explained. "Why not try getting in touch with the accountant at that car place? You said he liked your aunt and offered to help. If he still has the files, he'll have her social security number. They might divulge something to a business that they wouldn't to you. It's worth a try."

She couldn't hide her excitement. "Oh, you're so clever. It just might work. He was a nice little man."

"How do you know he was little?" he teased her.

"He had a little voice, that's how," she told him smugly, and stuck her tongue out for good measure.

He grabbed her to him. "Now, you're going to do penance for sassing me like that. I order you to kiss me three times, young lady."

Naomi giggled and happily complied.

Percy Wing, the accountant at McFarland Motors, was keen to help. When she asked if he still had Aunt Edna's file he laughed and allowed that he never threw anything away; he should have her social security number somewhere. He wasn't sure how much information he'd be able to get, but there was a woman at the social security office he spoke to often. He thought she might help.

Naomi said she'd be grateful for any information he could gather. She secretly hoped he'd come up with an address, no matter how old, but doubted he would. If they would only tell him if Aunt Edna had drawn a pension, it would narrow the search down to Canada. And if they said she was still drawing it, they'd know Edna lived on. But where? Naomi didn't relish the thought of searching province by province. It would have to wait until the book was finished, that is unless Louise wanted to do it.

She gave Percy Wing her e-mail address, but also gave him permission to call her collect if he had any news. A few days later, he called.

"Hello, Naomi, Percy Wing here. Well, I've got some news for you. My contact at social security was very helpful, but she wouldn't give me an address."

"Damn," Naomi muttered under her breath.

But Percy Wing had better news. " She did, however, say that Edna Cavenish was still drawing a pension, so your aunt is still alive."

"Oh, what good news," Naomi said enthusiastically.

"Yes, and listen to this: I pressed her some more, and she still wouldn't give me an address, but she said the payments were direct deposited to a bank in Arizona."

"Arizona!"

"Yes, no wonder you couldn't find her in London. She's been right under your nose all the time. I imagine you can find her now, don't you?"

"Oh, yes, Mr. Wing, that's wonderful news. I don't suppose she told you what city in Arizona?"

"No, miss, she'd already overstepped her boundaries."

"Well, there aren't that many cities in Arizona, so it shouldn't be too hard. Oh, I do thank you so much."

"You're very welcome, and don't forget to give your aunt my regards."

Naomi picked up the phone and called Ben immediately. It was only after she hung up, the realization of the role he'd assumed in her life occurred to her. Normally, her first call would have been to Louise. Now Ben was first in her thoughts. A trickle of fear ran through her.

Louise's excitement echoed Naomi's when she heard the news.

"Arizona! Wow, we'd never have thought to look there or anywhere in the U.S. for that matter. I wonder what made her move there?'

"I don't know. She obviously never married, because her pension goes to Edna Cavenish. Let's hope she has a listed phone number. It shouldn't be too hard to trace her."

"Where are the main retirement centers down there? Phoenix and Tucson?"

"Yuma's another one. I doubt she'd be in Flagstaff, it gets colder there."

"How about if I get on the web and try to find her phone number? I know you're busy, and I've got time this afternoon."

"That would be great, Lou. Give me a call when you find it, then we'll have to decide what to do next."

Naomi tried to return to her writing, but the latest developments with Aunt Edna kept surfacing. I wonder if she's been in Arizona all the time, she thought, or did she go to England first? Certainly, the hot desert climate would have drawn her in old age. Did she live there alone? How would she respond if we called her? Do we even want to call her?

Aunt Edna had chosen to cut herself off from the family. Why? Did she have something to hide? If so, she wouldn't relish two nieces showing up on her doorstep. When, and if, Louise found their aunt, Naomi understood they'd have some serious decisions to make.

Louise called in the evening. A decision wasn't necessary.

"Hi, sis, I can't find a thing. I've tried all the major cities and some smaller towns: no Edna Cavenish listed."

"Do you suppose she's got an unlisted number?"

"No, they tell you if that's the case, but all I got was 'no listing under that name.' She surely couldn't be living without a telephone?"

"I wouldn't think so. You don't suppose she has the money deposited there, but lives somewhere else do you."

"Why would she do that?"

"To avoid detection," Naomi sighed, "Oh, I don't know, Lou, am I being paranoid?"

"I think so," said Louise. She let out a long sigh. " Leave it to Aunt Edna; by all accounts she was always difficult. Well, she certainly has our work cut out for us. The question is: where do we go from here?"

Chapter 14

Edna

At the tail end of August 1952, Edna had the unenviable job of manning a kiosk on London's Paddington Station. She stood on her feet all day dispensing tea—a little more than lukewarm—and a vile liquid chicory concoction posing as coffee, to a steady stream of weary travelers.

"Quarter to bloody six in the morning," Edna muttered to herself, as she hurriedly opened up her kiosk. There were already customers waiting for a hot drink. Well, they'd just have to wait, she wasn't about to kill herself on their account. On the other hand, it was all money in the bank. Edna speeded up her preparations.

With the first wave of customers taken care of, and another train not due for three minutes, Edna had time to take a breath. She pulled a small mirror out of her bag and began preening herself. First, she touched up her bright, red lipstick, exaggerating the bow on the upper lip, as the movie stars seemed to be doing. Her already rouged cheeks were touched up next. Then she turned her attention to her hennaed hair. She hated the little cap and hairnet British Rail made her wear, and did her best to cover it with wisps of hair. Satisfied with the result, she studied her reflection. Her face was a bit rounder than she liked, but she did think her blue eyes looked terrific framed by her red hair. She knew she wasn't pretty like her sister Violet, but she made the best of what she had. Her figure wasn't bad; a bit boyish perhaps, but if she stuffed enough toilet paper in her brassiere, she didn't look half bad. So what was she doing here, she wondered. She was trying to make the best of it, but she chastised herself over and over again for the stupid move that put her here.

A few months ago, she was living the life of Riley down in Surrey. She'd taken the job of housekeeper as a last resort; cleaning house was not Edna's forte. But once she'd started the affair with Dr. Seymour, she didn't do much cleaning, that's for sure. It had been easy to persuade him to hire a cleaning girl. It had been easy persuading him to do a lot of things—mindful that Mrs. Seymour wouldn't take kindly to him dallying with the help.

She tried to think back to how it all started, but was a bit fuzzy on the details. The first time she slept with him was when Mrs. Seymour took the kids up to Yorkshire to visit her mother, she was sure of that. He'd been sneaking a kiss or a little slap and tickle for weeks prior to that, though. Edna supposed she'd flirted with him, but only because he'd shown an interest. Besides, Mrs. Seymour was a cold fish, so it served her right. It wouldn't have hurt her to say something pleasant once in awhile, but she treated Edna like the servant she was: something Edna didn't like to be reminded of. Dr. Seymour was at least civil to her, right from the beginning. He was quite amusing really, although you'd never know it when he was around his wife.

No, she wouldn't feel sorry for Mrs. Seymour. What was a girl supposed to do stuck out in the country, where cows outnumbered available men? Their country estate they called it. London hadn't been bad; at least there were places to go on her days off. At the farm, they wouldn't let her use the car. She was stuck, unless she rode a bicycle into the village. It was almost as bad as Spruce Creek. If she'd known they were going to spend so long in the country, she wouldn't have taken the job. But then again, maybe she would. Her previous job with the Caldwell's was awful. She'd been glad to be shut of them. The Bannisters, who'd brought her over from Vancouver after the war, were the best ones. But Mr. Bannister had up and died, so she'd had to move on.

It was that bitch Mary who'd caused all the trouble for her. She never should have insisted they get the cleaning girl. She had eyes in the back of her head, that one. She'd once had the gall to ask Edna if she was fooling around with the doctor. Edna treated it as a joke, but she wondered what Mary had seen to make her ask. The girl had obviously seen something, and just been waiting her chance to use it against Edna.

Her chance came on a Wednesday in July. Every Wednesday, Mrs. Seymour went to a neighboring town to have her hair done. Dr. Seymour spent Wednesday afternoons playing golf—except on the frequent occasions he snuck back to the farm for a roll in the hay with Edna. And it was just that: a roll in the hayloft, away from prying eyes. Not that there were any. Mary had the day off, and the farm help went to market on Wednesdays.

On this particular Wednesday, Mrs. Seymour's car broke down on a country road a few miles from the village. As luck would have it—lucky for Mrs. Seymour, not for Edna—the cleaning girl, Mary, was out for a bicycle ride with her cousin. Coming across her stranded employer, Mary offered help. She agreed to ride into the village garage, and have Mr. Wainwright send out a tow truck. Mrs. Seymour asked Mary to call Edna from the garage, with instructions for Dr. Seymour to pick the children up after school. Mary had ideas of her own.

"Dr. Seymour may already be home, Mrs. Seymour."

"No, Mary, he plays golf on Wednesdays."

"But Mrs. Seymour, I often see him going home on Wednesdays, and I'm sure that was him went by earlier," she said with mock innocence.

Mrs. Seymour weighed up the information. On second thought, she told Mary, she'd take care of it herself from the garage. When Mr. Wainwright arrived with the tow truck, he was only too pleased to take her home before towing the car. He dropped her at the road as she requested.

Edna, naked as a jay, was in the hayloft tickling the end of the good doctor's penis with a limp piece of hay, when Mrs. Seymour made her appearance. The memory of the next few minutes would stay with Edna forever. She vowed never to be caught in such a compromising position again: thrown out on her ear, with nothing to show for it. Next time, if there were a next time, she'd make sure she feathered her nest as part of the bargain.

Now, here she was on Paddington Station, working a job she would have quit long ago, if not for the profitable side business she'd created. It was all very clever really, as she'd often remind herself, while tallying up the profits in her flat. After the initial training period, she received very little oversight by the station management. She began quite simply, baking a few things at home, selling them at the kiosk and pocketing the proceeds. Over the course of several months, she'd upped the selection to candy bars and packages of potato chips. More recently she'd been buying and using her own tea and coffee—always careful to keep the station's profits at a stable level. This usually meant selling two cups of theirs to every one of hers. Next year was the coronation, and she figured her profits would soar with all the extra tourists.

It was a bit of a bookkeeping nightmare, but Edna was up to the task. Her bank account was growing nicely, and she had a definite goal in sight. When she'd saved enough money, Edna intended to leave England. She'd go back home for a visit, but she wouldn't settle in Canada. Her sights were set on America: land of opportunity.

It was a little after four on another dreary day, when Estelle came into her life. She waited on the tiny woman in her usual cheery way—it was good for business.

"Would you like an Eccles cake with your coffee? They were fresh baked this morning." A lie, she'd baked them last night.

"Ah, certainement, chéri, I love Eccles cake. The coffee I don't love, but it's better than English tea."

Edna noted the French accent. "You're French, no wonder you don't like our coffee. It's the best I can do for you, I'm afraid. Are you here on holiday?"

"No, my dear, I live in London, almost twenty years now. London I love. How about you, you have American accent, not much, but I can detect?"

"I was born in Canada, actually."

They chatted a minute or two more, before Edna had to attend to more customers. She saw Estelle a number of times after that, but always as briefly. The Frenchwoman was very well dressed, Edna observed, and she spoke beautifully. She looked to be 50ish, but may have been older under her impeccably applied makeup. She also had red hair, a deeper red than Edna's.

Their acquaintanceship may have remained at the same level, if Estelle hadn't missed her train one Friday. As luck would have it, Edna was about to finish her shift. She'd already packed up her supplies, and was about to pull the blinds down. This was late in the day for Estelle to be traveling, and the woman was obviously agitated. Edna pointed out where Estelle could go for coffee, and was surprised when she offered an invitation.

"You come with me, chéri, you finish work now, yes? I have to wait one hour for my train. I need someone to cheer me up. You always have a smile for me. I will buy you coffee."

They sat in the station's cafeteria restaurant. Estelle insisted on paying for Edna's coffee. She seemed genuinely pleased that Edna had joined her. She was annoyed at someone for causing her to miss her train, but she didn't say who it was. She was, Edna noticed, a fidgety, highly-strung woman, obviously used to things going her way. Edna envied the Frenchwoman's self-assurance. She also envied her clothes. The suit Estelle was wearing wasn't bought off the rack at Marks and Spencer, that's for sure. Her red hair had to be professionally done; it always looked perfect. The only bad thing about her was her teeth; they were a bit horsey. Other than that, she was an attractive woman.

Edna learned that Estelle's train journeys were to see her mother, in a retirement home west of London. Estelle herself had a flat in Kensington and came to the station by taxi. All of these things—the elegant clothes, the Kensington address and riding in taxis—meant only one thing to Edna: money. Estelle looked so out of place in the working-class cafeteria. She must be well off, Edna thought, and wondered what she did for a living. There was no wedding band, and she hadn't mentioned a husband. Edna would like to have fished for details. But Estelle wanted to hear all about Edna: where she was from in Canada, how long she'd been in England, was she married, did she have a boyfriend?

Edna laughed at the last question. "Not any more, I don't."

"Oh, chéri, what happened?"

"He broke it off very suddenly." The way Edna's cheeks flushed as she said this wasn't lost on Estelle.

"Ah, I think I understand, his wife found out, yes?"

"How did you…" Edna started to say, but Estelle's knowing expression gave the game away and they both burst out laughing.

"Chéri, I have been there," Estelle explained. "Believe me, these men are such fools. They can hide all manner of things in business, but can they hide a mistress from their wives, no. But you are over it, yes?"

"Yes, it's not like I was in love with him. I was bored and just having fun, really." She felt a need to save her reputation. "He's the only married man I've been with."

"But, you've had other lovers, yes, a girl as pretty as you?"

Edna flushed. She felt uncomfortable with the personal question, and just nodded her reply.

"Come, chéri, I'm French; love is like breathing to me. I am not shocked, but perhaps I pry too much. Tell me about your British Columbia, I have never been there."

Edna skipped Spruce Creek and painted Estelle a rosy picture of Vancouver, with its backdrop of snow-covered peaks and the beauty of Stanley Park. She described Victoria, on Vancouver Island, and told of watching Orcas from the ferry, their black and white bodies glistening as they breached. In the telling of it, she suddenly found herself missing home. Estelle noticed it too.

"Ah, you are a little bit homesick, chéri. You have family there?"

"Yes, but we're not very close. My dad died, but mum is still living, and I have sisters and a brother. I don't write much, and neither do they."

"Oh, so sad. You will go home one day, yes?"

"I suppose so, but I won't stay there. I want to go to America."

Estelle raised her eyebrows. "Why America? Don't you love London as I do?"

"There's so much opportunity there; in America I mean. I suppose London is all right. I just hate my job."

"Are you trained for other work, Edna?" The way she pronounced Edna was quite amusing.

"No, all I've done is childcare. Oh, and I worked in the shipyards during the war. I'm trying to save enough to go home, but it's hard on what I make."

Estelle looked thoughtful. "I'm sure it is, chéri."

The hour had passed, and it was time for Estelle to board her train. Edna still hadn't found out anything about Estelle. Was she married, did she work? Before she stood to leave, Estelle handed Edna her card.

"If you ever need anything, chéri, you call me, all right. I have enjoyed our little coffee. Perhaps I'll see you again next week."

Then she was gone, leaving Edna marveling at how much information the little woman had got out of her. She certainly asked a lot of questions. I wonder what her story is, Edna wondered. She looked down at the card in her hand, but it revealed only a name and telephone number: Estelle Martinique, KEN7-425.

Chapter 15

Naomi, Ben and Diana sat in the kitchen at Diana's, kept inside by a soft, but incessant summer rain. As she nibbled at fresh-baked cookies and sipped her tea, Naomi thought how much she loved this room. It was her favorite room in the old farmhouse. A red brick fireplace was angled across one corner. The walls were covered in birch paneling—the real stuff, not the composition substitute sold today. The kitchen cabinets were all handmade: a work of art, with inlaid copper door panels, punched with different designs. Age had given them a wonderful patina. It was a large room, meant to feed large farm families. Ben had described family gatherings in this room while his grandparents were alive. She could only imagine the warm, secure environment he must have grown up in.

She watched him now sparring with his sister over which one of them had the most farm chores while they were growing up. It was a good-natured squabble, and she could see the strong bond of love between them. They shared so many physical characteristics. Diana had Ben's hazel eyes and square jaw. Her hair, peppered with gray, was thick like Ben's. Naomi thought, not for the first time, she was so happy fate had thrown her together with these good people.

Talk turned to Naomi's family. She told them Louise called yesterday to say she couldn't find a listing for Aunt Edna in Arizona.

Diana had an idea. "I've been thinking; what if your aunt is in a nursing home? You said she's 80 odd. They don't always have their own phone lines, especially if they're senile. You could try checking them out."

"Would they tell me if she's there? Maybe that's an invasion of privacy," Naomi asked Diana.

Ben jumped in. "Here's what you do: don't ask if she lives there, simply ask to be put through to her room. If she doesn't live there, they'll tell you. If she does, they'll ask who's calling, etc."

Naomi looked thoughtful. "It just might work. I wonder how many nursing homes there are in Arizona?"

"That's the bad part," Diana ventured, "there's bound to be loads of them. Old people flock to the warm states. How about dividing up the main cities between you, Louise and me? The three of us should be able to manage it that way."

"That would be wonderful, Diana, if you don't mind helping. Let's see, how about you taking Tucson, Louise can take Prescott and Yuma and I'll have Phoenix and Sedona. If we don't find her in one of those, we'll have to start on some of the smaller towns. It sounds like an enormous project."

"Yes, but it's going to be fun. I've always fancied being a detective." Diana's excitement showed. "Now give me all the particulars again, and then you two clear off so I can get started."

"Fine, just cast us out in the rain," Ben said, feigning offense. "Come on, Naomi, we know where we're not wanted."

Naomi had just finished emailing Diana and Louise a list of nursing and retirement homes in their cities. Despite Diana's enthusiasm to get started, Naomi had insisted she get the list from the various chambers of commerce, thereby cutting down on phone calls. The chambers responded promptly to Naomi's inquiry, and she now had all the cities covered. As she expected, Phoenix had the lion's share. She'd have to find some way of categorizing them, and start out calling the most likely first.

She'd already called half a dozen places in Phoenix without any luck, when the phone rang. It was Louise.

"This is hard, sis, I've made nine calls already without any results. Do you think it's going to work?"

"I don't know, Lou. I've struck out so far too. It's just a matter of hitting the right one. I think Ben's idea will work, but it's going to take time—unless we're incredibly lucky. You should see the size of the Phoenix list I'm working on."

They agreed to continue, at least for the time being. Naomi knew they'd both feel like giving up at some point. Her eyes fell on the short list for Sedona. Perhaps she'd do those few next. It would eliminate one city, and she'd feel as though she were getting somewhere. Now that she'd made a few calls, she was relaxing more and there was no nervousness apparent in her voice. She'd give a breezy good morning, and asked to be put through to Edna Cavenish. She was also used to the response: no Edna Cavenish living here. That is, until the third call to Sedona.

"Good morning, will you put me through to Edna Cavenish, please?"

There was a pause at the other end, as though the person was measuring her response. Then, in a very businesslike tone, "May I tell her who's calling?"

Naomi gulped: pay dirt! "Yes, it's her niece Naomi, calling from Oregon." Naomi was panicked. What would she say? She hadn't thought that far ahead.

"Have you spoken to her before?" The voice on the other end of the line was still businesslike, though not unkind.

"Not for a long time," Naomi admitted.

"I thought not. Miss Cavenish isn't able to take calls anymore; she gets confused, I'm afraid. Can we try and give her a message for you?"

"Not really, I think she'd be surprised I'd called. We'd lost touch with her, you see, and we honestly didn't know if she was still living. How is she?"

"Your aunt is very frail, I'm afraid. She's lost her sight and most of her hearing. She's confined to bed, but her spirits are still pretty good. Are you thinking of coming to see her?"

Naomi was taken unawares. "I don't know. I'll talk to my sister about it."

"Only if you are," the woman continued, "I would make it soon. Frankly, I don't think she'll be with us much longer."

Naomi asked if she thought her aunt would remember her.

"I don't know," the woman said, "you're the first family member we've heard from. To tell you the truth, we didn't think she had any. Let us know if you do decide to come, so we can prepare her."

Naomi lost no time in calling Louise to give her the news. Louise was jubilant they'd found Aunt Edna, and relieved she wouldn't have to make more calls. The sisters talked at length over what direction they should take now. They had been so intent on finding Aunt Edna; they hadn't given any thought to what they'd do if they found her. Since they couldn't talk to Aunt Edna on the phone, Louise was keen to leave for Arizona at the first opportunity. Naomi needed more convincing.

"If she doesn't know us, what good is it?"

"I'm not sure, sis, but if we don't go, we'll never know, will we?" Louise said persuasively.

"I suppose you're right. We might not learn anything, but then again, it's our only chance, isn't it?"

"Yes, let's do it. We could fly down to Phoenix and rent a car. Let's treat it as a mini-vacation. I know you're a bit strapped for cash, so I'll pay for the car and our motel, if you can manage your fare. We only need one or two nights. Sam and the boys can manage by themselves for that long. Let me scope out the best deal on everything. I suppose one day is as good as another for you. Can you spare the time away from writing?"

"Yes I can; just go for the cheapest prices. If my neighbors can't feed Spike, I'm sure Ben or Diana would. I'd better call Diana now and let her know we have mission accomplished. I'll bet she's losing her enthusiasm at this point too."

It was a long, hot drive between Phoenix and Sedona. The sisters got a very early start, but were glad of the air-conditioning in the rental car by the time they reached their destination. The flight down from Portland had been uneventful. They spent the whole time planning how they would approach Aunt Edna. In the end, they decided it was something they really couldn't plan—so much depended on how senile their aunt was, and if she remembered them.

It was a good stretch of road up to Sedona. Naomi and Louise took turns driving. This part of Arizona was new to both of them. Their father had driven the family to the Grand Canyon once when they were very young. Louise had returned there with her family more recently, but hadn't continued south. The desert cacti fascinated the sisters, and they spent the trip marveling over the size of them. Before reaching their destination, they became accustomed to the dryness surrounding them, and were pleasantly surprised at the lush oasis of Sedona.

"Wow, sis, this is nice," Louise said with enthusiasm. "Look at the art galleries. We must make time to visit them."

They stopped for a bite to eat, and a quick look around, before asking directions to The Village at Red Rock, where Aunt Edna lived. Flowers apparently loved this climate; they were abundant in beds and window boxes all over town. The stuccoed Spanish buildings made the perfect backdrop for the brilliant colors. It was obvious to Naomi and Louise that this was an affluent neighborhood: a far cry from Spruce Creek. What manner of circumstances had lead Aunt Edna here, they wondered.

Directions to 'The Village' were easy to follow: about a mile out of town on the left, you can't miss it. The sisters were expecting a clinical looking facility, with maybe two or three buildings and a small garden area. What greeted them was so far removed from that image they were stunned.

"Holy cow," Louise stammered, "It looks like a five-star resort."

The term 'village' was aptly applied to the project. In addition to the nursing home, there was senior housing, a golf course, tennis courts, clubhouse, swimming pools and a small commercial area.

They followed signs to the care center: down a long, sweeping driveway fringed with flowering oleanders of pink and white. The building was tucked discretely in a quieter corner of the village, but retained the quality they saw elsewhere.

Louise turned to Naomi with a grin. "Well, here goes. One thing's for sure, Aunt Edna couldn't afford this place on a nanny's salary. I think we've just found the Cavenish inheritance."

"I'm not sure how that makes me feel," Naomi said with a lukewarm smile, "I guess I'm hoping she won the lottery, better that than cheating the family."

Louise patted her hand. "Let's go find some answers."

They were expected and were asked to wait in a small sitting room for the charge nurse to brief them. A pleasant looking woman soon joined them, introduced herself as Joanne Melrinck, charge nurse. After exchanging greetings, she asked them a few questions. Naomi realized she was verifying their identities, and then, apparently satisfied, she turned the subject to Aunt Edna.

"Your aunt is typical of people with senile dementia," she explained in a gentle tone. "She has good days and bad days. It's hard to say how much she remembers, because she never talked about family. Did you say she was from Canada? I'd never have guessed it, she sounds so English."

"She lived in London for a few years," Naomi offered, "but she was born and grew up in British Columbia. How is she doing? We were told she's blind and deaf now."

"She has some hearing, but you have to shout. There's no way she would wear a hearing aid." The nurse chuckled. "She's quite a character, this aunt of yours. Have you seen her paintings?"

"She paints!" Louise registered surprise.

"Well, not anymore, but she used to be quite good. I'll tell you what, I'll give you Marge Jenkins address and number; she is your aunt's best friend. Marge is ten or twelve years younger than Edna, and is still very much with it. She has most of Edna's paintings, and I know she'll enjoy showing them to you."

"Does she live in Sedona?" Naomi asked.

"No, here at the village."

"Did my aunt live here before coming to the care center?"

"She's lived here for many years. She had a beautiful home overlooking the golf course. Persuading her to move here was not an easy task for Marge."

Naomi and Louise exchanged meaningful glances.

The nurse stood up. "Well, let's go and see her, shall we? I haven't told her you're coming. Not much point, really, she wouldn't remember."

The wizened old woman propped up in bed looked nothing like the Aunt Edna the sisters remembered. The hair was the giveaway: still a bright, orangey-red, although thin now, to the point of looking ridiculous. It reminded Naomi of paintings she'd seen of Elizabeth I. Aunt Edna moved her head much like a bird, trying to follow sounds with her limited hearing.

The nurse motioned for them to come closer to the bed, then took Edna's hand and spoke. "Edna, dear, it's Joanne. You have some visitors."

"Who is it?" The strength of her voice surprised the girls.

"Your nieces have come to see you."

"The police have come to see me!" Edna sounded astonished.

"No, dear, your NIECES."

"What nieces?"

Louise bent over the bed. "Aunt Edna, it's Louise and Naomi, we're May's daughters. Do you remember your sister May?"

"May, May," she turned the name over in her mind. "The name does ring a bell. Did Daddy know her?"

The girls were perplexed. They exchanged puzzled glances. It was looking as though their aunt was too senile to be of any help. Aunt Edna obviously couldn't make the connection with their mother, May. They glanced at the nurse, who said softly, "She talks a lot about Daddy, but we don't think it's her father. Do you have any idea who it could be?"

Louise answered for them. "We don't have a clue. Perhaps her friend Marge could help you."

“We’ve tried asking her,” the nurse explained. “ She said it would be Edna’s father. The staff is convinced it’s not.” Her voice dropped to a whisper. “ You see she’s made some off-color remarks about him.”

“What sort of remarks?” whispered Naomi.

The nurse leaned close to them. “Sexual remarks.”

Louise locked eyes with Naomi. They both had expressions of surprise. When amusement started welling up in Louise’s eyes, Naomi had to look away quickly. There would be time for laughing later.

“Let’s see if we can activate any memories.” The nurse was trying to be helpful. “ What town did you say she was from in Canada?”

“Spruce Creek.”

The nurse leaned close to their aunt. “Edna, these girls are from Spruce Creek. Do you remember Spruce Creek?”

At the mention of Spruce Creek, their aunt screamed out in a mixture of anger and terror. “Get them out of here. There’s no way they’re taking me back to Spruce Creek. They know I killed Daddy. They just want the money. Get them out, get them out. I’ll never go back there, I’ll never go back. It’s my money. I worked for it. Get them out.”

Louise and Naomi, visibly shaken by their aunt’s outburst, were ushered out of the room as the nurse tried to calm her. They stood in the hallway dumbfounded at what was happening. The nurse, Joanne, rang for assistance: she was having difficulty calming Aunt Edna.

“What do you make of that?” Louise hissed at Naomi.

Naomi just shook her head, unable to put words to what she was feeling.

There was no consoling the old woman and it became necessary to give her a sedative.

Nurse Joanne was apologetic. “I’m sorry, she’s just so frail, we had to calm her down. She obviously didn’t remember you, but she sure remembered Spruce Creek. Bad memories, apparently.”

“It was a dismal place to grow up in.” Naomi explained. “It’s a shame she didn’t know us, we hoped to tie up a few loose ends for the family tree.”

“Maybe Marge can help you there, she and Edna are pretty close. Why don’t you call on her?”

Marge Jenkins was their only hope. They called her before leaving the care center. She was expecting to hear from them. The care center had told her Edna’s nieces were coming to visit. Marge said she would be happy to see them and show them Edna’s artwork. She had an appointment to get her nails done at one. Could they come later? They settled on 2:30 p.m., which gave them plenty of time to return to Sedona for a look around.

They were glad to leave the care center. Aunt Edna’s outburst had been both puzzling and disturbing. Over lunch, they tried to make sense of it all.

“Did you catch the ‘they know I killed Daddy bit’, Lou?” Naomi asked with her mouthful. “What do you suppose that means?”

Louise looked uncomfortable. “I’m not sure. We know she had nothing to do with Granddad’s death: he was killed on the job. The nurse seemed sure it wasn’t her father she talked about when she said Daddy.”

“Precisely. I was thinking, what if she meant her mother, and had got it mixed up because of her dementia. We could well have our answer, you know.”

“You’re jumping the gun, Naomi. It could be nothing more than the ramblings of a senile old lady—maybe part of a dream she had.”

"What about the money, then? She was convinced we'd come to get it. You only have to look around to know she has plenty."

Louise nodded. "Yes, that place doesn't come cheap. What did she mean saying 'I earned it'? If she'd got it legally, why would anyone be coming to take it away from her? After all, we were just anyone to her. She couldn't understand that we are her family."

Naomi looked pensive. "I feel sorry for her, in a way. I know she was difficult to get along with, but to be dying here without family. I can't believe she didn't try to contact Mum as she got older."

"Well, it doesn't sound as though she was unhappy. You heard the nurse say she was quite a character. That usually means someone who enjoys life. Her friend Marge can probably fill in some of the blanks." Louise pushed her plate toward Naomi. "Here, try the tuna salad, it's really good."

Naomi complied, nodding her approval. "How much are we going to tell the friend?"

"I don't think we can plan much before we see what she's like. Let's just play it by ear, see how friendly she is. She sounded great on the phone." Louise fumbled in her purse. "I'm going to call Sam before we leave, see how the boys are doing. I'll let him know we're spending another night in Phoenix. Okay with you?"

"Yes, we'll have to. Just as well we booked the flight tomorrow. I'll call Ben after you're finished. I told him we'd take an earlier flight, if we could, but there's no way we'll be finished in time."

Louise was only gone a few minutes. She couldn't reach Sam, so had left a message. She'd also called the motel to book another night.

"I'm going to order a piece of pie while you call Ben. Do you want some?" Louise asked.

"No, I'll pass this time, but save me a bite of yours," Naomi responded as she pushed back her chair. "I hope I can reach Ben. See you in a minute."

Ben answered on the first ring. Naomi felt excitement at hearing his voice.

"I knew you'd call," he said. "So, how's it going? Have you learned anything?"

She told him about Aunt Edna's outburst and how uncomfortable it had made them feel.

"I can imagine. A bit of paranoia there, I'd say, as though she'd always suspected someone would come after her money. Did the nurse think that's what you were there for?"

"No, I'm sure she didn't. She gave us Edna's best friend's number. We're going to see her this afternoon. That's why I'm calling, really, to let you know we can't make it home tonight. We're hoping the friend can shed some light on things," Naomi explained. "I was wondering when Edna said she killed Daddy, if she meant her mother and just had it mixed up. It's funny, Louise is still reluctant to deal with that side of it, although she wants to find out about the money."

"You know I have misgivings on that score too," he said earnestly. "Whatever you find out could trouble you more than the uncertainty of not knowing.

"You're saying, what you don't know can't hurt you."

"Something like that. There could be no justice and, personally, I'm not convinced it's a crime to help a dying person meet their maker."

"I'm not either," Naomi agreed, "but where there's disappearing money involved, it rather alters the picture, don't you think?"

"Possibly. Let's hope the friend can fill you in on where your aunt's money came from. I hope you're taking notes; it'll make a good book."

Naomi laughed. "You bet I am. Well, I'd better get back before Louise eats all the pie. I'll call again tomorrow."

"Naomi, I miss you."

She felt a warm glow. "I miss you too."

They were still avoiding the 'love' word, she noticed, but it didn't matter. One day, if circumstances allowed, they could declare their love openly. For now, I miss you would have to suffice.

Chapter 16

When Marge Jenkins opened the door, Louise and Naomi could see immediately why she and Aunt Edna had connected. Their aunt's friend looked like she'd stepped through a portal from the 40s: hair bleached flaxen, set in tight waves, and heavy makeup, with an emphasis on big lips. Only the clothes—denim shorts and a Nike tee shirt— had any connection with the nineties. She was a pretty, gregarious woman, and welcomed the sisters enthusiastically.

"I was so surprised when the care center told me you were coming," Marge explained, holding out a freshly manicured hand. "In all the years I've known her, Edna never had a visit from family."

"Does she ever talk about her family?" Louise asked.

"Not much. She was sure they didn't like her. I know she hated where she grew up. Once or twice when she'd had too much to drink, she'd talk about her little sister—Fay I think it was. Anyway, she was the only one she seemed to have any feelings for."

"That will be our mother: May," Naomi explained. "She died recently."

"Oh, I'm sorry, dears. Edna would be too if she could understand. She's not as hardhearted as she would have everyone believe. I think it's her way of dealing with never having been in love: the one thing money can't buy. It's been a lonely life for her, really. Still we had some good times together," Marge finished, smiling at the thought.

"How long have you known her?" Louise asked.

"We met in '65; we were both living in Phoenix at the time. My husband, Earl, had just died. I joined a golf club to get out a bit. That's where I met Edna. Although she was older, we hit it off immediately."

"And then you both moved here?" inquired Naomi.

"Not right away. We both bought lots as soon as the development was approved. Edna built first; that would be in 1983. Her home was just around the corner. I built mine two years later." Marge paused. "I've got some iced tea made. Let's take it out on the patio, then we can talk more."

They sat under a bougainvillea-covered trellis, in a corner of the yard heavily shaded with palms and other heat-loving plants. A kidney-shaped swimming pool dominated the well-manicured yard. Marge told them, with pride, she swam laps every morning at seven.

Naomi waited for an opportunity, and when it came asked, "Do you remember what Aunt Edna had to say about our mother?"

"Not really. To tell you the truth, the times she talked about her family, I'd tied one on too." Marge laughed heartily. "There was a time we could really knock them back, but we slowed down as we got older. No, I can't bring to mind what she said, other than she was happy for her." Marge paused. "I'm not sure why."

"Probably because she was able to join our dad in Oregon after Gran died," Naomi suggested.

"Maybe. I really can't remember," said Marge.

"Did she say anything about her mum's death?" Naomi persisted.

Marge looked puzzled. "Not that I remember. Was it an accident then?"

Louise jumped in quickly, "No, not at all. Gran lived to a pretty good age. Edna's getting up there, too, isn't she?"

Naomi noticed Louise had cleverly changed the subject, but let her continue.

"They told us at the care center you had some of Aunt Edna's paintings, I'd love to see them before we leave."

Marge responded eagerly. "Well, come on, let's do a gallery tour. I have several up on the walls, but most of them are in the back room." She turned to the girls with a twinkle in her eye. "Now don't be shocked, you're going to see plenty of boobs and butts—especially men's butts."

Naomi and Louise laughed with delight. They were enjoying this lively woman.

They toured the house first, looking at Edna's paintings Marge had displayed. They were well done. Louise poured over them, as only another artist would—checking technique and exclaiming over the use of color. She noticed a similarity in composition with her own work. She paused at one painting of a particularly handsome, nude man. "Wow, I'll bet Aunt Edna enjoyed working with this model," she said playfully.

"Isn't he something," Marge chuckled. She was obviously having fun with the sisters. There was melancholy in her voice when she said, "Oh, I wish you girls had visited before Edna got like this."

Naomi explained how they'd only just found out Aunt Edna was still living. She told about searching for her in England. "The family always assumed she'd died there," she finished.

"Well, I suppose it's her fault for cutting herself off from you all," Marge said wistfully.

As they moved about the house, Naomi was impressed with the quality of the home. Sumptuous wasn't quite the word to describe it, because it reflected the clean lines of homes built in a hot climate—open space, lots of tile and easy access to the outdoors.

Naomi told Marge how much she liked her home.

"If you think this is lovely, you should have seen Edna's. Now *that* was lovely."

"Did she sell it?" Louise inquired.

"Yes. She first went to an assisted living apartment over near the care center; I talked her into that. The house got to be too much for her, with her eyesight failing. She couldn't bear to part with her stuff, though; she gave me a lot. The rest is in storage. I'll have to go through it all one day," Marge explained. "I'm executor of her trust. She's leaving a lot to charities. If I find any family stuff, photos and the like, I'll send them to you girls. You must remember to give me your addresses before you leave. Now, let's go in the back room and see the rest of the paintings."

There were somewhere between 15 and 20 canvases stacked in the back room. When they finished looking through them, Marge surprised them.

"Now, I want you both to choose a painting to take home with you. I imagine the plane can handle it, if you don't choose a large one."

They tried to refuse, but Marge was adamant. She'd been instructed to sell them and give the proceeds to the humane society, but she declared, "I know if Edna were here, she'd do the same thing. You take them and enjoy them."

Naomi chose a desert scene, because she said it would always remind her of Aunt Edna living out her life here. Louise's choice was more complex: an abstract entitled, "Who says I can't?" The title, she explained, personified Aunt Edna to her; while the composition was so uncannily like her own, she couldn't resist it.

Marge seemed happy with their selections.

They returned to their shady spot on the patio, and began talking about their aunt again. They asked Marge how much she knew of their aunt's life, and where she'd lived before coming to Phoenix.

"She lived in London for years, but I think she'd been in Canada for awhile. Her mum had died a couple years before I met her, if that helps any. We had some fun in those early years," Marge reminisced. "That Edna, she was a wild one. I didn't really notice the age difference until recently. We used to go all over together: Italy, Greece, Spain, you name it."

"Have you no children, Marge?" Louise inquired.

"No, honey, I married a wonderful man, almost 20 years my senior. He provided well for me, but the one thing he couldn't provide was a child. We had been thinking about adoption when he died." She paused, trying to wring the sadness from her voice. "I could have remarried; I was still young, but the right man didn't come along. After a while, I stopped looking. Earl, my husband, had left me with plenty, bless his heart. Then I met Edna and started having fun again."

Naomi had been wondering how they would approach the question of Aunt Edna's money, and was relieved when Louise jumped right in.

"One thing we've wondered about Marge, is how Aunt Edna could afford to live like this," Louise spread her arms to encompass the plush surroundings. "She grew up in poor circumstances, and to our knowledge never married. Did she win a lottery or something?"

Marge threw back her head and burst out laughing. "She won a lottery all right, but I don't know if I should tell you about it," she paused, looking at them closely. "You really don't know her secret, do you?"

Louise and Naomi shook their heads, eager to hear what they'd come in search of.

"She hid it from her family so well. What the hell, it can't hurt her now," Marge emphasized. "Let me tell you about our girl Edna."

Chapter 17

Edna

Traveling first class on British Airways, Edna decided, was how she'd always go in the future; no more cramped coach with dirty restrooms. Yes, my girl, she told herself, it's first class all the way now. A satisfied smile stretched from ear to ear.

She caught a man across the aisle eying her with more than a little interest. Yes, she thought, I do look pretty darn good. She wore a periwinkle blue linen suit, with a short, boxy jacket and tight fitting skirt, off-white stiletto heels and matching purse. Her hair, not yet the garish red she'd adopt in later years, was softly curled around a butcher boy beret—all the rage with the fashionable set. She'd let the staff at Harrods dress her for this big occasion: her exile from England. Well, not exactly exile, but she had promised not to return. A promise she'd keep for many years.

They'd been in the air thirty minutes. Edna felt the gin and tonic taking effect. She reclined the seat and closed her eyes, but sleep didn't come. There was too much to think about, it had all happened so fast. Now here she was flying back to Canada. There hadn't been time to let her family know she was coming. Well, there had really, but she preferred it this way. She'd get settled in an apartment in Vancouver before going up to Spruce Creek. She'd get a car, too, although her driving would be a bit rusty. She might have to take a few lessons. Then again, she wouldn't want to take the car to Spruce Creek. It's best the family didn't know about her newly acquired wealth, that way she wouldn't have to explain how she got it. She'd need to work in Vancouver for a couple of years. That should be time enough to get her U.S. green card, she thought, and for her money affairs to be settled. Then it's Arizona here I come!

Daddy, poor old Daddy, bless his heart, he'd set her up for life. It had been eight years since Estelle introduced them. She hadn't been keen on the idea at first, but soon warmed to it. In fact, when Estelle first made the suggestion, Edna remembered feeling revulsion and a little fear. She smiled at the thought, and surprised the man across the aisle: he thought he'd been watching her sleep.

Edna's days on Paddington Station came to an abrupt end. It seemed British Rail did check up on their employees from time to time. It happened on a particularly cold November day, about three months after she first met Estelle. Her customers ate more when it was cold, Edna observed, so she'd baked up some sausage rolls along with the Eccles cakes. They were moving very nicely. When a man in a smart navy blue overcoat asked if they were fresh, she replied proudly, "I baked them myself, this morning."

To which he replied, "I was not aware we employed you as a baker." He revealed his identity: British Rail Inspector #26. Edna couldn't think fast enough, too late to gather up any more incriminating merchandise. She stood mute and complied mechanically as he asked for a sack to gather up his evidence. He stuffed the sausage rolls and Eccles cakes into the sack, told her to carry on as usual, and strode away toward the main office.

She realized with a sense of relief he hadn't looked around to see what else she might have added to the meager selection usually sold at the kiosks. Edna began quickly stuffing into bags the candy bars, potato chips, tea, coffee and sugar that she'd brought from home. She reached for the duffle bag she carried her supplies in, but stopped in her tracks. "Oh, bugger," she said aloud. It had just occurred to her they might search her, before letting her go. They were bound to fire her, that much she knew.

She looked around frantically trying to decide what to do. She knew time was running out, he'd be back in minutes. Nothing for it, she thought, and scanned the platform until her eyes fell on a poorly dressed couple, with two snotty-nosed children trailing them.

"Excuse me," Edna practically yelled at them. Several people stopped to look. She beckoned to the couple. The man, looking perplexed, pointed to himself. Edna nodded vigorously. They approached warily.

She held the bags out to them, explaining hastily, "Look, I have to get rid of this food in a hurry. No questions, all right? Will you take it?"

The wife stuck her nose in one bag. She looked worn, maybe ill, and spoke with a strong Cockney accent. "Will anyone come after us?" she asked Edna.

"No, it's my stuff, honest, but get it out of here quickly."

They needed no more convincing, and had just disappeared from view when the inspector returned with his manager.

It didn't take them long to fire her. She played dumb, said she didn't think it would hurt to sell a few cakes now and then. It's not like she was stealing from them, she explained innocently. They'd already checked the books, and could see that profits had remained stable. Whether they believed her act or not, she'd never know. They paid her wages, checked her bags and marched her out of the station. Just like that.

A couple of weeks later it finally hit her. She had no references, and couldn't get a job. She'd applied for a few, but was never called back. The rent would be due soon, and she didn't want to dig into her savings again. How much did she have left? Edna rummaged in her bag, looking for money that may have lodged in a corner. There was no money hiding, but she did come up with Estelle's card: Estelle Martinique, KEN7 – 4256.

She toyed around with the idea of calling her, but couldn't think what she'd say. How could Estelle help her? The Frenchwoman had said to call if she needed anything. Well, she needed a job. Then it occurred to her: Estelle moved in wealthy circles, she might know someone who needed a housekeeper. Edna hung her head in despair. She didn't want that kind of work again, but what else could she do. If she was ever going to make it to America, she had to get working again quickly.

Edna stood looking up at the building in Kensington that housed Estelle's flat. It was beautiful: a Georgian terrace, elegantly maintained. She saw the curtains stir, and knew Estelle was watching her. She'd dressed with care for this meeting: her best gray wool suit, over a soft green blouse. She'd pulled her hair back in a French roll; decided it made her look too young, but didn't have time to change it. To compensate she'd applied more makeup than usual, but that didn't look right either so she'd rubbed a lot off.

She felt nervous as she rang the doorbell. She wasn't sure why. Estelle had been friendly enough on the phone. She thought she might be able to help her find work, and had suggested she come around.

They hadn't seen much of each other since the day they had coffee together. Estelle was always rushing for a train, and only had time to exchange a few words. Today, she greeted Edna with a peck on both cheeks, took her hands and pulled her into the flat. Edna's eyes darted around the room, taking in the rich brocade furniture, heavy velvet curtains, silver tea service and ornate wall hangings. It looked like a room that might be featured in one of the upper crust magazines she'd perused while working at the train station.

Edna's reaction wasn't lost on Estelle. She could see the impression her flat was making on the younger woman. "You like my little home, chéri? It's elegant, yes? I am so happy here."

Edna nodded her approval. "It's beautiful Estelle, it's a lovely home." But even as she said it, Edna noticed something missing. Homes had photographs. Estelle's beautiful living room had not a one. And another odd thing; she could smell cigar smoke.

A whistling teakettle took Estelle to the kitchen. It gave Edna a chance to look around more. The smoke she smelled would have been pipe tobacco, for the pipe sat on a side table. There was a well-stocked bar behind glass doors. If not married, Estelle must have a gentleman friend, she thought. It shouldn't surprise her; Estelle was a trim, good-looking woman.

They were finishing up their coffee before Edna had her answers. The first half hour it had been all about Edna: Had she found a boyfriend yet, did she have many friends? The last question gave her pause for thought. She realized that the closest thing she had for a friend was the woman sitting opposite her, and she hardly knew Estelle. When it came to why she left Paddington Station, Edna found herself telling all. She had no one else to talk to, and it was a release to get it off her chest. Only when she'd finished did she have a sudden thought.

"Oh, Estelle, I hope you don't think I'm a bad person. I always treated my employers right, and I wouldn't let you down if you found me a housekeeping position."

Estelle had been sitting quietly, studying Edna. She sat forward suddenly, apparently having made a decision.

"Chéri, you have told me your little secret. Now I will tell you mine. Our secrets we don't tell to anyone else, okay?"

Edna nodded, curious to hear what her new friend had to say.

"I think we are a lot alike, you and I," Estelle explained. "You have ambition like I had at your age. I admire that. My sisters married men with nothing, and struggled to pay the rent. That was not for me. When I saw an opportunity, I took it."

The confession that followed, at times had Edna with her mouth open. Estelle was twenty when an English 'gentleman' came to her village in the south of France. He had rented a local chateau for the summer. He was out for a hike without his family when he stopped in the corner shop where Estelle worked. He was obviously smitten with her, and returned many times over the next few weeks. Eventually they'd met in back of the shop, where she'd let him kiss her, play with her breasts, lift her skirt and fondle her 'til she was damp.

"He wasn't bad," she explained, "a little old, a bit pudgy, but not bad looking. If I closed my eyes, he could have been anybody." She saw the look of shock on Edna's face. "Chéri, he had something all the local boys lacked: money, lots of money."

Edna swallowed hard and tried not to be judgmental.

When the 'gentleman' returned to England, he sent for Estelle, and set her up in the Kensington flat. He was, she told Edna, a prominent man, but she could never reveal who he was. He provided well for her, and now for her widowed mother. She saw him every two weeks or so, and had actually grown quite fond of him.

Edna sat in shock. What followed shocked her even more. Estelle reached out and took her hand.

"Chéri, look around you. You could have all this, it's the easiest job in the world," she continued as Edna's eyes widened.

"My gentleman has a friend, he is looking for someone, a lady friend. I think he'd like you."

Edna squirmed uncomfortably. "I don't think…" she began, but Estelle cut her off.

"Don't worry, chéri, if you don't like him, you wouldn't have to go through with it. You could at least meet him." She patted Edna's hand. "You need a little time to think about it. Call me tomorrow."

Edna made the phone call around ten. It was the flat that finally decided her. She looked around her dingy, musty smelling flat; with its decaying shared bathroom—shared by the alcoholic upstairs—and saw a way out. Her prospects of finding another job were so slim, and besides, who would know. She had no friends to speak of, and her family was a continent away. If she did it just long enough to accumulate a small nest egg, it would be okay. She managed to convince herself.

She had another meeting with Estelle. This time Estelle served cocktails. After the second one, Edna felt light-headed. Estelle was explaining the man in question—obviously married—was also a prominent member of society; his identity would not be revealed. If Edna liked him, they'd have their first rendezvous at Estelle's. Then, if things went well, he'd have Estelle set Edna up in her own flat.

"How do you know he'll like me? Edna inquired.

"I'm just about sure he will, but I need to see you naked. Take your clothes off," she practically ordered Edna. She brushed aside Edna's protests, "You can keep your panties on, but I have to see your breasts."

"Why?"

"He likes young girls. I have to see that your breasts aren't too large."

"How young?"

"Young"

"Estelle, I'm in my thirties, for Christ's sake." The drink had loosened Edna's tongue.

"Yes, but you look so young, chéri. If your body's young, we can make you look even younger. Trust me."

Edna reluctantly stripped off. She felt foolish standing in front of the little Frenchwoman, but Estelle nodded her approval.

"Just as I thought, chéri, your body is boyish; small breasts, no sagging, a little more bottom than I would like, but you'll do." She pulled the front of Edna's panties open and peered in. "We'll have to shave that bush," she said, and laughed heartily at Edna's horrified expression. "Here, chéri, you need another drink."

Edna saw the funny side of the situation and laughed with her. "And I suppose he'll want me to wear a school uniform?" she said in jest.

"Probably."

"You must be joking!"

"Don't worry, chéri, I can make you look like a teenager. I'm going to set up a meeting, but you'll come here first so I can dress you," Estelle said, smiling at Edna. "This could be fun, chéri."

Edna's smile dimmed. "If you say so."

The meeting was to take place at the Regents Park Hotel in London's West End. Estelle had booked a table for tea. It was the classiest place Edna had eaten in. She eyed the plates of pastries being wheeled between tables. At any other time, her mouth would have been salivating, but not today. Her stomach was doing flip-flops. She knew the man in question wouldn't be there for another half hour, but that didn't do much to ease her tension.

Estelle sensed her anxiety and squeezed her hand, "Relax chéri, you look like an adorable schoolgirl."

Edna knew she was right. The transformation had been amazing. She wasn't wearing a school uniform, but a youthful print dress supplied by Estelle. It de-emphasized any womanly curves, but Estelle still insisted on no bra. Her shoes were flat, and to her embarrassment, Estelle had made her wear ankle socks. She was ready to resist if Estelle had wanted to braid her hair, but she didn't. It went without saying there was no makeup.

Checking herself in the mirror before they left Estelle's flat, Edna couldn't believe the transformation. She could probably get children's fare on any bus in the city.

They'd only been in the restaurant thirty minutes or so when Estelle leaned toward her with a smile. "You passed, chéri."

"What do you mean? " Edna was confused. She looked around. "Is he here?"

"Relax, little girl, he's gone already. But not before giving me a nod that he liked you."

"But I didn't see him." Edna was annoyed.

"We couldn't meet him in public, chéri. Now you will meet him at my place. Are you ready?"

Edna was shaken. "I wish you had told me."

"Then you would have put on an act. I wanted you to look like a nervous schoolgirl. Come on, now let's see if you like him." Before standing, she gripped Edna's hand. "Now remember, chéri, you're not going to marry him.

Butterflies took over Edna's stomach. "He won't want to do anything today will he?"

"I'm not sure, probably not," but her words were said without conviction.

Chapter 18

Naomi and Louise sat forward on the edge of their chairs listening to Marge's amazing story about their aunt. They hadn't interrupted with questions; the truth was they were speechless.

Marge was enjoying herself, and she liked to think that Edna wouldn't mind. She'd always found Edna's past colorful. She could tell by the girls' expressions that Edna had been successful in keeping the truth from her family. Her siblings were all gone now, so it wouldn't hurt to let the story out.

She paused to pour more iced tea and let the girls catch their breath.

Louise broke the silence. "Wow, who'd have thought, Aunt Edna a call girl."

"Not a call girl, honey, she'd be the first one to correct you on that. A mistress; there's quite a distinction. A call girl sleeps around, I don't think Edna would have done that."

"Well, was this Estelle a madam, setting her up like that?" Naomi joined the conversation.

"Turns out she was, somewhat. She was apparently the one all the politicians called when they wanted a bit on the side."

Naomi pounced on that piece of information. "Ah, so they were politicians."

"Yes, most of them; Edna's certainly was, and he had a title.

"You mean Sir something?" Louise asked.

"Try Lord something," Marge responded.

Naomi and Louise said 'wow' simultaneously.

Marge continued telling them about Estelle. "Edna only found out all this about Estelle much later. But the funny part; she wasn't even French! It was all an act. She was born in Hackney. Doesn't that just crack you up?" Marge laughed heartily. "Hackney in London."

"But the story about meeting her 'gentleman' in France?" Louise asked.

"Made up. It worked though. Edna said it made her more accepting of the idea. She was certainly a cool customer, that Estelle."

"But did she have a gentleman? Was she someone's mistress?" Naomi wondered.

"Oh, yes, he was for real, and that's really how she got into it," Marge laughed again. "It was just another way of supplementing her income."

"So they paid her?"

"Not in cash. Some stock would change hands. She was no dummy, that's for sure." Marge finished.

Louise wondered if Edna had kept in touch with her after she left England.

"Oh, no, they were on the outs a while before Edna left," Marge explained. "She'd found out too much for Estelle's liking. I think Estelle was jealous of the way things turned out for Edna."

"How did they turn out? Did she like the guy? I'm assuming she did." Naomi was anxious to hear more.

"I'm not sure like is the right word," Marge said thoughtfully, "I'm not even sure how Edna would describe it."

Chapter 19

Edna

Estelle had to practically push Edna into her living room. He had helped himself to a drink, and was sitting on the sofa when they came in. Getting up was a struggle, and Edna saw why—to her dismay. Estelle had described him as a little portly, but Edna knew a potbelly when she saw one. In his sixties, Estelle said. More like pushing seventy, Edna thought. He was tall for an Englishman, and had the large nose prevalent in the land; in his case, laced with a network of broken blood vessels. He is impeccably dressed, and he does have hair—that's a plus, she thought sarcastically.

She was ready to reject him on the spot. But when he spoke, he had a surprisingly gentle voice, with a slight Scots brogue. Estelle had been sending Edna stabbing little looks, warning her not to respond too hastily. She'd promised she wouldn't, so tried to calm down.

The introductions were made. His palm was somewhat sweaty. Oh, God, Edna thought, if his palm's sweaty, what's the rest of him like. She was in danger of losing it. Estelle, perhaps sensing it, excused herself and ducked out before Edna had time to react.

"Come sit down, let's get acquainted," he patted the sofa next to him.

She approached the sofa as though it were a bed of nails and sat out of arms reach. They chatted a little. She found herself trying to sound young, as Estelle had instructed, and wondered why she was bothering. There was no way she could go through with this.

"Would you like a little drinkie?" He was up before she could respond. "A wee gin and tonic, perhaps?"

She nodded, glad to have something to keep them both occupied. Oh, how she wished Estelle would hurry back. Wouldn't she have something to say to her, ducking out like that without any warning. He handed her the drink with a gentle smile. She noticed his hand shook a little. When she tasted how strong he'd made it, she knew Estelle had prepared him well.

They had made it through the first drink and were partway through the next. He was beginning to look better; had actually made her laugh a couple of times. Later, she couldn't remember what they talked about. In what seemed no time at all, his driver was buzzing the doorbell. When he got up to respond, she realized with relief that he wasn't planning to have a go at her today. She thought she was home free. But he returned to the sofa, and beckoned her to come closer. She could see perspiration on his upper lip.

"Now, wee lassie, I have to go. I'll come and see you again, is that all right?"

She found herself nodding approval and again wondered why. Had she taken leave of her senses? Was where she lived that important?

"Good, " he said, "Before I go though, you've been a naughty girl having a wee drinkie. I'll have to spank you for that."

She couldn't believe her ears; surely he was joking. But to her astonishment, he pulled her over his knee, flipped up her dress and pulled down her panties. She felt his hand caress her buttocks before he spanked them. He didn't do it hard, just enough to turn them pink. Edna was speechless, and when he stopped was gasping for breath. He mistook it for crying, and tried to bend and kiss the flushed areas. His belly got in the way, so he caressed them again repeating, "Daddy will make it better, there, there, Daddy will make it better."

And then he was gone. Edna was so shaken; she poured herself another stiff drink. She lay out on the sofa, and was on her way to being completely smashed, when Estelle returned.

"Now that wasn't so bad was it, chéri? He is a nice gentleman, right?" She hugged Edna. "I'm to take you looking for a flat tomorrow. We'll find one in Kensington, like mine. You'll be so happy."

Edna, speech slurred, tried to get out a thought, "But I don't think I…"

Estelle jumped in quickly. "Look, chéri," she held out a 50 pound note, "he didn't want to give it to you, he thought you might take it the wrong way. He wants you to treat yourself. What a nice man."

The next morning, Edna awoke with a dreadful headache. She asked herself, "What am I doing?" The 50-pound note lay on her bedside table. She picked it up and studied it. Was she really capable of doing this for money? There had to be other work out there somewhere. She climbed out of bed, resolving to phone Estelle and call the whole thing off.

Edna hadn't slept well. The drunk upstairs had created a racket around 2 a.m. Then she heard him fall out of bed closer to three. She made her way to the shared bathroom. The door was open, and the smell emanating from the windowless room was overwhelming. The drunk had puked by the toilet again. Edna covered her mouth and nose with her hand; she had to pee. In the middle of relieving herself, she made a final decision.

The die was cast. The next day they found a furnished flat in Kensington, much like Estelle's, and only a few blocks away. Edna received her instructions: No family photos displayed—it made them uneasy, no other visitors to the flat—ever. She was told to keep the bar well stocked and herself available. That didn't mean she couldn't go anywhere, Estelle explained. She would only see her 'gentleman' every two weeks or so, and a pattern would soon be established. Estelle added a few more instructions tailored for Edna: Keep your pubic hair shaved, act like a girl and even wear a school uniform if he wants you to.

Every time Edna started to doubt her decision, she looked around her new flat and told herself she did the right thing. It was beautiful, and the bathroom was all hers. She knew Daddy's first visit would be difficult, but she'd get through it with her eyes closed. She thought of him as Daddy, because she didn't have another name, and that's how he referred to himself.

His first visit took place sooner than she'd expected. He gave her an hour's notice. Time enough to shave and put on one of the girly dresses she'd bought. And time enough to swallow a huge gin and tonic.

It was awful. He'd obviously had to sauce himself up to give him courage for their first encounter. His journey up the short flight of stairs to her front door had been nothing short of a miracle. She'd saved him the trouble of finding her doorbell by opening the door herself. Edna thought in his unsteady state he'd more likely sleep than fool around. She was wrong.

"Hello little girlie, Daddy's home. Let's go and help Daddy get comfortable." He patted her bottom as she walked through the door ahead of him.

She didn't offer him a drink, although afterwards she wished she had—one more might have put him over the edge. He flopped on the sofa and told her to take Daddy's shoes off. Next came the clothing, layer by layer. She unbuttoned his shirt and caught her breath. My God, she thought, he wears a girdle! The thought of the belly being even larger than it appeared made her struggle to stop from vomiting. She stopped at his briefs. She just couldn't do it.

"Oh, my wee girlie's shy. Well let me show you what Daddy's got for you."

He dropped his briefs and stood before her. His potbelly, though it protruded, didn't hang—giving her a clear view of what he'd got for her. Edna had never seen a penis she considered beautiful, but this one took the booby prize as far as she was concerned. It was large, drooping, and covered in bulging veins. Close your eyes, Edna, close your eyes, she told herself.

He'd arrived with a paper sack tucked under his arm, and now held it out to her.

"Here, I've brought you a wee present, go and put them on," he instructed.

She hurried to the bedroom, tore open the bag and almost laughed out loud. A pair of navy-blue flannel panties, like young schoolgirls wore—really young schoolgirls wore. She pulled them on, and reluctantly went back to him.

"Now we're going to play a game," he said.

The game consisted of him on all fours crawling around the room looking up her skirt. First, she had to climb on the coffee table, then the sofa. Then she had to stand over him, pull aside the elastic leg and let him have a 'wee peep.' Then a 'wee touch.' Finally, he pulled off her knickers.

Then suddenly he was "Daddy" again, not the young boy he'd been pretending to be. Daddy was horrified to see her with her knickers off. He bent her over the chair, and whacked her bottom with his semi-limp penis. Then he tried, without success, to penetrate her. Either the drink or his nervousness over their first encounter kept him from holding an erection.

After many failed attempts, the doorbell buzzed. His ride! Thank heaven for small mercies, Edna thought.

Estelle called before the hour was out.

"How was it, chéri, not too bad, eh?" She said with fake cheerfulness.

"I survived," Edna responded without enthusiasm.

"Each time gets easier, you'll see. Now, get dressed up, we'll go and celebrate."

Celebrate, Edna thought, *celebrate*; not a word I would have chosen.

Estelle was right; it did get better with time. Daddy's visits were a variation of his first one. She was always a girl, which satisfied her. She didn't have to act amorous and fake orgasms. At first, she thought his actions perverse, but came to see it differently. At least he wasn't out preying on an actual young girl, she told herself.

Edna gave herself a year, but the year came and went. They had settled into a routine, and her bank account was growing. She loved her flat, and had found companionship and sexual satisfaction in a most bizarre fashion. Not with Daddy, with Gordon.

It was no coincidence that Estelle found Edna's flat so quickly, she would later learn. Daddy owned the building, and she was not the first 'wee girlie' he'd had ensconced there. Age or indifference had necessitated a turnover. Upstairs resided Gordon: Daddy's trusted confidante, financial adviser, and the son of an old friend. In his late forties, Gordon's family had stopped trying to marry him off. He was too shy for his own good, they surmised. He became Daddy's perfect alibi. "Off to see Gordon on some financial matters, my dear," was an off-used expression in Daddy's household.

It was inevitable that Edna and Gordon would meet. His shyness didn't protect him; Edna seduced him on their fourth meeting. Theirs was a strange friendship, but satisfying to both of them. They would sit and talk late into the night. It was from Gordon that Edna learned the basics of finance. One of Gordon's tasks was to 'pay' Edna. Money couldn't change hands: too easy to trace. His methods were complex, but eventually Edna would get her due. She let Gordon invest for her; something Daddy didn't know about.

Daddy also didn't know Edna knew his true identity. It didn't take her long to discover. A snippet on the evening news showed parliament debating an official date to celebrate the new queen's birthday. Her eyes weren't on the screen, but his voice drew her attention. There was her 'daddy', a member of the House of Lords. She gave a satisfied smile; the information might help her someday.

That day was a long time coming. Almost eight years into their relationship, Daddy died on her, literally. As she would tell her friend Marge years later, " It didn't seem funny at the time, but it was like something you see in the movies now."

"Didn't you have any inkling it was going to happen?" Marge had asked.

"No," Edna explained to her friend. "We were on the bed, he was on top. His legs had started giving out if he stood, but he still liked to be the aggressor. Anyway, Marge, he couldn't get it in, he struggled and struggled, got redder and redder in the face. Suddenly he gave a big moan, I thought he'd come, but then he went limp. God was he heavy: I couldn't breathe."

When Daddy went limp, it took Edna a minute or two to realize what had happened. He didn't respond when she talked to him. When the truth hit her, she was horrified.

Daddy was lying dead on top of her! She tried rolling him off, but the bed was soft and his dead weight was too much for her. She screamed for Gordon with all her might, hoping, frantically, that he was home.

Edna and Gordon were on their third drink. It had been quite a day. They'd had to call the police. They did think briefly about trying to move him to Gordon's flat, to avoid a scandal, but Daddy's size made it impossible. She had wanted to dress him, but Gordon said what's the use, he's on the bed, they'll put two and two together.

The police interview had been embarrassing in the least. When they'd asked for Daddy's name, Gordon took them aside and explained the situation. Eventually, an ambulance was called and Daddy, wearing nothing more than a blanket, left Edna's flat for the last time. She stood at the window in her robe watching the ambulance crew at work. A car pulled up, the occupant, a youngish man in a business suit, jumped out and hurried over to get a look at Daddy. He glanced up at the window and Edna hastily withdrew. Later she found his business card in her mail slot. He was a reporter for one of the sleazier newspapers. He'd obviously recognized Daddy. Gordon wasn't surprised.

"Those chaps chase after ambulances, especially in this area, where every other person is someone in the public eye."

"And he wants my story," Edna sounded thoughtful.

"You bet he does, and he'd pay you well for it," Gordon said with concern.

She smiled at him. "I wouldn't want to tarnish Daddy, or rather Lord Robert's reputation, but it's tempting."

"Edna, you wouldn't?" Now he was alarmed.

"No, I probably wouldn't, but what do I do now."

They sat quietly for a while, Gordon deep in thought. When he broke the silence, he had a plan.

"I think I've worked it out, Edna. Lord Robert couldn't put you in his will, but I know he would want you to get a settlement," he explained. Then he laid out a plan: the family lawyers would be told Edna was contemplating telling her story, but would consider a settlement. Gordon had ideas on what that should be, and asked Edna to trust him.

"Gordon, I don't want you to destroy your relationship with the family," she said, "after all he was your father's friend."

"My father may have tolerated his conduct, but I found it loathsome. Revolting even."

She'd never seen him so riled up.

He continued. "He may have been a good politician, and, yes, I liked him. But it's hard to overlook this side of him."

And so she agreed to his plan, and so did Lord Robert's family. The settlement was too complex for her to understand. She knew stocks and bonds were involved, and Gordon was in charge of it all. He said it could take a couple of years to finalize everything. She trusted him because of his reaction to the family's demands of her. He didn't have any problem with the first one: she must call the reporter, feign surprise at him leaving his card and tell him innocently that Lord Robert was, of course, visiting his friend and financial advisor who lived upstairs. She knew the reporter didn't believe her, but with nothing else to go on, the matter was dropped.

The second demand Lord Robert's lawyers made clearly upset Gordon: Edna must leave the country quickly, and promise not to return. Gordon's reaction confirmed a growing suspicion she had; the man was in love with her. She didn't love him. She was fond of him, yes, but she didn't love him. Rather than let him see it, she pretended to be upset. They could meet in Canada or America, she told him, knowing he'd never take her up on it.

Now here she was winging her way westward, a woman of means. It would take longer than she anticipated for the money to come through. She'd have to work at something for a year or two. Then the world was her oyster.

Edna beckoned the stewardess. "I'd like some champagne, please."

"Certainly, madam, I'll be right back."

The stewardess returned, poured Edna's champagne and asked, "Is there anything else I can get you, madam?"

"Not a thing," Edna responded. She waited for the woman to leave, and then raised her glass to the window. Gazing out at passing clouds, she said in a whisper, "Here's to you Daddy, wherever you are."

Chapter 20

Naomi had her bare feet propped up on the wicker table she kept in her sunroom. Three weeks had passed since the Arizona trip, and now it was a warm day in Oregon; warm enough to have all the windows open. A slight breeze tousled her hair, and she blew a wisp away from her eyes. Spike stretched out on the floor beside her trying to cool himself. Naomi, reaching for her iced tea, gave his belly a rub with her bare toes. He gave a small purr, but didn't move a muscle.

"Lazy old cat," she said affectionately.

After working all morning on her book, she was taking a break. It felt good to get away from the computer for a while. She was riffling through the package from New Zealand, briefly looking at the photos, but the letter her mother had written was what she wanted. Something was troubling her. Going over the letter again, she tried to come to some conclusions. Along with the mention of money, her mother had remarked on Edna's fancy new clothes. That was probably why I'd jumped on Edna as the suspect, Naomi thought. After the Arizona visit and all that Marge had told them, it was obvious Edna had no motive. Naomi felt so bad that she'd been so ready to convict Aunt Edna. On the flight back from Arizona, she'd talked about it with Louise.

"Don't feel bad, sis, I was convinced she'd run off with the money too," Louise admitted. Then she giggled. "How were we to know she was gainfully employed?"

Naomi laughed too. “Oh my, I wasn’t prepared for that, were you? In your wildest dreams could you even imagine doing that?”

“In my wildest dreams…yes.” Louise said with dramatic flair. “It was fun though, wasn’t it?”

“Yes, it was.” Naomi’s brow furrowed. “ I feel sorry for Aunt Edna never falling in love. Do you think she would have gotten together with Gordon if he hadn’t died so soon?”

“I doubt it. Marge said they corresponded up until he died. If Edna had wanted him, knowing her she’d have got him. No,” Louise said with conviction, “she obviously wasn’t in love with him. Poor old Gordon.”

“Well, he certainly set her up for life, didn’t he?”

“He and Daddy both. Now why couldn’t you and I have met a duo like that?” Louise joked.

Naomi laughed. “I’d take Ben and your Sam any day. I’ve been thinking, Lou, I’d like to do something for Aunt Edna, but I don’t know what. We can’t send her flowers she couldn’t see. What can we do?”

“Difficult, isn’t it?” Louise agreed. “How about sending Marge flowers instead, and explaining our dilemma to her?”

Naomi liked the idea, so that’s what they did.

Well, Naomi thought, packaging up the letter, Aunt Edna is eliminated as a suspect. Mum wasn’t to know who financed the fancy clothes, but that left only Gwen and Violet as suspects. We may soon have the answer on Gwen, Naomi realized. There had been a message on the answering machine when she got back from Arizona. Her cousin Michael in Canada was ready to arrange a family reunion. Naomi called Louise and they’d agreed on a date. It was agreeable to the cousins. Now Michael, his wife Jean, their cousin Susan and her husband, Paul, were coming to Oregon late in August. Michael had a timeshare at a resort near Redmond, so they would be staying there. The reunion would take place at Louise and Sam's. They would stay up to four days; there would be plenty of time to learn more about Aunt Gwen and Uncle Bill.

An old oak cabinet in the living room housed all manner of things Naomi hadn't found a home for yet. She was putting the New Zealand package back on a shelf when Ben called.

"Bad time?" he asked.

"No, perfect, I was just taking a break. How about you, have you finished the stinky statistical stuff?"

Ben's environmental analysis sometimes got him holed up at home. He practically withdrew from the world as he struggled with mind-boggling statistics. Naomi hadn't seen much of him for a few days.

"It's not stinky statistical stuff, it's all necessary—um," he searched for words, "stinky statistical stuff," Ben finished, to the sound of her giggles.

"Told you."

"Okay, smarty-pants, maybe I won't tell you why I called."

"But then again, maybe you will. You're dying to tell me, I can hear it in your voice. What's up?"

"Are you at a place where you could take a couple of days off?"

"I think so, it's been going well."

"Well, see what you think of this: Peggy called, there are a number of things at the ranch I need to see to. How about driving out there with me? I can show you the ranch, then drive you to your sister's and pick you up the next day. I've wanted to meet Louise, Sam and your nephews. What do you say?"

"It sounds great. I'd like to meet your sister, too. Peggy will be there, right? We still need a chaperone you know," she teased him.

"Yes, she'll be there, but who's going to protect your virtue on the drive over?"

"You'll need both hands on the wheel for the Santiam Pass, and I'll only authorize one stop."

"Where's that?"

"Mill City for ice cream. It's against the law to go through there without getting one, you know," she continued her teasing.

"For you, a double scoop," Ben responded.

They agreed to leave the day after next. She assured him Louise wouldn't mind the short notice. The drive over would take the best part of three hours. They'd never been alone that long, but not a lot can happen when you're driving, Naomi assured herself.

The drive over was sheer magic, Naomi thought later. They'd listened to good music, held hands a few times, shared childhood experiences and even talked about the future. Talking about Elaine wasn't easy for Ben. He admitted to losing hope that she would ever come out of the coma. Her doctor wouldn't say as much himself, for some brain activity had been detected. Now so much time had passed, Ben sensed the doctor was losing hope. Ben finally said for the first time he would welcome her death. The revelation caused him to choke up. Naomi squeezed his hand tightly, and gently steered the conversation in a more positive direction.

They made only one stop on the way over: at Mill City where she settled for a single scoop of huckleberry ice cream. She was familiar with Sisters, the closest town to Ben's ranch, but had never been up the side road leading to his home. Naomi loved the ranch even before she saw the house. She could see why Ben was so drawn to the place. The setting was perfect: tall ponderosa pine, a large pond with willows, lush, irrigated pasture for the horses and llamas, and a wonderful view of the Three Sisters mountains.

They were thrown a curve when they got to the front door. Peggy had pinned a note to the screen. It seemed her daughter in Eugene had been rushed to hospital with appendicitis. She apologized for her absence, but had to hurry over there. There followed a list of things Ben should attend to.

The air was charged with tension as they absorbed the fact they were here alone. Naomi couldn't meet Ben's eyes. She was unsure what his next move would be. It would be better if I act nonchalant about the situation, she thought.

"Well, do you want to give me a quick tour of the place before we head to Louise's?" she asked.

"Sure thing, the tour starts here." He was quick to pick up her tone. "But we'd better say hello to the dogs first."

The dogs, Gertie and Bart, were ecstatic to see Ben. They were in a run attached to the barn. He let them out and had to restrain them from slobbering all over Naomi. She hugged them, and told him not to worry they'd soon settle down. Gertie, a golden lab, was the most rambunctious of the pair. Bart, a basset hound, would definitely be described as laid back. He lay on his back, inviting Naomi to rub his belly. She did so, looking up at Ben and laughing. Ben's expression caused her cheeks to flush. She saw so much desire in his face it unnerved her.

"Better get that tour underway," she said quickly.

His jaw was clenched as he nodded in agreement.

To own a log home had long been one of Naomi's dreams; one she hadn't shared with Ben. It hadn't seemed appropriate. This house was everything she'd want in a log home. The logs were large, and a warm honey color. A covered porch ran the length of the house, both front and back. The metal roof and trim were painted a dark, rich green. Inside, logs were exposed sparingly, mostly on some lower walls. There were a number of sheet-rocked walls, giving the house a light, airy feeling. All the large ceiling beams were left exposed, and the ceilings themselves were ten feet—with the exception of the kitchen and breakfast nook. The great room, with a wonderful river rock fireplace, had a cathedral ceiling, opening to a loft.

"It's beautiful," she assured Ben.

He nodded. "The truth is, it's hardly been lived in. Peggy's spent more time here than we did. Elaine was traveling so much, I took to staying out in the cabin near the dogs."

"The cabin?"

"Come on," he said, "I'll show you."

The cabin was just that: a one-room log structure—with bathroom—nestled into the pines on the back portion of the property.

Ben swept his hand across the forest view beyond the fence. "All that's public land: Bureau of Land Management. It goes on for miles."

The inside of the cabin could be described in one word: cozy. A single bed, with plaid wool cover, sat against one wall. The opposite wall, housed a small Swedish-style woodstove. The only other furniture in the room was an old oak rocking chair, an end table and a tiny set of drawers. The log walls and ceiling in the cabin made it rather dark but gave it an intimate feel.

Naomi poked her head in the bathroom and withdrew.

Ben grinned. "You missed something."

"What?" She looked puzzled.

He walked behind the bathroom door and pointed to a cabinet. "The kitchen," he said, pulling on the door. It dropped down into a shelf, revealing a coffeepot, hotplate and a meager supply of food items.

"That's the smallest kitchen I've ever seen," she laughed, returning to the main room. She sat in the rocking chair, enjoying the feel of the smooth wood arms. Ben stood in the doorway, back to her. They stayed this way for a few minutes, not talking, both reluctant to leave this special place. She didn't need to see his expression to know what was going through his mind; she could feel the torment from across the room.

"We should go," he said hoarsely.

"I could stay here forever," Naomi responded, regretting the words as soon as they were uttered.

He turned to her. "Oh, God, Naomi, we must go," he implored her, and walked outside.

Naomi struggled to regain her composure. She lost the battle. Throwing caution to the wind, she walked over to the bed and threw back the plaid cover. It was a hot day and she was wearing a white gauzy dress, with matching loose slip underneath. She removed everything, and then feeling self-conscious put the top layer of her dress back on. It buttoned down the front and she hastily fastened a few buttons.

Ben had walked out behind the cabin and was leaning on the back fence watching the dogs play. Her feet crunched on the cinder path and he turned to face her. She had the sun behind her, he could make out every curve of her body, and the way the breeze was blowing her hair around. It wasn't until she was at his side that he saw her state of undress.

He gasped. "Naomi, don't ask this of me, please." He had an arm out as though to ward her off.

She pushed his arm away and pressed a finger to his lips. "Ben, all I'm asking for is to live for this moment. No commitments, no guilt. I need you to make love to me. Don't make me have to beg for it, I can't help myself anymore."

She saw and felt his resignation as he pulled her to him.

" Naomi, oh, Naomi." He was kissing her all over her face. "I want to be able to say I love you, you know that, don't you?"

She was nodding with tears in her eyes. Their lips met and they kissed with a passion she'd never felt before. His tongue sought hers and her body trembled. His arms were on her shoulders, now they ran down her back and cradled her buttocks, pressing her to him.

Then he forced her away from him and stood looking at her. The wind and their passion had loosed all the buttons on her dress. She stood before him totally exposed.

"My God, you're beautiful," he gasped. "Even more beautiful than I'd imagined." Then he touched her breasts gently, running his hands over her body as though it were a blown glass creation. He cupped her breasts and bent to kiss them. Her nipples stood erect; his lips found them. Suddenly he gave a moan, picked her up in his arms and strode toward the cabin.

They arrived at Louise and Sam's a little later than expected. It had been so hard tearing themselves away from the solitude of the ranch. They were so absorbed with each other; both sensing this was a one-time occurrence.

Introductions had been made and now Sam and Ben were outside looking over the property. Louise grabbed Naomi to help get drinks for everyone. In truth, she could hardly wait to get her sister alone.

"You did it!" Louise said jubilantly.

Naomi was astounded. "How did you know?"

"How did I know? You positively sparkle, that's how." Louise turned to teasing. "So, what happened to—we're just going to be friends?"

Naomi smiled. "We were finally put to the test. Hormones won out, Lou."

"Well, I'm glad they did. I like him, sis, he seems real nice. You didn't tell me he was so good looking. Well, maybe you did, but you didn't say he had a great bod."

"Oh, Lou," Naomi scolded. "You're not supposed to notice things like that, you're a married woman."

"Okay, but I'm not blind. Those Wrangler butts just drive me nuts."

"Lou, cut it out," Naomi said laughing.

Louise smiled at her sister. "Seriously Naomi, he seems very nice. The boys sure took to him."

Craig and Brian could be seen through the window, doing their best to get Ben's attention. Later, over a meal, they opted to sit on either side of him; an honor usually bestowed on Naomi. Both boys loved to camp, and listened intently as Ben told of a close encounter with a bear on his last trip out. They asked what seemed like a million questions, and Naomi was impressed with Ben's patience. Sam and her nephews appreciated Ben's knowledge of the wilderness, which was closely linked with his profession. Naomi caught Louise studying Ben, and could sense her approval. It wasn't that she needed her family's approval, but it was nice to see they liked him.

It was late when he left. The boys had been sent up to get ready for bed. Sam, about to go and check on them, turned to Naomi.

"He's a real nice guy, Naomi. I sure hope it works out for you."

"Thanks, Sam, so do I."

Louise was quiet. She busied herself about the kitchen, obviously deep in thought. Naomi knew she wanted to say something, but hadn't found the words yet. They worked side by side for a few minutes. Finally, Naomi couldn't stand it any more.

"Okay, out with it, Lou."

"No, it's nothing," Louise explained, "I was just thinking about life's ironies. I wish, oh, how I wish the situation could be different. But what I keep coming back to is that he's just right for you."

Naomi's eyes filled with tears. "Yes, but I can't have him."

Louise put down the cans she was holding and hugged her sister. "I know, I know, that's what I mean. What a cruel twist of fate." Louise patted Naomi's back, like a mother soothing a baby. She said gently, " It might not always be this way, sis, just take it a day at a time."

Chapter 21

The post office wasn't busy. Naomi entered almost walking on air. Under her arm, she clutched the finished manuscript. Nothing could spoil her happy mood, not even Kevin's cousin Angela working the counter. She had never cared much for Angela, and was sure the feeling was mutual. Still, she greeted her in friendly fashion, and when the business had been taken care of inquired about Kevin.

"Have you seen Kevin lately? Have they had the baby yet?"

"She's got a couple of months to go, but she's having problems. They may do a C section soon," Angela replied, with hardly an expression.

"Oh, I'm so sorry, I do hope everything turns out all right," Naomi was sincere. "If you see him, be sure and tell him I wish them the best."

Angela gave a sarcastic sneer. "I'm sure that will help."

The slight was like water on a duck's back to Naomi. Her manuscript was on its way; a weight had been lifted from her shoulders. She drove home with the radio loud, singing along with the Pointer Sisters.

When she got home there were flowers on the doorstep. Ben's card read, "Just to complete that euphoria you're feeling, Love Ben." She'd called him before she left for the post office. Their relationship had changed since they made love six weeks ago. They hadn't done it again. The tension had been released, and now they were content to go back to where they were. There was an unspoken love between them. Naomi felt guilty for practically seducing him, though she knew he wanted it as much as she did. She hoped Elaine could forgive her, should that day ever arise.

They hadn't talked about the future again. It was far too painful for Ben. There was no change in Elaine's condition. Ben was in limbo: waiting for a woman he loved to die, and free him to begin a life with a woman he also loved. Naomi felt a deep compassion for him and knew, no matter what the future brought, she would always love him. She had loved Kevin, still did after a fashion, but making love to Ben was like doing it for the first time. A depth of passion she never achieved with Kevin. Soul mate was the buzzword these days. Kevin was a wonderful friend, but she'd never quite thought of him as her soul mate. There was no doubt in her mind: Ben was her soul mate.

She hadn't talked to Louise much over the past six weeks. It had been a goal to get the book finished before the upcoming family reunion. The family mystery, as they'd taken to calling it, had been put on hold, at least as far as Naomi was concerned.

She called Louise later in the day. "The dirty deed is done."

"Yea, way to go, Naomi. I'll bet you're feeling thirty pounds lighter. What do you think? Were you happy with the way it turned out?"

"Yes, I think I am. There was a point were I thought I wasn't able to immerse myself in it enough to make it good. But in the last six weeks, I pulled it off."

"And we all know what happened six weeks ago, don't we?" Louise teased her.

"Lou, trust you to jump on that."

"Hey, whatever works. See, all that release of tension left you free to create. Anyway, I'm glad you called; I wanted to call you, but didn't want to interrupt."

"Why? What's up?"

"My friend in England e-mailed me. She's waded her way through a pile of documents on the Cavenish estate. From what she can make out, the government confiscated the entire estate over a hundred years ago."

"What for?"

"She said it's hard to fathom out, but it appears to be connected to royal gaming."

"Did she say what that is?"

"Something to do with setting aside land for the royals to hunt on. The government apparently felt the Cavenish acquired the land illegally. Anyway, back in the fifties a Cavenish—don't know how he's related—took it to court. He was seeking just compensation for the heirs.

It sounds as though he was a lawyer. He died in '65, by the way."

"So that's where the money came from?"

"It could be," Louise explained, "but there was apparently appeal after appeal. Pat, my friend, is still trying to wade through it. She can't spend a lot of time on it at the moment, she's involved in a pretty big case."

"Well, at least she's proved there was an estate involved. Since the government were looking for Granddad, it must have gone in the heirs favor, don't you think?"

"Not necessarily. They may have been rounding up the heirs, pending the outcome. It might have been required. Anyway, we're at a standstill at the moment, so on to other things now. About the reunion; will you be bringing Ben?"

Naomi wasn't ready to move on, but she responded to the question. "No, Lou, it wouldn't be appropriate."

"I didn't know if he might want to go to the ranch, then just pop over to have a barbecue with us."

"He'd probably say yes if I asked him. But I can't start including him in family activities until I know he's free to be part of the family."

"Still no change, huh?"

"No, it feels like it's going to go on forever, Lou."

"I know, sis, but one day at a time remember." Louise tried to comfort her sister.

They did more planning for the weekend's reunion. Naomi waited her chance to return to the family mystery.

"Lou, how well do you remember Aunt Violet?"

Louise hesitated. "We're not back to who killed Gran, are we?"

Naomi chose her words carefully. "I was just wondering if you remembered her as I do: so sweet and pretty."

"She was, and no I don't think she'd have been capable of killing anyone, in case you're also wondering that." Louise sounded peeved.

Naomi ignored her sister's tone. "Perhaps Michael and Susan will have more insight into how she ended her days. They seem to have been close to her. Michael said she used to send them postcards."

"Perhaps. I know Gwen and Aunt Violet were quite close; they would go to church together. I'm hoping the cousins can fill us in on a lot of family details."

"Like where Michael got all his money," Naomi added.

"That would be interesting, but I want to know about his dad. Uncle Bill was always a bit of a mystery."

"How so?"

"Well, Aunt Gwen seemed more like family than he did. I was always a bit afraid of him. He didn't smile much."

"That's what Michael said. I wonder what his problem was."

"Maybe we'll find out. But promise me one thing, Naomi; don't bring up Gran being euthanized. They'll think you're nuts." Louise waited for Naomi to respond, but she didn't, so she continued. "Gran died, sis, she just died."

The conversation ended soon after. Naomi looked pensive as she hung up the phone. Maybe Louise didn't believe their grandmother was euthanized, but their mother thought so. She'd told Naomi in as many words. Perhaps she'd thought they were all to blame: Aunt Edna, Aunt Violet and Aunt Gwen. Naomi just didn't know. She wondered again why she cared so passionately. Louise didn't. Why her? What hold did her grandmother have on her? They had so few years together. When she thought of her grandmother, she didn't see her face with any clarity, just her hair, her long, gray hair. But she had to see this through. Their mother had planted the seed, and whether Louise approved or not, Naomi vowed she would find an answer.

Chapter 22

Gwen

The hospital cafeteria was almost empty at this time of night. Gwen liked working the night shift. No matron hovering over you, waiting for your every mistake. The nursing sister was easy to get along with. She seemed to understand that some rules could go by the wayside, given the situation. Every bed was filled with the sick and wounded. Lately they'd been getting Canadian lads too. Gwen felt so sorry for them, fighting a war so far from home and having no one to visit. She'd do her bit to cheer them as she went on her rounds. For their part, they'd respond warmly to the little Welsh nurse.

Except the boy they'd brought in with appendicitis. There had been complications and he'd been here two weeks already. Gwen had never seen him smile. He was nice-looking and at first Gwen had tried to flirt with him. She soon gave it up as a lost cause. If he wasn't interested, that was his tough luck. There were plenty of other fish in the sea. She was always getting asked out. Her smile was what drew men to her, not her looks. She was short, with what she'd heard described as an ample figure. Her round Welsh face, with pale blue eyes, was framed with dark brown hair. She wore her hair in a pageboy except on duty, when it was pinned up under her starched cap. She was always smiling and this, coupled with her soft Welsh voice, the young soldiers found irresistible.

She finished her tea and hurried back to the ward. Beds were lined up along both walls, ten on each side. These weren't critical cases; the patients were well on the way to recovery. From here, they would be released back to their units. A young redheaded lad in the third bed beckoned her.

"Nurse, the chap in bed seven could use you. I think he's had some bad news."

Bed seven was the soldier who wouldn't smile: William Cavenish from Canada. She went straight to him and saw with alarm he was crying. After drawing the curtains around the bed, she sat beside him and took his hand. She didn't say a word just let him cry. He held on tight to her hand and in time the sobbing subsided.

"Bad news?" she asked quietly.

"My brother," he said. "Mum's letter only just reached me. He was killed a month ago."

"I'm so sorry, pet," she said sincerely. "Where was he?"

"France, up near the border."

She nodded; the casualties had been high from that battle. He continued to hold her hand as they talked. She asked if he'd seen action yet. He hadn't. His appendix ruptured soon after he reached England.

"Were you hoping to meet up with your brother?" she asked.

He nodded. "I figured they'd keep the Canadian troops together. Frank didn't know I was coming. I was going to surprise him…" his voice trailed off.

"I'm sorry, pet," she said again, squeezing his hand. She waited a few minutes before asking him about his family in Canada.

He talked of British Columbia, and of Spruce Creek. He had to paint a picture for her of where Spruce Creek was. She still couldn't place it. She kept him talking to keep his mind off his sorrow. He told her he was a lumberjack and described what that was like. She was called away a couple of times, but returned to him when time allowed. The second time back, he greeted her with a smile.

He looked so nice when he smiled, she could see why she was attracted to him. The first time she saw him out of bed she was surprised at how tall he was. He was a bit on the skinny side, but most of these young men were. His hair was very dark, and his eyes a lovely hazel. She thought his nose a little long and thin, but his smile seemed to shrink it.

They talked well into the night, and she saw a side of him that others would seldom see. He was discharged a few days later and went back to the Aldershot Barracks until they could figure out what to do with him. It was only a short distance from the hospital, covered quickly on a borrowed bicycle. He'd wait for her in the cafeteria, and soon the other nurses were calling him her boyfriend.

Their first formal date was when he asked awkwardly if she would like to go to the chippy for fish and chips, then perhaps to the pictures. They saw "This Happy Breed" and she noticed Bill didn't laugh as often as she did. Perhaps it's because he's Canadian, she thought, they might not understand the humor. She wore her green wool coat and a perky little hat to match. Bill told her she looked nice.

It was weeks before he plucked up the courage to kiss her, and she had egged him on at that. When his posting came through, he stammered, stuttered and finally blurted out a proposal. Gwen didn't hesitate; she had found things to love about Bill Cavenish. The hospital chaplain, with only a handful of people to witness it, married them. There was no time for Gwen's family in Wales to attend. They had known each other five weeks, four days. That was February 1942 and Bill shipped out the next day. He managed to get home on leave twice, but it was June 1945 before they were reunited.

Gwen spent the three years nursing a succession of young, lonely, battered men. There were times when she regretted her decision to marry in haste, times when she had trouble bringing her husband's face to mind. But after his first leave, things were better. It was considered bad luck to talk about the future, so they didn't. Bill wasn't in the line of fire, so they both knew instinctively they would have one together.

Their 'honeymoon' was spent visiting Gwen's family in Wales. Her father, Alynn Davies, and his sister Blodwen raised her, her mother having died in childbirth. The brother and sister were short, stocky look-alikes, with ruddy complexions characteristic of outdoor life. They lived on a farm in the Rhondda Valley, where her father tended his sheep and grew market produce. It would have been an idyllic setting, if not for the coalfields on the horizon.

Gwen and Bill spent three awkward days there, trying not to get underfoot. Noticing Gwen's folks were getting on in years, Bill tried to help. But he was not a farm boy and hadn't a clue how to handle sheep.

"Get a hand under her chin, boy," Alynn would shout out excitedly. "She's not going anywhere with you hanging on now, is she."

Gwen would stand and laugh at the sight of Bill hanging on to the sheep for dear life. Her father didn't suffer fools gladly, and he'd figured this was some fool she'd married who couldn't handle a sheep. Bill confided to Gwen that the smell alone made him ill.

"Oh, that's nothing, pet, wait 'til Dad has you help with trimming the dung locks," she teased him.

"Gwen, I couldn't do it," he said earnestly.

She laughed and told him she was only teasing. "Dad wouldn't ask you to do that. It's all right, pet, I knew I wasn't marrying a farm boy."

It was a sad farewell: they were both so old. Gwen clung to the auntie who had been more like a mother to her. She'd given her life to raising Gwen, never having married. Even on this solemn occasion, Auntie Blodwen would not suffer tears. Always a 'cut and dried' person, she lost no time in telling Gwen to stop her sniveling.

"Now you mind you go to chapel, and keep up your singing in the choir, Gwen. And don't forget to write us, regularly." She turned to Bill; "You take good care of our girl for us, young man. She's all we've got, you know."

Gwen watched Bill through a veil of tears. He assured them he'd be a good husband to her, and he'd send her back to see them as soon as he was able. Then he shook hands with them both.

Her father wouldn't want a lot of emotion; Gwen knew that. So she tried to make it brief: a kiss on the cheek and a short hug. He grabbed her hands and pressed something into them, whispering in her ear, "In case you want to come back, pet."

Bill helped Gwen onto the bus, and they waved and waved until the two little figures disappeared from view. Gwen had a premonition she wouldn't see them again in this life. She looked down at the pile of money in her hand and watched her tears stain it.

When they arrived in Spruce Creek, she got her first glimpse of the private nature of the man she'd married. He hadn't told his family about her. They were shocked, but obviously pleased. His young sisters, Kath and May, were especially excited. His mother seemed a little put out that she'd been kept in the dark, but she soon got over it and welcomed her new daughter.

Gwen could immediately see why Bill hadn't painted her a detailed picture of Spruce Creek. She'd seen Powell River first and thought it lovely. Just the right size town, she thought, and the views across the water, toward Vancouver Island, were beautiful. As they drove toward Spruce Creek, she felt the world closing in on her. It was all the tall trees. Gwen was used to the naked, rolling hills of Wales—where even on a stormy day, the light could reach the ground. The ground at Spruce Creek was perennially damp and dark.

Gwen had expected a town, but Spruce Creek was more like a hamlet, carved out of the surrounding forest. The forest itself was beautiful, but she got the feeling it could reach out and engulf the town overnight. It would be hard to be happy here, but she'd try for Bill's sake.

Around the dinner table, talk turned to the future.

"Will you go back to logging, son?" Bill's mother asked.

"No, Mum. I'm going to use my benefits to go to college, pick up some business courses. I might work in the office, but I'm done cutting trees."

"There's no college around here," she responded.

"No, we'll go to Vancouver for the time being. I'm not looking to get a degree, just enough training to get me into the office," Bill explained. "I'm sure Mr. Stewart will give me a chance. Does he still run the place?"

May piped up, "Yes, my friend Mamie works for him. Do you want me to talk to her?"

"No thanks, May, I'll go in and see him before we leave."

"Before you leave, Bill," his mother said, "there are some of Frank's things that you might want."

Gwen noticed, at the mention of Frank, the happy mood was quelled. That was the first time she realized how closely Bill walked in his brother's shadow. The second time was when he came home from a meeting with Mr. Stewart.

"What did he say, Bill?"

Bill's face was a study of resentment. "He said any brother of Frank's would be welcome to come work for him again."

"Well, that's good, isn't it, pet" she asked timidly.

"No, it's not good," he exploded. "He could have said he'd like me to work for him because I always did a good job, because I did. But, no, it's because I'm Frank's brother." He pounded the table. "Frank, Frank, Frank, they've even erected a memorial to him, for Christ's sake."

Gwen had never seen him angry like this. He walked out without meeting her eyes. He almost bumped into Violet, who was just about to come in.

Violet looked at Gwen and asked quietly, "Is Mum here?"

Gwen shook her head, "She's next door." The words were no sooner out of her mouth than she burst into tears.

Violet hugged her new sister-in-law, waiting for an explanation. She heard Gwen out, and then started talking to her gently. "Gwen, it's really nothing you said. Poor Bill has had to live in Frank's shadow all his life."

Gwen looked mystified.

Violet continued, "You see, Frank was a big, lovable guy—the life and soul of the party type, if you know what I mean. Everyone in town loved him, even though he was a bit of a rascal. Bill was always quiet and rather shy. You could depend on him, but he was overlooked when Frank was around. You can imagine what that was like."

Gwen nodded.

"You know what was probably the hardest thing," Violet explained, "going off to war. He didn't have to go, you know. He was Mum's only son at home and Dad was dead. Bill could easily have got a deferral. But everyone at the lumberyard would bait him with, 'Frank's gone, when are you going.' He did it just to save face," she finished.

Gwen finished mopping her tears. "Thanks, Violet, I've just never seen him like that before," she explained.

"You won't often, it takes a lot to rile Bill. He's a good man, Gwen, I know he'll make you a good husband." She patted Gwen's hand. "I for one am glad he went to the war, because he met you."

When Bill returned they talked it out. He was sorry he'd upset her. She told him she understood. She said living in Spruce Creek might be difficult for him, she'd be happy living in Vancouver. Maybe after college he could get a job there or, better yet, Powell River. He agreed that it would be better for him to get away from Spruce Creek. Gwen didn't let on the relief she felt.

They set out optimistically for the big city, where they rented a studio apartment—not big enough to swing a cat around in. Bill did a nine-month crash course at the university, passing with distinction. Gwen had never seen him so confident. To add to his happiness, she found she was pregnant. Life looked good.

Bill's confidence soon turned sour. There were more returning troops than there were jobs. With a baby on the way, he needed to get working soon. Optimism gave way to despair. Gwen hated to see him do it, but he reluctantly accepted a position with Spruce Creek Logging. The only bright spot in the situation was when they set up house in Powell River. It was another tiny apartment, but they had a view of the water. Spruce Creek Lumber was only a starting point, Bill assured her, and they shouldn't let it spoil the excitement of having their first child.

They were happy in those days. Gwen loved her little apartment, and she made friends easily with other young mothers. Powell River was everything she thought it would be.

Although she worried about her dad and Auntie Blodwen, she wasn't homesick. In the summer, she would often make a picnic for Bill and they'd go down to Willingdon Beach. They'd watch the children play as they munched on sandwiches.

As Bill worked his way into management, Gwen made a good friend of Violet. It was Violet who helped her when Michael was born, and again with Susan. The two women went to church together, where Gwen sang in the choir. Gwen was glad of Violet's friendship, because over time she and the children saw less and less of Bill.

When he'd bought the little car, she'd pictured them taking short trips, going on family outings; but it didn't happen. Bill was so determined to come out from the shadow of his brother, that he worked relentlessly at the logging company. It didn't take him long to work into management, but it was at high cost. He provided well for his family and was not unkind, but Gwen noticed with a sense of helplessness that he grew more and more serious as time passed by. He still lived for the day he could quit Spruce Creek Logging. Of late, he was talking about working for himself.

"If we only had a bit more money, Gwen, I could open an insurance office in Powell River."

"We hardly see you now, Bill," Gwen said tentatively, "What would it be like with your own company?"

He looked a little surprised at her statement. "I'm only doing what a man must do, we've got two children to send to college, don't forget. There's no way in hell they're going to work for Spruce Creek Logging. Don't you want better for them than that?"

"Of course I do, pet. I just meant it would be nice if we could do more things as a family—go on picnics or go fishing. You know," her tone turned pleading. "I'd love to take a vacation, Bill, go south of the border. I've never seen America. The kids would love it."

Bill considered her request. "We'll do it one day, Gwen, I promise, but we can't afford it now. I'm going to start studying insurance so I'll be ready when the time is right. There's a lot of money to be made. We'll even have money to go to Wales and see your dad."

Gwen didn't say anything. Bill had been putting the Wales trip on hold for years, reluctant to spend the money. Her Auntie Blodwen was long gone, and now her father was ailing. She had resigned herself to the fact she would never see him again.

If Bill noticed her silence, he didn't let on. He was still trying to figure out ways to start his own business. "If I could only figure a way to get hold of some capital," he said tensely.

Gwen patted his hand. "We'll get there, pet," she assured him.

Chapter 23

The laughter could be heard across the canyon: The family gathering at Louise and Sam's was in full swing. The last to arrive, Naomi was greeted with a hug from her cousin, Michael. Jean, his wife, followed suit. It had been years since Naomi had seen Susan, Michael's sister, and she had never met Susan's husband, Paul. She greeted them now with enthusiasm. She had always liked Susan, and could tell the feeling was mutual.

It was a warm day, perfect sitting on the deck weather. The Canadian cousins hadn't been in this part of the country before, and found the view of so many snow-capped mountains awesome. Sam was surprised.

"But, you have tons of snowy mountains in B.C."

Michael explained the difference, "Yes, but ours in Vancouver seem to go straight up. You can't stand back like you can here and see such a wide panorama. What's the big one on the right, again?"

"That's Mt. Jefferson. Mt. Hood is taller, but we can't quite see it from here," Sam explained. "They're all volcanoes. We'll take you out to the lava fields tomorrow. It's incredible how far that stuff flowed."

They sipped on cool drinks, and caught up with each other's lives. The tales Susan and Paul told of life in Guatemala fascinated Naomi. Her cousin seemed very happy with the path she'd followed, Naomi thought. Michael was in fine form; so different from the serious boy she remembered. He and Louise were sparring back and forth, causing them all to laugh often.

Naomi had been watching her nephews, Craig and Brian, pitching horseshoes over by the barn. Finding an opportunity, she slipped away to join them.

"Hey, you guys, the burgers are almost ready."

The boys looked rather dejected.

"What's up?" Naomi asked, and then answered her own question. "Not much fun for you guys, huh?"

"There's no kids," eight-year-old Craig responded.

"Yea, it's boring, all grown-up stuff," Brian, the ten-year-old added.

"I know," Naomi sympathized, "I'm sorry I don't have some little cousins for you. Couldn't you have the neighbor boy over?"

"Mum won't let us," Craig pouted. "She won't even let us play on the computer."

"I wish you'd brought Ben with you," Brian said, "He was fun."

"Why didn't you?" Craig added.

Naomi didn't like to lie, but her nephews were too young to understand the situation. "He wasn't able to come this time, but I will bring him again. The only thing is he'll beat you at horseshoes," she teased them.

"No way," they said in unison.

"Aunt Naomi, who's the fat guy?" Brian asked.

"That's our cousin Michael from Canada. Didn't your mum introduce you?"

"Yes, but if he's a cousin, how come we've never seen him before?"

Naomi thought for a minute. "I suppose it's because they live in Canada and we live here. Your mum and I have lived in Oregon since we were very young. We didn't get to know our cousins well. Now we're making up for lost time."

She glanced across at her cousins: Michael on the short side and stocky like his mother, Susan tall and slender as a reed, her father to a tee. The cousins were having such a good time getting to know each other. It always amazed Naomi that from her grandparents' six children, she, Louise, Michael and Susan were the only offspring.

Naomi turned back to the boys. "I tell you what, you guys…"

Louise interrupted by calling out that the burgers were ready.

"Okay, let's go chow down," Naomi suggested, "and I'll see if I can get Susan and Paul to tell you about living in Guatemala. They have all kinds of weird and funny things happen to them."

Later in the afternoon, Louise had finally relented and let the boys on the computer. She and Sam had taken Michael, Jean and Paul to the barn to see the horses. It gave Naomi her first real opportunity to talk to Susan.

"Naomi, I read your book. Michael sent it to me." Susan said.

"Dare I ask what you thought?"

Susan laughed. "I thought it was good, entertaining."

"That's what I'd hoped for," Naomi explained. "I've just finished the second one. I'll send you a copy this time. You are going back to Guatemala, right? Is it home to you now?"

"For a while longer at least. The clinic can manage without us now. We've recruited other doctors, so Paul has some relief. And the Lion's Club has helped us out with ophthalmologists, so I'm almost redundant. I think we'll eventually move back to Canada and just do fundraising for them."

"Was it your idea to open the clinic?" Naomi asked.

"No, Paul's really. I met him in college. He'd been down there with his church—helping to construct houses, actually. Anyway, he saw the need for health care and made it a goal. We were able to do it soon after we graduated."

"It must have cost a bit to get started?"

"It did. We wouldn't have been able to do it without Mum and Dad."

Naomi's ears perked up. "Your folks financed you?"

"Not completely, we'd been able to raise donations through the church and businesses. But Mum and Dad put the frosting on the cake, so to speak."

Naomi was about to ask how, but the group from the barn joined them and the conversation took another course.

Michael and Jean opted out of hiking into the canyon to see the Deschutes River up close. Louise stayed back at the house with them, which left Naomi, Sam, Brian and Craig to lead Susan and Paul to the water's edge. It was a beautiful hike: down a series of benches, studded with old growth juniper and interesting rock formations. The air was fragrant with the smells of juniper and sage. The two boys led the way, eager to get to the water's edge and hunt for frogs. Susan and Naomi lagged behind the men, deep in conversation.

"I was sorry to hear your mum had died, Naomi, it must have been hard on you girls."

"It was; it happened so suddenly. She was just beginning to enjoy life, without responsibilities. I hadn't seen a lot of her the last year. She was going here, there and everywhere with her girlfriends. At least she had fun for a while."

"I'm glad. You know my dad never did. "

"That's what Michael said."

"Sad really. Mum wanted so much to go back to Wales, but they never did. He kept putting it off, and putting it off, 'til finally Mum's dad died. She never really forgave Dad for that."

Susan plopped down on a rock to rest. Naomi followed suit, mopping her brow.

"How sad for your mum, Susan. She was an only child, wasn't she?"

"Yes. They were old when they had her, in fact, her mother died during childbirth."

"I wonder your folks didn't have her dad move out to Canada."

"They thought of it after his sister died—she lived with him. But he had the farm and there was no way he would leave it. My dad was thoughtless not to let Mum go on a visit. It's not like they couldn't afford it. He was just work, work, work. No matter how much he made, it was never enough. To tell you the truth, Naomi, I used to worry Michael was going to be just like him."

Naomi nodded. "I know what you mean. I was so relieved to see how he'd changed when I visited them. He's like a different man."

Susan smiled. "We can thank Jean for that. I know he found God, but he wouldn't have done it without her. That's the difference; my mum was timid and would never challenge my dad. Jean can hold her own."

They resumed their hike. The men were some way in the distance, but Naomi knew the trail. It was a warm afternoon and there was no need to hurry. Naomi was about to return to the subject of Susan's dad, but Susan asked about Naomi's divorce.

"I didn't hear about your divorce until I got here. Kevin seemed like a nice guy. I guess I was surprised. Was it something you both wanted?"

"He is a nice guy, Susan, and I was just as surprised as you were when it happened."

Naomi found it easy to confide in Susan. She gave her all the details, including the fact she blamed herself for most of it. Susan stopped walking, turned and took hold of Naomi's arm.

"Naomi, you're taking too much of the blame; letting Kevin off too easy. Perhaps you weren't giving him as much attention as he deserved, but there was a compelling reason. On the other hand, here he was meeting someone he never told you about, and then starting a romance with her. I'd say he should be shouldering most of the guilt. You don't sound too bitter, though."

"I'm not. Oh, at first I was, then mum got sick and I didn't have time to think about it. Now I look back and think we were more like two friends living together. It's hard to remember much passion. It really happened for the best, Susan." Naomi paused, before asking, " Did Louise tell you about Ben?"

"No, who's Ben, a new beau?"

"After a fashion," Naomi said. She told Susan about meeting Ben, and how their relationship had developed. Explaining Elaine was difficult. Susan was ten years older, and Naomi wondered how she would take it. She saw concern flit across Susan's face.

"Oh, Naomi, that's a hard one."

They walked on in silence for a few minutes. She knew Susan was struggling with what to say. Her cousin was deeply religious, and this would be a moral dilemma for her. The men up ahead had paused, waiting for them to catch up. Naomi broke the silence.

"I didn't mean it to happen, Susan. I fought it as long as I could— we both did."

"That's not what concerns me, Naomi, although maybe it should. I just worry that he is reaching out in his grief, without knowing his true feelings. He told you he loves his wife. If she came out of the coma tomorrow, where does that leave you?"

Naomi couldn't respond. They were fast closing the gap between them and the men. Susan reached out and held onto Naomi's hand.

"You must face the fact that it could happen—it happens everyday. I just don't want to see you hurt again. Think about it, Naomi, you must think about it."

Naomi was shaken. Susan was trying to make her focus on something she'd been avoiding. Louise had voiced the same concerns, but not as strongly as Susan. Louise had met Ben, and the optimist in her wanted things to turn out right. Susan was viewing the situation from more of a distance.

As they joined up with the men, Susan gave Naomi's hand a squeeze. "I shall be praying for you, cousin. Let me know if I can help."

It was getting late in the evening. Craig and Brian were given a special privilege to stay up late, and were back at the computer. The adults were all sprawled around: the results of a large meal. Sam and Louise had taken them all to the Mexican restaurant in town. Everyone had eaten too much—everyone except Naomi. She just picked at her food, and it hadn't gone unnoticed by Louise. The sisters were in the kitchen making coffee when Louise brought it up.

"What's up, sis, you hardly ate your dinner? Are you sick?"

"No, Lou, it's just something Susan said. I told her about Ben. She doesn't share your optimism. It's kind of depressed me. I'll try and snap out of it."

Louise gave her sister a knowing look. "That's why I didn't mention Ben to her," she whispered, "I knew she'd have difficulty with it. Don't let it get you down, sis. Come on, let's get them going on the family mystery."

They returned to the living room with the coffee, and Louise lost no time in diving right in.

"Hey, Michael, I suppose Naomi told you we were wrong about Aunt Edna and the embezzlement," she said.

"She did, what a surprise. Just goes to show how things can get distorted."

"What embezzlement?" Susan asked.

They filled her in on the details.

"Did you know, we'd been to see her in Arizona?" Naomi asked Susan.

"Yes, Michael wrote and told me. She threw you out, or something."

"Did she ever," Louise laughed. "We felt like criminals, didn't we, Naomi?"

Naomi nodded. "She was yelling that we'd come for the money. The staff were beginning to look at us a bit strange."

Michael joined in. "That's something I've been meaning to ask you: where did she get her money from? You said she was living in a fancy place."

Naomi and Louise exchanged glances. They had kept Aunt Edna's background a secret until now.

"It can't do any harm, Naomi," Louise said. "I think we should tell them. Sam, check and see the boys are out of hearing range."

Louise told the story. Naomi knew she'd do a colorful job of it, just as Marge had. They all found themselves laughing at Aunt Edna's antics. When she came to the end, and how "Daddy" had died, Michael laughed so hard he had a coughing fit.

"Can you just imagine it," he roared with laughter. "Poor old Edna laying there yelling for help. Oh, the indignity," he finished, laughing anew.

When the laughter finally quit, Susan remarked, "It's funny, but Aunt Edna was always the odd man out. She didn't seem to fit in with the family. She was the only redhead, too."

"Did she get along with Gran?" Naomi asked.

"Not very well. She seemed to resent being born into a poor family," Susan explained. "She always had grand ideas. I suppose she achieved her goals, albeit in a strange way."

"Her goal was the same as the rest of them," Michael added, "Just to get out of Spruce Creek. I wonder Aunt Kath didn't take a nanny's job like Edna did."

"She didn't want to go that far away from the family," said Louise. "She got away for awhile, working in the shipyard, but she came right back after the war."

"It's probably because she didn't marry until she left Canada. She was a more sentimental type, and needed family around her. I remember, though, she did get a job on the island, didn't she, Louise? You would know that. " Michael asked.

"Yes. She didn't get home often in those years. My mum sure missed her; they were very close. That's why she followed us to Oregon. She married a guy my dad knew, and they ended up living in Prineville. That's a bit east of here. We saw quite a lot of her after her husband died, didn't we, Sam?"

Sam nodded in agreement.

"Do you guys know much about the Cavenish side of the family? Like where they came from. Did they have money, things like that?" Naomi asked.

"Scotland originally, Dad told me," Michael said. "He said his grandparents came over with no more than the shirt on their backs. I guess it was very tough for them."

"Do you know if their family back in Scotland had much?"

"Money?"

"Yes, or landholdings."

"Not that I'm aware of. How about you, Susan?"

"I never heard of anything," Susan acknowledged. "Why, have you uncovered something, Naomi?"

Naomi looked at Louise.

"We're not sure," Louise explained. "There is an old Cavenish estate in Scotland, complete with castle—in ruins, I might add. We're trying to get to the bottom of a centuries old lawsuit. It looks like the heirs were due reparations for the government's illegal takings of the estate."

"No kidding!" Michael exclaimed.

"We were hoping you two may know something about it," Naomi added.

"It's news to me," he said. "Are they still fighting it out?"

"Well, that's the odd part," Louise was choosing her words carefully. "It looks as though Gran would have received whatever money there was. Mum never mentioned it to us. Did your dad ever say anything to you?"

"No, in fact Dad used to slip Gran a little money now and then. She helped him get ready to set up his own business with a small loan, and he was forever grateful," Michael explained.

"Could that have been the money?" Naomi asked.

"Heavens no," Michael assured her, "it was only a couple thousand the logging company collected for her when Granddad died. Dad used it to take classes in insurance, and then when the inheritance came through he launched his own business. He paid Gran back every penny and more."

Louise looked puzzled. "Inheritance?"

Michael looked at his sister. "That's right, they probably don't know about it."

Susan explained. "My folks kept it a secret from the family—Dad's idea, he was afraid they'd want to borrow from him. Especially Ralph, Violet's husband, he was a scoundrel. To tell you the truth, I didn't realize it was still a secret, I felt sure your mother would know. I know Dad sent her some money when your father was killed."

"We didn't know that, either," Naomi explained. She listened intently as Susan went on with the story.

It seemed that the coal company whose holdings bordered their grandfather's farm in Wales, had been trying to acquire the farm for years, Susan said. The old man had held out, but he was no fool. Suspicious that mining was going on below ground on his side of the fence, he sought the help of a lawyer to prove it. When they had their proof, they offered the mining company a deal: buy the land for a very large price or deal with a lawsuit. The company settled quickly. Within months, their grandfather died and everything went to their mother, Gwen.

"It wasn't a fortune, but Dad invested what he didn't use for the business startup. He did very well; put us kids through college for one thing, and gave Paul and me money to start up the clinic." Susan finished.

"Susan wouldn't split the money evenly when he died, because we had the two kids," Michael explained.

"And I'd already had a chunk for the clinic," Susan interjected.

"Anyway, it left Jean and me well set." He gave a big grin. "You girls were probably wondering where the money came from for my house, right?"

Louise and Naomi looked uncomfortable.

"It's okay, who wouldn't wonder. Dad was less than honest keeping it from the family. But I'll say this for him: he saw to it that Gran was comfortable. He used to pay the district nurse on the side to get her to go more often than she was allowed. He worried it was getting too much for your mum. I remember hearing him discuss it with my mother. Perhaps he redeemed himself," Michael finished up.

Naomi and Louise were in the kitchen washing coffee cups. Their cousins had returned to their timeshare. They would be back in the morning for a day of sightseeing.

"Well, there we were with egg on our face," Louise said.

"He seemed to take it with good humor though. I think they understood how suspicious it looked."

"Yeah, serves his dad right for hiding it like that."

"Well that lets out Aunt Gwen as a suspect. You realize what that means."

Louise grimaced. "Not dear Aunt Violet. Oh, sis, it can't be her. Everyone loved Aunt Violet."

"But no one liked her husband."

"I didn't think of that," Louise gasped.

"I didn't either, until Susan called him a scoundrel just now. This may seem far fetched, but how's this for a scenario: Gran tells Aunt Violet about the inheritance, Ralph gets the information out of Aunt Violet..."

"And he coerces her into cheating Gran out of it," Louise jumped in.

Sam walked in carrying a stray coffee cup. "Are you girls hatching up Naomi's next book?"

"Oh, Sam," Louise gave him an agonized look. "It looks as though Aunt Violet did it."

Sam shook his head in wonderment. "You two need a touch of reality. First of all, you're still not sure there was any money; second, you heard what Michael said: his dad was giving your grandmother money. Why would she need it if she had an inheritance?"

"Because rotten Ralph had already got it," Louise explained.

"Then call up rotten Ralph and demand it back," Sam teased her.

She threw the dishtowel at him. "Go to bed, you of little faith."

"Gladly, or the next thing you know, I'll be the prime suspect." Sam said goodnight and beat a hasty retreat.

"What do we know about this Ralph character?" Louise asked.

"Here's the bad part, Lou," Naomi said sadly, "Michael said he died in a fire soon after Gran died."

"That's not so bad if he *was* the sleaze ball everyone says he was."

"No, not that. It's Aunt Violet; she apparently traveled all over. Michael said she sent postcards to them."

"And where did she get the money for that?"

"Exactly!"

"Hmm, we'll have to find out all we can about Aunt Violet tomorrow." Louise changed the subject. "Are you feeling better, sis? What exactly did Susan say about Ben?"

"Nothing I didn't already know. She said I have to think more about what will happen if Elaine comes out of the coma." Naomi paused, gathering her thoughts. "I can't do it, Lou. I have to keep it out of my mind or I'll go crazy."

Louise nodded in agreement. "Let's face that hurdle when, and if we come to it," she said reassuringly. She looked at the clock. "We'd better turn in, we've got a full day planned tomorrow."

They started the day of sightseeing by driving south, through Bend, to Lava Butte. Susan and Paul rode with Naomi, who followed Sam's Suburban to the top of the butte. Here Sam, enjoying his role of tour guide, gave vivid descriptions of the volcanoes erupting and the resulting lava fields below them.

Naomi sat with Michael while the rest of the group walked out on the lava flow. His back couldn't handle it, Michael said, he was saving it for the cave they would visit later. They sat among pines, whispering in the wind, chipmunks scampering at their feet. Michael was talking about his plans for retirement.

"We're thinking of going back to Powell River. We both like it there. It's more conducive to old age than Vancouver, and the air will be good for us."

"Have you been there lately?" Naomi asked.

"We went up about a month ago. It's growing, but still has its charm."

"Did you go to Spruce Creek?"

"No, the place has no meaning to me: I was born in Powell River. We only went to Spruce Creek to visit Gran. I tell you who we did see in Powell, though, Sharon Dukes: they lived next door to Gran."

" Sharon, is she Mrs. Dukes granddaughter?"

"Yes. Her mum, Eileen, wasn't married, so Mrs. Dukes more or less raised Sharon. She works in a bakery on the north end of town. Her grandma died years ago, but her mum still lives in Spruce Creek. She said the place hasn't changed much."

"I'd like to go again one day soon. I don't have a real sense of a family place, having grown up down here," Naomi explained.

"You won't get it in Spruce Creek, I think you'd have to go back to Scotland for that."

"Maybe I'll do that one day, too."

Susan got fifty yards into Lava River Cave before yelling to Naomi, "I can't do this, Naomi, I'm too claustrophobic, I've got to go out."

"Okay" Naomi yelled back, "just turn around, you'll see daylight in a few yards. I'll just make sure the others know we're going out, then I'll catch up with you."

She found Susan sitting on a bench hugging herself, trying to get warm.

"Brr, it was cold in there. No wonder you said to bring coats."

"Amazing isn't it. Let's go find a patch of sunshine to sit in until the others get back," Naomi suggested.

"Will they be long?'

"It's over a mile, if they go all the way. Michael might not make it that far."

"Paul probably will—Brian and Craig will see to that. It's great country, Naomi, so much to see and do."

"Yes, I like it too. I've been toying with the idea of moving here. I'd like to be closer to my nephews."

"They would love that; aunties are special."

"You had a close relationship with Aunt Violet, didn't you, Susan?"

"Yes, she was so sweet. My mum and Aunt Vi were good friends."

"Did you ever go to her place? I was wondering what her husband was like. You called him a scoundrel yesterday, so I guess he wasn't too nice."

"I don't like to speak ill of the dead, but he was an awful person. He would beat on poor Aunt Violet. She would show up at our place with bruises. We never went to her house; nobody did. No one in Spruce Creek liked him."

"I wonder why she married him."

"Dad said she was too shy; she didn't know how to fend him off. She was very pretty, you know. He was a handsome man, too, so she probably liked the look of him. He hadn't been in Spruce Creek long. Nobody had figured out what he was like."

"Didn't she work in Powell River?"

"Yes, that's why we saw so much of her. He would never have let her come over otherwise. She used to get off work early and stop by. Rotten Ralph never knew. The man she worked for was a lovely person; he understood the situation. I can see him now," she laughed. "When we went by his office, I'd look at his name on the window. It was in gold lettering: Etienne Chartier, Solicitor. I thought it so romantic—that is until I saw him. He was short, tubby and bald."

Naomi laughed. "Etienne Chartier, yes it does have a nice ring to it. Did she work for him until her husband died?"

"Yes, I think so. Her husband died in a house fire, you know—their house. Aunt Violet was lucky she wasn't home."

"Do they know what happened?"

"They said he used to squirt lighter fluid in the woodstove to get it going. It must have blown up the house, but I'm not sure how."

"And Aunt Violet left on her travels soon after. Michael said you'd get postcards from all over. Whereabouts in France did she settle?"

"It was in Sete, on the southeast coast. I've got the address somewhere at home. I was going to visit her when I got word she'd died."

"Poor Aunt Violet. A sad, little life really, going through all that, then dying alone."

"Yes, poor Aunt Vi."

Chapter 24

Violet

That she presented such an endearing picture sitting on the beach was totally lost on Violet. She had never fully understood her beauty. Now at 65 she could still turn a man's head. Her hair was completely white and she wore it long, tied at the nape of her neck with a filmy scarf. She didn't wear a hat at the beach since she'd taken to coming down late in the day—when all the tourists went for their evening meal. Her skin was only lightly tanned, and provided the perfect backdrop for her sad, blue eyes. They had called her the pretty one back in Spruce Creek. What would they call her now, she wondered. Her health had been so bad lately. When she looked in the mirror, she saw an old woman—a frail, old woman. Her weight had stayed the same all these many years: 105 pounds. But now her bones were brittle and she must be careful.

She hunched up her knees and spread her gauzy skirt out around her. Her eyes were locked on the horizon, searching for something that would never come. All the years she had lived here and she still missed the sunset. Sunrise on the Mediterranean could not compare to the sunsets back home. It was one of the hardest things for her to get used to in her adopted home: no sunsets over the water. She had such vivid memories of scarlet, purple and peach dipping into the waters of the Strait, before creating a silhouette of Vancouver Island in the distance. But the beach here at Sete was lovely: white sand stretching as far as the eye could see. They called it the seven-mile beach in the travel brochures. It was a lovely, quiet place when she moved here. Now the tourists had discovered it, and it wasn't quite the same. Nothing was the same now she was alone.

Her eyes fell on her bag, with the postcard sticking out. That's right, she was going to write a postcard to Susan, her niece. She scribbled a few lines—always just a few lines. There was so little of her life she could share with them. The address presented a problem: Susan had written she would be spending the summer in B.C. After some thought, Violet decided to mail it to her brother in Powell River; he would see Susan got it. You could always rely on Bill. She wondered what he looked like these days. And Gwen, her dear friend Gwen, who she'd, had to leave in the dark when she left Powell River. It still hurt Violet to think about it. Gwen and Bill had stayed in Powell River all these many years. Powell River. Tears filled her eyes. Powell River: her sanctuary. This self-imposed exile hurt so much. Violet fought back the tears. She'd suffered enough at the hands of Ralph Braun.

Violet was still grieving for her brother Frank when Ralph Braun came on the scene. He was the right age for the draft, and should have been off fighting the war, but he never went. She failed to understand how he got out of it. The first time she saw him was in the company post office. He was tall and broad-shouldered, with a thatch of blonde hair, clipped short. His eyes were blue, but when he smiled, Violet noticed, they stayed cold. He had a cocky air about him, and stood brazenly looking her up and down before saying, "Well, hello beautiful."

She blushed to the roots of her hair and looked for an easy escape, but he blocked her passage.

"Wanna go for a coke?" he asked.

Violet kept her eyes on her shoes and shook her head.

"Aw, come on," he insisted. "It's your lucky day."

She managed to get out of it that time, but he got her name from the company clerk who ran the post office. He pursued her relentlessly over the following weeks. Everywhere she went he seemed to be there. The only place she could get away from him was at the office. She had a job: file clerk at Spruce Creek Logging. Ralph was not liked there; he was known as a troublemaker. He stayed away from her while she worked.

Denny Sullivan had tried to caution her about him. "Stay away from him, Violet," he said. "That guy's bad news." But then Denny had been sweet on Violet himself, until her brother chased him off. Frank chased off all the boys. She wished he hadn't with Denny; she rather liked him. Now Denny had got Joan Weber pregnant and was having to marry her.

Anna Schultz told Violet all the girls were jealous about Ralph. "He's so good looking, Violet, you're so lucky. You'd be crazy not to go out with him."

In the end, he won her over. He was a perfect gentleman on their first date. He bought her flowers; it was hard to get chocolates with rationing. Saying goodnight at her front door, he'd pecked her lightly on the cheek. She heaved a sigh of relief as she closed the door behind her. Perhaps the naysayers were wrong; Ralph had behaved perfectly. She had felt a tingle of excitement when his lips touched her cheek. Ralph Braun had won her over.

It was a very brief courtship. Ralph was anxious to move out of the single men's bunkhouse, and into a house of his own. He wasn't first on the list, but, through intimidation, managed to get a small place set back in the trees. It was a distance away from the other houses and very old. The company was going to condemn it, but Ralph promised to do a few things to improve it. They relented, more for Violet's sake than his.

They were married in Powell River by a justice of the peace, with her sister May the only bridesmaid. There was a war on, and the other girls were away in Vancouver working in the shipyards. She would have liked her brother Bill to give her away, but he was still in Europe. The honor fell to old Mr. Murdoch from the logging company. She could tell her mother wasn't keen on Ralph, but felt she'd get over it when she got to know him.

Ralph was supposed to have fixed up the house in the weeks prior to the wedding. When he carried her over the threshold, it was obvious he hadn't. The tiny living room was supposed to have a fresh coat of paint; instead, it was decorated with empty beer bottles. Violet tried to hide her disappointment. She started picking up the bottles in an effort to tidy up the place. Ralph had other ideas.

"Come here, Violet," he ordered, "that can wait. I want to make a woman of you."

She looked at him with a combination of amazement and fear. She realized he'd had a lot to drink at the small reception the neighbors had thrown for them.

"Can we wait a little while?" she asked timidly.

Ralph gave a coarse laugh. "Hell, no, I've been waiting for weeks to pop that cherry. Get over here."

She did as he asked, and without a word, he began ripping her clothes off. A couple times his fingernails dug into her flesh. She winced, but bore it in silence. When he had her breasts bared, he grabbed them roughly.

"Not much of a mouthful," he snickered, before sinking his teeth into them.

Violet cried out in pain, "Ralph, you're hurting me."

He pulled back then, belched and said with a hint of sarcasm, "That's right, you're a first-timer. I'll be gentle with you."

Somehow, she knew he wouldn't.

The next day when he left for work, Violet sat at the kitchen table, with head in hands. She had a bed pillow under her; the soreness made it painful to sit. But the pain in her body was nothing compared to the pain in her heart. She rocked back and forth wondering whatever she'd seen in Ralph Braun. He'd treated her so roughly. How could she ever find love for him now? People had tried to warn her; Denny had tried to warn her. Oh, how she wished she'd listened. Now it was too late; she was his wife and would have to bear the consequences. Perhaps in time he would soften.

But he didn't. He never made love to her; he just used her. Violet dreaded every encounter. Soon he read it in her eyes and made her pay for it. She wasn't to know those early weeks would be the best part of her marriage. Ralph had plenty of work to keep him occupied. But after awhile the heavy rains came and he couldn't work. He cursed and moaned at the weather, and each day his drinking got heavier and heavier; like a dam backing up. Violet had a premonition of what was to come. She tiptoed around him for fear the dam would break. On the fifth day it did, and she wasn't prepared.

She walked the quarter mile to work each day. On this particular day, she stopped at the company store after work to pick up groceries and the mail. It had rained on and off all day long, and as she hurried along, trying to balance the food sack and her umbrella, the heavens opened. Denny Sullivan—on his rounds as the logging company's security guard—came cruising by. He rolled down his window and offered her a ride home. It was only 200 yards. Violet saw nothing wrong in it.

Ralph was waiting behind the door. She barely got across the threshold, when he pushed her to the floor. The groceries went flying. The side of her head landed in the eggs—her rationed eggs.

From behind her, she heard him yell 'slut' as he came at her. With the whites and yolks of egg dripping down the side of her face, she tried to sit up. His work boot made contact, and she saw the egg splatter like the spokes on a wheel as she slid to the ground. She didn't pass out, but pretended to. It worked. Ralph found his beer and staggered to the living room. Violet lay still as long as she could, hoping he would pass out. When she finally heard him snoring, she got up, gingerly.

She didn't cry. Even when she looked at herself in the bathroom mirror, she didn't cry. What she did do was start building a level of hate for the man that would eventually consume her. Her face was swelling rapidly, and she worried how she would hide it from the people at work tomorrow. Then she remembered it was Friday: had he remembered it too. By Monday, the swelling would be down, and she could try to hide it with her hair. Violet just hoped her eye wouldn't blacken.

The next morning, Ralph was sweetness itself. He made her coffee and told her he was sorry; he wouldn't drink like that again. But he did, over and over again. She blamed the bruises on walking into a door, falling over the sewing machine or falling off her bicycle. And when she ran out of excuses, she explained she had a balance problem. She knew people weren't fooled. Occasionally, someone would say something to her, trying to help, but she brushed them off. She was too afraid of Ralph to accept help.

Two things happened to make life more tolerable for Violet: The war ended, and her brother Bill came home, bringing with him a new wife, Gwen. Gwen would become Violet's best friend. The second event: a fall from her bicycle, lead to a new job, and a new life—of sorts.

Violet liked Gwen right from the start; kindness just oozed from her. Bill and Gwen were staying with her mother for the time being, and Violet used any excuse to get away from Ralph and visit with them. Her mother's health was beginning to fail, so Ralph couldn't complain too much. It was weeks before he got over to meet Bill, but Bill had heard all he needed to know about Ralph Braun. After the meeting, he took Violet aside.

"Violet, I've heard what he's like. You don't have to stay with him. Why don't you leave him?"

She shook her head. "You don't know what he's like, Bill—what he's capable of. He'd never let me go, his pride wouldn't let him." Her eyes filled with tears. "He'd hunt me down, that's for sure."

Bill never broached the subject again. Soon he and Gwen left for Vancouver and college. Violet missed Gwen terribly, but, as luck would have it, Ralph was sent to a logging camp far off in the forest. He would be away three or four days. Violet asked for a day off work, and took the opportunity to ride her bicycle into Powell River. It was a lovely spring day, with fleeting clouds. The clouds took her attention away from the road, and before she knew it, her wheel struck a rut and she landed on the pavement. Her leg was grazed and bleeding, but other than that, she was all right. She was sitting on the curb, searching her pockets for something to stem the blood, when a man came running out from the building behind her.

"Mon Dieu, mademoiselle, are you hurt?"

Violet tried to assure him she was all right, but he caught sight of the blood. "Please, come, I have bandage in my office," he motioned to a door. Violet saw etched in the glass in gold lettering, Etienne Chartier, Solicitor.

"I am on the telephone," he explained, inching his way back to the door. "Follow me, s'il vous plais."

She watched him through the window pick up the telephone and begin talking animatedly with his hands. He beckoned her to come in. Violet couldn't see anyone else in the office, but he looked harmless enough. She judged him to be in his fifties. He was short, balding and wide around the middle. By his accent, she guessed he was French-Canadian. She limped into his office just as he hung up the phone.

"I am so sorry," he explained. "My secretary left me without warning, I am trying to do everything myself. Wait, please, I have a first aid kit in the bathroom."

He returned with supplies, and would have cleaned the wound himself if Violet hadn't insisted she could do it. He offered her coffee and she accepted, glad for a chance to ease the stiffness in her leg. He seemed kind and they talked for a long while. She learned he was 48, not French-Canadian but French. He'd lived in Canada many years, he explained, having left France after a divorce.

Violet told him a little about herself; really very little, mostly she talked about her family. She was usually shy around strangers, but found it remarkably easy to converse with him. He was one of those people you thought you already knew. She was surprisingly relaxed in his presence. When he found out she did office work at Spruce Creek Lumber, he was delighted.

"Violette, do you believe in fate?"

She raised her eyebrows in surprise.

He answered for her. "Of course you do. I need a secretary so badly; why else would you fall off your bicycle right outside my door? You have been sent to me."

Violet laughed, thinking he was joking. But he wasn't, he was very serious. She was flummoxed. "But I'm only a file clerk, I couldn't do it."

He wasn't to be dissuaded. "Can you type?"

"Only with two fingers."

"Good enough. Can you answer a telephone?"

"Yes."

"Then the job is yours," he said with finality.

Violet shook her head. "No, no, there are problems. My husband would never let me work in Powell River. Anyway, how would I get here?"

He could tell she was interested. "I will give you an advance; you can buy a little car. Can you drive?'

Violet nodded.

"Good. We'll talk about salary in a minute, but I will pay you so well, your husband can't say no."

Violet looked at him with her sad, blue eyes. "Why are you doing this?"

He gave her a charming smile. "I could say it's because you have the most beautiful eyes I've ever seen. But the truth, Violette, is that I cannot find anyone. With the war over, so many women are marrying and moving away. Please say you'll do it," he implored.

She was never quite sure why she agreed to it; fear of Ralph should have stopped her. Perhaps it was Etienne himself. He was so easy to talk to; she liked being in his company. Whatever the reason, she left his office with a job, a very generous salary and a new sense of optimism.

Dealing with Ralph turned out to be a lot easier than she expected. He was more interested in how she met Etienne, than he was in the job. Violet told him the truth about the bicycle accident—she had the scars to prove it. She also stressed her new employer was old, bald and fat. As soon as she mentioned the salary, she knew she'd won him over: money came close to beer in Ralph's affections. He had a little problem with Violet having a car, but she pointed out there was no way around it. He relented. All the same, she knew he would watch her closely. She'd have to be careful not to anger him.

Violet loved her new job. It soon became obvious to her that Etienne's practice was not a busy one, but checks came from France each month and helped keep him afloat. They developed a comfortable working relationship. Violet managed her tasks and soon gained confidence. Etienne trusted her completely, leaving the office in her care when he went to Vancouver or Victoria on business. Over time, she could see he was attracted to her. What surprised Violet was that she felt an attraction for him. Things may not have progressed beyond that point, if Ralph hadn't forced the issue: he beat on her again.

When Etienne saw the bruises, he showed such concern she broke down crying.

"Oh, Violette, my Violette," he said, taking her in his arms.

She clung to him and let him stroke her hair.

"What can I do to this man," he said angrily.

"There is nothing you can do, Etienne," she assured him, "he would only do worse."

"Then you must leave him, Violet. I beg you come to France with me."

She was touched by his concern. It was the closest he'd come to a declaration of love. She told him gently how much she appreciated his offer, but she couldn't leave now. He understood by her choice of words that one day she would leave Ralph. He would ask her again one day, he said, and kissed first her cheeks and then her lips. She didn't resist. They had broken the barrier. It was an easy step to take it further, to take it all the way.

From the safety of a backroom at the office, they carried on an affair for years. Etienne would periodically try to get her to leave Ralph—they could go to France he'd say. Her fear of Ralph wasn't the only thing stopping her now. Her mother had become very ill; she couldn't leave her sister May with all the responsibility. Then there was Gwen and Bill. If she went to France, she'd never see them. If she went to France, no one must know where she'd gone. Gwen might guess, because she'd confided in her about her relationship with Etienne. Ralph, she knew, would put two and two together and track her down—for in his own warped way he did love her.

No matter how she looked at it, Violet became convinced that she couldn't leave while Ralph lived. And Ralph didn't deserve to live, not after what he'd taken from her. She'd just been biding her time, but one day she'd make him pay. When the circumstances were right, she'd make him pay.

She was 31 when Ralph had sealed his fate. Violet, to her great joy, found out she was pregnant. There was no doubt in her mind as to the father. Since the first time he'd hit her, Violet had always taken precautions with Ralph. He didn't know it, but there was no way she would bear his child. This was Etienne's baby in her belly. She kept her condition secret from everybody, even Etienne, as she tried to work out their future. She was in her third month, and still no closer to figuring it out, when Ralph attacked her again: this time with devastating consequences.

He'd been sent home from the job for failure to follow safety rules. It was his third offense, and management was trying to teach him a lesson. His fury filled the little house. By the time Violet got home from work, he was not only furious, but also drunk. As soon as she saw his condition, she attempted to leave, but he grabbed her from behind. He'd learned something since the early days when he'd hit her. Now he went for the areas covered by clothing, hiding his cowardly acts from the world at large.

Violet fell to the ground quickly, and rolled in a ball to protect her stomach. He pulled at her hair to turn her over, saying, "Look at me, you slut." She resisted with all her might, but it wasn't enough. She felt a rib break from the force of his boot, but forgot about it the instant she felt the impact on her belly. He kicked her twice there, and it was enough. They told her later at the hospital, it had been a baby boy.

Ralph was beside himself. He cried and cried. "Violet, you should have told me. I never would have done it. Now I've lost my son."

He never once said he was sorry. She ached to tell him it wasn't his son, but was afraid for Etienne. The doctor told her it was unlikely she would ever conceive again. When she left the hospital, she made a silent vow that one day Ralph Braun would pay for what he'd taken from her. That day came in the autumn of 1964.

Chapter 25

Naomi hung up the phone, grabbed her lemonade and plopped down on her sofa, legs outstretched. It was late in the summer, one of the dog days—too hot for comfort, yet so precious, knowing the gloom of winter was to follow. She held the cool glass to her forehead. It was hard to think in this heat, maybe that's why Louise had sounded so crabby. How to figure Louise? What was making her so changeable? Her call had posed more questions than it answered. She seemed so hot and cold on the family mystery. Two weeks ago, when the cousins were visiting, she seemed so keen to solve the mystery. Now today, she was urging Naomi to give it up.

Perhaps Louise couldn't bear to think Aunt Violet had euthanized Gran and taken off with the inheritance. But Aunt Violet was the only suspect left. Who else could it be? Louise knew their mother said only the three women were there the night Gran died. They had eliminated Edna and Gwen. Naomi had to admit Aunt Violet was the most unlikely of the three. If she did do it, that husband of hers forced her into it, Naomi felt sure. That he died so soon afterwards, was his just reward. Maybe Aunt Violet had left Spruce Creek because she felt so guilty. She never returned, not even for a visit. Naomi found that suspicious.

Louise had told her she didn't want to think about it anymore. If her friend in England turned up anything on the Cavenish estate, she'd let Naomi know. She urged Naomi to put it out of her mind. That shouldn't be too difficult right now,

Naomi thought, forcing herself to get moving. She'd just that morning found a note in her mailbox; the post office had a package too big for the box. It would be her manuscript, and she needed to go pick it up. Her editor promised the revisions were minor. Naomi was anxious to see if she was right. One way or another, it would need all her attention for a few days, maybe more.

She drove to the post office with the car windows open, and stood in line feeling rather disheveled. Kevin's cousin, Angela, was working one window. Naomi hoped she didn't get her. She didn't, but was at the next one over when Angela leaned over and told her with a smug look, "Kevin and Star had a little girl."

"Oh, how nice. Are they both doing all right?"

"They're fine, and all as happy as clams. Kevin loves being a father."

Angela emphasized the last comment, Naomi noticed. She was probably looking for a reaction, but Naomi wouldn't give her the satisfaction. It wasn't until she was sitting in the car, that she explored her emotions. She was happy for Kevin, she really was. It was no good thinking it should have been her child. She was sterile, not Kevin. Nonetheless, she couldn't help feeling a little sorry for herself. She would call Ben when she got home; he always made her feel better.

When she got home, there was a message on her answering machine from Aunt Edna's friend, Marge Jenkins.

"Naomi, dear, it's Marge Jenkins, Edna's friend. Would you call me, please?"

She forgot to leave a phone number, and Naomi spent a few minutes hunting in her desk before it turned up. She had a good idea why Marge was calling; her voice sounded so emotional. Naomi called her right away.

"Marge, it's Naomi. Is it Aunt Edna?"

"Yes, honey, she went this morning, about two o'clock." Naomi could tell Marge had been crying. "I would have called you earlier, but I was up all night,"

"I'm so sorry, Marge. Poor Aunt Edna, did she have an easy passing?"

"Easy for her, hon, but not for me. Her mind was so far gone, I couldn't even tell her goodbye. Still," her tone became more positive, " she wouldn't want me to grieve. She'd be the first one to say go mix yourself a double. I just might do that now that I've talked to you. I couldn't get Louise, will you tell her?"

"Yes, of course I will, Marge. We should come down for the funeral."

"No, honey, she didn't want one. I'm to have her cremated and spread the ashes out at Red Rock. She was adamant about that. There's no sense you coming all this way. I have a new gentleman friend, he can help me."

"Well, Marge, let us know if there's anything we can do. Please, I mean it. It should be our responsibility."

"Don't worry yourself, Naomi, we worked all this out between us years ago. Edna would have done the same for me if I'd gone first."

"Can I send flowers?"

Marge thought for a minute. "Better than flowers, why don't you make a donation to a woman's shelter. Edna would have liked that idea."

"I will, Marge, and again, I'm so sorry you've lost your friend. We'll keep in touch."

"Yes, dear. I'll start going through her things when I feel like it. There's bound to be photos you'd like to have."

Naomi knew she'd have to call Louise. She hoped her sister would be in a better mood than this morning.

"Lou, did you get a message from Marge Jenkins?"

"I don't know. I just walked in. The light is flashing. What's up?"

"Aunt Edna died this morning."

"Oh, how sad. Was Marge with her?"

"Yes. She said her mind had gone, so she couldn't tell her goodbye."

"She's going to miss her. What about the funeral? "

Naomi told Louise their aunt's wishes and Marge's suggestion for a donation. They discussed the possibility of Marge finding any family photos in Aunt Edna's effects. Their aunt hadn't been sentimental as far as family was concerned, but they both hoped she'd kept some photos. Changing the subject, Naomi told Louise about Kevin's baby.

"How nice for them. Are you all right with it, sis?"

"I am happy everything turned out all right for them. It made me a little sad. I would like to have been a mother, Lou."

"I know, sis, maybe…" Louise stopped.

Naomi knew she'd been going to say maybe one day you will be. Then she remembered Ben. Her prospect of becoming a wife, let alone a mother, was something neither of them wanted to address right then.

The next three weeks Naomi worked long hours on her manuscript revisions. They weren't too extensive, but she found it difficult, as she had with her first novel. Knowing a better book would result from her labors, she kept at it. She was reaching the end, when something occurred to take her mind off it completely.

A letter arrived by registered mail. She had just signed for it and saw it was from Marge Jenkins, when the phone rang.

Louise sounded excited. "Did you get a letter from Marge?"

"I just signed for it, but I haven't opened it yet. It doesn't feel like photos."

"It's not. Open it, open it," Louise could hardly contain herself.

Naomi pulled out a letter, unfolded it and a check fluttered out. She stooped to pick it up, glanced at the check and let out a gasp.

"Holy cow."

Louise laughed. "Want to sit down, sis?"

"Did you get one too?"

"Yep."

"Louise, mine's for $20,000!"

"So is mine."

"We can't accept it."

"That was my first thought, but read the letter. Call me back later and we'll discuss it. I've got to run Brian to the doctor; his allergies are playing up."

Naomi was glad to sit down; her knees were feeling a little weak. She had never been able to handle surprises well. She opened the letter and started to read, shaking her head in disbelief as she progressed.

Dear Naomi,

First let me say I'm writing a similar letter to Louise. You'll find enclosed a check for $20,000. As you know, Edna left me everything she had that wasn't earmarked for charities. It's a lot and I don't really need it. Also, I don't feel right taking it knowing she still has family. You girls were kind enough to come down here and check on her, so I feel you should have some of it. If she'd met you before she went senile, I know she would have felt the same way. She was fond of your mother, so let's say it's for her also.

I won't take no for an answer on this, so don't even try. Do with it as you wish. As I said, she already gave a lot to charities.

My friend and I are off on a cruise. When I get back, I'll start going through Edna's things.

God bless you both,

Marge.

P.S. His name is Harry, by the way. Wish me luck!

Naomi sat for a long time going over things in her mind. Mostly she felt a profound sense of guilt. They had gone to Arizona to find out if Aunt Edna had stolen Gran's money, not to check on her welfare. It just wouldn't be right to accept the money. Granted, once they were there, they would have done anything they could to help their aunt and said as much. Marge had refused all offers. God knows I could use the money, Naomi thought. Even if this book is as successful as the first one, it will likely be two years before I feel secure again.

Try as she might, she couldn't justify accepting the gift. No sense talking to Louise, she thought, my mind is made up. She dialed Marge's number, formulating in her head what she would say to this generous friend of her aunt. But she didn't get to say it: there was no answer. She tried several times throughout the day, and concluded that Marge had already left on her cruise. Naomi knew she couldn't put off calling Louise any longer.

"Well, have you got over the shock yet?" her sister asked.

"No, it's unbelievable. What did Sam say?"

"He wants a statehood conferred on Marge."

"No, seriously, Lou, does he think we should accept it?"

"He thinks it's a little embarrassing, but he says you can't look a gift horse in the mouth. I'm inclined to agree with him, but I sense you're not."

Naomi told her sister she'd tried to reach Marge and refuse her share. "I feel too guilty, Louise. We didn't go down there with good intentions."

"Partly we didn't, but we also wanted to check on her welfare. Do you think if we'd found her in dire circumstances, we wouldn't have helped her? We offered Marge help, remember, but she refused. We're not bad people, Naomi."

"I know, but it still doesn't seem right." She thought for a minute. "You know what I'd really like to do, Lou, is tell Marge why we went down and how I feel. What do you think?"

Louise took her time responding. "All right, sis, I suppose I'd always feel some guilt. Let's compose a letter together, and mail both checks back to her. That way she can do what she wants." Louise paused before adding, "Boy, that's big of us, I just hope she mails them back, little sister."

"If she does, I promise not to bug you about it again."

It was a couple weeks before they heard back from Marge. She'd been cruising the Caribbean with Harry. Now Harry was moving in, and Marge was on cloud nine. She began her letter with a row of capitals: I SAID I WOULDN'T TAKE NO FOR AN ANSWER! Their guilt was unfounded, she said. After reading their explanation, she'd have suspected Edna too. As far as guilt goes, she thought Edna guilty for cutting off her family. In her position, she could have helped her mother more. And the sister she was most fond of, Louise and Naomi's mother, May, certainly could have used paid help in caring for their grandmother. Don't feel bad, she urged, it makes me feel good doing this for the two of you. Then she finished by encouraging them to go visit her soon.

So it was decided: they would keep the money. Louise couldn't hide her delight. She'd wanted to start a summer riding camp for blind children, and the money would make it possible. Naomi approached Ben with the idea of contributing to the program Elaine had been championing when she had the accident. He was touched.

With the question of the money settled, and her manuscript returned and accepted, Naomi felt a wonderful sense of relief. When Diana called with an invitation to dinner, she accepted with a light heart. Ben would be there. It was well into September, but they were experiencing an Indian summer and the nights had yet to pick up the chill of fall. She chose a blue dress that echoed the color of her eyes. Her hair had grown over the summer and now more than brushed her shoulders. She swept it up in a clip, letting a few tendrils snake down the sides of her face. Her makeup she kept to a bare minimum. Stepping back from the mirror, she sized up her appearance. Not bad, Naomi assured herself. The light tan she built up over the summer gave her a glow of health. She gathered up flowers picked from her garden and headed out the door, confident and happy.

Diana, as usual, prepared a delicious meal, with as much fresh produce as her garden could muster. She treated Naomi like family these days and welcomed help when it was offered. Ben automatically performed chores he'd probably been doing in this kitchen since he was a boy. Naomi watched him with affection. Feeling her eyes on him, he looked up and held her gaze, while the energy flowed between them.

Diana wasn't blind to the situation. "All right, you two knock it off. Let's have another glass of wine before we tackle the dishes."

She headed for the living room and Naomi was about to follow suit, but Ben caught hold of her. He pulled her to him and whispered in her ear, "You're irresistible tonight, in your gown of blue. It matches your eyes. Kiss me before the chaperone returns."

Naomi laughed, wrapped her arms around him and they kissed. A wave of happiness swept over her. Was it Ben or the wine? She didn't really care; she just wanted to feel this way forever.

Diana succeeded in getting them into a game of Scrabble. Ben told her she was suicidal going up against two writers. She said she'd take her chances, and sought Naomi's help in keeping him honest.

"You have to watch him, Naomi, he'll put in these nonsensical words and claim they are legit science terms."

"She's a sore loser, Naomi," he said in defense.

"I'm not sure I should get in the middle of this sibling rivalry," Naomi responded. "Besides, how many scientific terms do you expect me to know, Diana?"

"Just wing it," she said.

Ben won the first two games. The girls put their heads together and decided to ban the use of any scientific words they didn't know. It didn't help much; Ben won the third game too.

They had started what they decided would be their final game, when the phone rang.

Diana held the phone out to Ben with a questioning look on her face. "It's for you: the hospital."

Naomi detected a flicker of concern as Ben took the phone. In the next few seconds, his face went ashen and he looked over at her in alarm. Naomi and Diana exchanged glances. All they could do was to listen to his side of the conversation.

"How long ago did you notice it?"

"What kind of signs, can you explain?"

"Have you called her doctor?"

"Yes, of course I will. I'll be right there. Thank you."

After he put the phone down, they all stood rooted to the spot. Ben was silent for what seemed an eternity to Naomi. In reality it was only a minute or so. When he spoke, his voice was unusually gruff.

"They think Elaine's coming out of the coma. There is eye and body movement." He looked at Naomi, a pained expression on his face, "I have to go, Naomi."

"I'm coming with you," Diana said without hesitation.

Naomi pulled herself together. "Yes, go, please. I'll clean up here."

Naomi could see Ben's heart was breaking as he headed for the door. He turned to speak to her. "Naomi, I…"

She shook her head, stopping him mid-sentence. "Go," she said gently, fighting back tears.

Diana followed Ben outside, turned and told Naomi, "I'll call you."

"Please," Naomi whispered.

Later Naomi couldn't remember cleaning up the kitchen. She must have done so in robotic fashion. She did remember standing there before she left, savoring the feel of the room she'd come to love. It would likely be her last time in the house. How could Diana keep up a friendship with her under the circumstances?

Once home, she knew there was no point in going to bed. How could she sleep? She wanted her sister's comfort, but knew it was too late to call Louise. All she could do was to sit and wait for Diana's call. Ben, poor Ben, what was he going through, she wondered. Naomi cradled her body and rocked, trying to block out the terrible anguish she felt. Everyone had told her this day would come. They'd wanted her to prepare for it, but how could you prepare for something like this. You can't turn love on and off; it has to fade like her love for Kevin.

Would she one day only feel a faded love for Ben? She didn't see how that could be. She loved him with such intensity. Life was not fair; life was not fair at all.

Spike jumped on her lap. Her tears created a pattern of spots on his fur. He suffered the dampness for a while before jumping down. She wanted some tea, but lacked the ambition to get it. Memories of that first cup of tea with Ben came flooding back, and she cried some more.

Around two a.m., she had finally cried herself out. When the phone rang, she had herself together enough to answer it. Diana sounded tired. She apologized for the late hour, but said Ben insisted she call: he was worried about Naomi. When she heard that, Naomi almost came unglued, but managed to hold on. There wasn't a lot of news. Elaine's movements had stopped minutes before Ben and Diana got there. Tests revealed there were changes, and her doctor felt she likely would regain consciousness soon. There was nothing to do but wait.

Naomi asked how Ben was taking it. Diana hesitated before answering. When she did finally speak, there was sadness in her voice.

"It's the first time I've seen him in such pain. Even when Elaine had the accident, he wasn't like this. Then he was anxious, scared, on tenterhooks; but now I see he's in deep pain. I think he'd already begun to grieve his loss of Elaine, thinking her dead already. Then you came along and helped him through the process, and now this. He's struggling, Naomi."

Naomi fought back tears; tears for Ben, not herself. "Diana, promise me this: If Elaine comes around, tell Ben not to call me. We can both handle it better that way. Tell him I know he loves me, but he loved Elaine first. Tell him, tell him…" she couldn't finish.

Diana said gently, "Naomi, let's just wait. We don't know what's going to happen. If there's any change, I'll call again. I will tell Ben you'd rather hear it from me, okay. Try to get some sleep."

Naomi did manage a little sleep. It was fitful and she woke often, but it got her through the night. There were no more calls from Diana. At seven, she made tea and tried nibbling a toasted muffin, but had no appetite. At seven thirty, she couldn't put off calling Louise any longer.

"Lou, it's me."

"Oh, sis, what's wrong?" Louise knew instinctively Naomi was in distress.

Naomi related the happenings of the night. She was near tears all the time, but managed to finish.

Louise, for once, didn't have a ready comment. She said something like, "Oh, wow," then paused to gather her thoughts.

"Naomi, get in the car and come over now. You need us around you, okay?"

"I can't, Lou. Diana said she'd call. I have to wait."

"Okay, but pack a bag and be ready to head out right away. Bring Spike if you need to." Her tone changed from authoritative to gentle. "We'll get through this, sis. Hang in there. Let me know when Diana calls."

Naomi packed a bag mechanically. Louise was right; it would be better to get away from here. She couldn't help Ben: he was in his own private hell. She uttered a silent prayer that Elaine would fully recover, if she came out of the coma. Ben deserved that. He had been vigilant and faithful all this time. It was she, Naomi, who had wronged Elaine. Along with all her other feelings, guilt was rearing its ugly head.

The long awaited call finally came at 10:23 a.m. Naomi's hand shook as she picked up the receiver.

"Naomi, it's Diana." Her voice sounded tentative. "It looks as if the hospital was right, Elaine is coming around."

"Can she speak?"

"No, but her eyes are open, and it looks as though she understands."

Naomi swallowed hard. “How is Ben?”

“I don’t think he’s had time to reflect yet. There are still a lot of complications. They’re running tests.”

Naomi wanted to say, has he asked about me, but knew that would be cruel. Instead, she told Diana she was going to her sister’s for the time being.

“I’ll tell Ben. Naomi, I really don’t know what to say. I want to say I’m sorry, but that doesn’t seem right. I feel somewhat to blame for bringing you and Ben together. Perhaps we can work out some kind of friendship after all this is over.”

“I can’t think straight right now, Diana. Perhaps I should move to Redmond, but then again, they’ll probably move back there. I don’t know what the answer is, but you do what’s best for Ben.”

Her voice was choking with tears. She said her goodbye and hung up quickly. So, that was it. The love of her life ended in a phone call.

26

Violet

The trauma of her mother's death brought back to Violet the pain of losing her baby, and the fact that life was passing her by. It was time that she and Etienne carved out a little happiness for themselves: time for Ralph to pay.

She planned it all very carefully. Ralph was home with a sprained ankle, and spent all day watching television and drinking. Violet knew by mid-morning he'd be passed out in front of the woodstove. He would probably have left the stove door open, and there would be a can of lighter fluid nearby. His dangerous habit of squirting it in the firebox was well known throughout her family.

She told Etienne she had a dentist appointment and left at ten. Once outside Powell River, she hid in the trees and changed into some of Ralph's clothes she'd brought with her. There was only one road to Spruce Creek, and she didn't want anyone to recognize her. There was not much she could do about the car, but there were a lot of black Austin's about. She left the road a half-mile before Spruce Creek, hid the car up an old logging road, and approached the house on foot. She could reach the back of the house without coming out of the trees. It was unlikely anyone would see her. Violet carefully peeked in the window. Ralph had his head back and mouth wide open. He must be out, she thought. Just to be sure, she scratched at the window with a twig several times. He didn't budge an inch.

Once inside, she moved quickly and quietly. Before she left that morning, she'd gone around and made sure all the windows were closed. Now she slowly opened the window in the undressing room—not a lot, but enough to give life to a fire. She moved as she'd rehearsed in her mind: a few more empty beer containers at his feet; newspaper placed as though fallen on the hearth, and around the other side of his chair—it had to look natural. Her heart was pounding so loudly she was sure it would wake him, but he didn't stir.

The fire wasn't burning as brightly as she'd hoped, but there were good-sized embers. Her hands shook as she carefully poured lighter fluid over the newspaper and into the carpet. She was relying on the carpet to produce enough smoke to kill him, before the sound of the fire woke him up. It was risky to spread the fluid too far, and she left enough in the can to make it look accidental. They were able to analyze fires so much these days, but she had to be sure it would work.

Only one thing left to do, and this was the most dangerous. She had to carefully remove a chunk of burning ember, and place it close to the soaked newspaper. From her pocket, she pulled a strip of newspaper she'd cut at the office. She laid it down to become a bridge between the ember and fuel-soaked paper. After glancing quickly at the path of her retreat, she turned for a last look at the face she despised. She thought she might feel remorse, but she didn't. The smell of smoke was already in the air before Violet reached the back door.

She knew she should hurry away, but she had to be sure, so she stood looking through the back window until she saw flames. With the house being set off so far from the others, it would be a long while before any neighbors noticed. Violet hurried back to her car, pulled off Ralph's clothes, and allowed herself two minutes to stop hyperventilating. She had to stay in control. Think of the future, she told herself. All the way back into town, she kept whispering to herself, "Think of the future."

Etienne was on the phone when she got back to the office. She put her hand over her mouth and motioned to the bathroom. He nodded, and continued talking. She hurried in, opened the toilet and heaved and heaved. When the bile finally petered out, she splashed her face with cold water, over and over again. She made sure she was calm and collected before she went back to her desk. Etienne mustn't know, mustn't be implicated.

Keeping her mind on work was difficult; she kept expecting the RCMP to arrive. Etienne thought her lack of concentration due to the tooth work. She was beginning to think her plan hadn't worked—that Ralph had woken up and escaped—when Denny Sullivan walked through the door. He was with the RCMP now, and would have only one reason for being there. Her heart was pounding wildly as he walked up to her desk.

"Violet, is there somewhere we could talk privately?"

She tried to register surprise, and motioned to the back room.

"I'll be back in a minute," she assured Etienne.

Denny followed her. She noticed he closed the door before he spoke.

"Violet, I've come to let you know that Ralph is dead. He died in a house fire this morning."

She kept her eyes down. That way he wouldn't see the lack of emotion.

"Your house is probably beyond repair," he continued, "I'm sorry."

Violet nodded, still looking at the floor.

"There are things you'll need to do. Shall I talk to Bill about that?"

"Please." Her response was barely audible.

Denny stood without saying anything for a minute or two. When he did speak again it was quietly.

"Look at me, Violet."

She did as he asked.

He took her hands. "It was my job to come here and tell you this, Violet, and today I'm here as a friend. When I come again, there'll be a detective with me and I won't be able to act as your friend."

She was paralyzed with fear. How could he know? She tried to speak, but her voice caught in her throat.

He saw the question in her eyes. "I was on the Spruce Creek Road this morning, parked up the old quarry cutoff, watching for speeders." He squeezed her hands. "I saw you, Violet—going both ways."

She froze, eyes locked on his. His expression told her he knew.

"Look, what I want to tell you is very important. Remember this, please." He looked emotional, but his tone was serious. "When we come back, we'll be asking questions; it's the usual procedure. Only answer exactly what we ask, Violet, don't add a thing. Not a thing, okay?"

She nodded.

"Ralph had a lot of enemies," Denny continued, "there's bound to be suspicion. Let's hope the fire investigators don't find anything." His expression turned to one of deep compassion. "If they do, I'll be powerless, Violet."

She stood mute; fear preventing her from thinking.

"The detective's a new guy; he's bound to be more thorough than someone who knew Ralph," Denny explained.

A tap on the door interrupted him. Etienne stuck his head around.

"Is everything all right, Violette?"

She tried to respond, but tears welled up in her eyes.

He was at her side in a flash; arms ready to hold her.

"Mon Dieu, what is it?" he asked Denny.

"Her husband died in a house fire this morning," Denny said.

Etienne looked like he'd just taken a punch to the chin. He was momentarily speechless. He reached for her blindly, held her to him and said over and over, "Oh, Violette, oh, Violette."

Denny, looking from one to the other, had a sudden flash of understanding. He gave them a few minutes, before addressing Etienne.

"I'll need to talk to Violet again, sir."

When he'd left the room, Denny turned to Violet. "Does he know where you were this morning?" he said, referring to Etienne.

She shook her head. "I told him I had a dentist appointment."

"Did you go to a dentist?"

She shook her head again.

"Oh, boy," Denny said worriedly.

Violet followed his train of thought. If they did question her, she'd need an alibi—she hadn't planned for this eventuality. She assumed they'd rule it accidental death, knowing Ralph's drinking history. She couldn't, she wouldn't drag Etienne into this. "I can't involve him, Denny. If he left on a business trip…" she suggested weakly.

"The sooner, the better," he responded.

Etienne left the day of the funeral. She'd had to tell him in the end, although in her heart she felt he knew. He wanted to stand by her, but she convinced him it was better this way. After they'd interviewed her, she'd leave on a cruise—probably to the Caribbean, she told him. She would eventually make her way to Europe, where they would meet up again. He wasn't happy with the arrangement, but she said she'd manage better without having to worry about him. It would be all right, she assured him.

She wasn't sure that it would be. Denny said they'd wait until after the funeral to contact her. She was staying at Gwen and Bill's, where there was little emotion over Ralph's death. Violet knew no one expected her to grieve. The one thing she couldn't do was go to the house. Bill salvaged what he could of her personal effects. Etienne had given her money for new clothes. She bought a few things in Powell River, but shopping was no pleasure—she'd wait until she got to Vancouver. But first, she had to get through the interview.

It went better than she expected. Denny arrived with Detective Michael Rawlings the day following the funeral. Violet tried to stay calm, but knew she must have seemed emotional. Not knowing her, Detective Rawlings probably put it down to her grief. She tried not to have eye contact with Denny, but could feel his eyes on her the whole time. The questions appeared to be routine, and she answered them as Denny had instructed, adding nothing. She felt an enormous sense of relief when they stood to go. The detective was beginning to unnerve her; he had a somber, Dragnet-like approach to his job. His last comment sent a river of fear rushing through her.

"Thank you, Mrs. Braun, that pretty much wraps it up for us. The fire people still have to file their report. I don't imagine that will be anything out of the ordinary, unless of course your husband had enemies." He gave what passed for a smile: it was an attempt at wry humor.

Thankfully, he turned away after he said it. Denny's eyes met hers. She thought she saw fear in them, and this guided her actions in the following days.

Gwen and Bill could understand her need to get away for a while. A cruise, they agreed, was the perfect solution. Since she didn't have much in the way of belongings now, taking everything she owned with her didn't seem out of the ordinary. The office, she explained, could be closed until Etienne returned; there was no pressing business with him away. It troubled Violet greatly that she couldn't take Gwen into her confidence; she had been such a good friend. But what she didn't know, she couldn't tell. She did know Violet and Etienne were having an affair, and that secret would be hard enough to keep if it ever came up.

Maybe one day she'd be able to return, Violet thought. One day when the fear left her. But it never did.

Chapter 27

Sam and Louise were so good to her, Naomi thought, as she perched on a rock overlooking the river. They surrounded her with love; yet let her have time alone to reflect. She'd been here three days already. After Diana's call, she had found Spike's travel cage in the garage, scooped him up and headed out. She drove out over Mount Hood and through Madras, wanting to stay away from the route she'd traveled with Ben.

The boys were back in school now, so she and Louise had plenty of time to talk. As usual, Louise helped her to see things a little more clearly. The guilt was the first thing her sister handled.

"Stop beating yourself, Naomi," she said. "It takes two to tango. Ben could have avoided the situation if he'd wanted to. Put yourself in Elaine's situation. Don't you think you'd forgive what happened under the circumstances?"

Naomi knew how she'd feel, but she wasn't so sure about Elaine. Louise did make her feel better about it though. They discussed the future at length, but couldn't come to a decision. What would be best: living in the shadow of Kevin or risking running into Ben and Elaine in Redmond? Louise didn't have the answer. Naomi still favored moving to Redmond, but maybe not for a while.

Sitting on the rock now, she contemplated what her next move should be. The book was finished. Thanks to Marge, she didn't have money problems. Perhaps she should take a vacation; she hadn't had one in years. The more Naomi thought about it, the more sense it made. She would take a month. That would give her enough time to make some decisions. Not enough time to get over Ben; that could take years, if ever.

The sun was beginning to set over the mountains when she went back inside to Louise and Sam. She joined them at the kitchen table, after calling goodnight up the stairwell to her nephews.

"Well, I've made one decision, you guys," Naomi said. "I'm going to take a vacation—thanks to Marge."

"Great!" Louise expressed approval.

"Sounds like a plan." Sam added, "Where will you go?"

"I haven't figured that out yet. Where is it good at this time of year? What do you think?"

"You could head south. It will have cooled off now." Sam suggested.

"We were just in Arizona, so I wouldn't want to go there. Perhaps I could go hike the canyons in Utah, I've always wanted to see them."

Louise, who had been quiet until now, offered an opinion. "That wouldn't be good, Naomi. You need to be around people, not off by yourself hiking."

"You're right," Naomi agreed. "Can you think of anywhere that fits the bill?"

"I'm thinking," said Louise. She got up to refresh her coffee. She puttered about the kitchen for a minute or two, before shouting out, "I've got it!"

Sam looked at Naomi. "We're not surprised are we?"

Naomi laughed. Louise always came up with a solution. "Well, let's hear it," she urged her sister.

"You're going to love it." Louise said with enthusiasm. "You can go and find Cavenish Castle. What do you think of that?"

Naomi registered surprise. “I never thought of going overseas.”

“Well, you can afford it now, so why not. My friend Pat can help with details. It would be great fun, and a good way to take your mind off things. I’d love to come with you, but the boys are in school. You’d have to take lots of photos.”

The more they talked about it, the more Naomi liked the idea. It would give her something else to focus on. She didn’t say so to Louise, but it was in her mind that she could also go to France and check up on Aunt Violet. Before they went to bed, they got on the web and checked airfares and accommodations. All Naomi needed to do now was pick a date. She’d need to make arrangements for Spike first, but the sooner she could leave, the better. Getting to sleep was still hard, but at least she had something else to think about besides Ben. Nevertheless, he was in her thoughts as sleep claimed her.

She awoke resolved to go home today and make preparations for her trip. Talk at the breakfast table centered on it. Her nephews were envious that she’d get to visit a castle. Naomi promised them souvenirs, and they went off to school happy. Sam was preparing to leave for work when the phone rang.

“Probably the office,” he said, grabbing the portable as he stuffed papers in his briefcase. His expression changed, and he glanced across at Louise before holding the phone out to Naomi. “It’s Ben.”

Naomi’s heart skipped a beat; she felt panic about to overtake her. “Lou, I can’t talk to him.”

Louise took the phone from Sam and walked outside. Naomi stood shaking so much; Sam walked over and put his arms around her. Louise was back right away, and surprised Naomi by holding the phone out to her.

Her face was expressionless. "Naomi, you need to talk to him." She pressed the phone into Naomi's hand. "It's okay, sis. Please do it."

Naomi, still shaking, walked outside. She managed to get out, "Hello, Ben," before choking up.

"Naomi," his voice sounded odd, and it took her a minute to realize he was crying. "I had to call. Elaine died last night."

"Oh, no, I'm so sorry," she almost whispered. "Oh, Ben, Ben…" she tailed off.

There was silence on the line, as they both tried to deal with their emotions. Eventually he spoke.

"I loved her, Naomi."

"I know you did. It must be very hard."

"I'm going to need some time."

"Yes, yes, of course, take all the time you need. I understand, Ben."

"I'm going out to the ranch for the time being."

"Okay." She could hardly hear herself for the beating of her heart. "Ben, I'll be here when you need me."

She wanted to say I love you, but knew it wasn't the time for him to hear it. He didn't need to hear about her trip either; she'd call Diana and tell her. She'd still go, it would give him the distance he needed right now. Naomi caught sight of Louise hovering at the window, her face a model of concern. She gave her a thumbs-up, and saw her sister's expression relax.

"We don't have to talk now, it's too difficult for you. I'll call Diana," she told him

He seemed relieved. "Thank you. Take care." And he hung up.

Naomi couldn't move. Her emotions were going haywire. A few minutes ago, she was contemplating life without Ben. Now she was to have him back, but at what price. I loved her, Naomi, he had said. She felt his pain. He must be allowed to grieve without her in the picture. It was a good thing she was going away for a month.

Ben hadn't said how Elaine died, perhaps he'd told Louise. She turned to go in the house and almost collided with Sam on his way out. He hugged her, and told her everything was going to be all right.

Louise pushed a mug of hot tea at her. "Here, sit down, you're so pale, you may fall down."

"Lou, I don't know how to feel. I want to be happy, but it doesn't seem right. Poor Elaine, did he say how she died?"

"No, just that she had. He only told me that because I said you couldn't talk to him."

"I'll call his sister in a minute. I didn't tell him about the trip either. He was crying, Lou, he loved her so much."

Louise patted her hand. "He's a good man, Naomi. He'll love you that way one day."

That set off Naomi's tears again, and Louise hurried to get tissues. They sat and cried together for a few minutes. It was a strange little scene, Naomi thought, here we are crying out with happiness and sadness.

She waited until she'd showered and had better control of herself to call Diana. It was a poignant conversation. Apparently, Elaine had regained consciousness, but no power of speech. They thought she understood some of what they said, but she wasn't able to give them any indication. She was doing fairly well for about 36 hours, and then something went horribly wrong. The doctor's speculated the renewed brain activity may have caused it. Ben barely had time to say goodbye to her before she lapsed into a coma again. Death came quickly after that.

Diana gave voice to what Naomi had secretly been thinking. It was a blessing she died, given she would have been severely handicapped. Ben felt the same way, Diana explained, although it was hard on him. It would take a while for him to get over it, she said, and the ranch would be the perfect place. He would be all right, knowing Naomi understood, Diana added.

Naomi told her about the planned trip. Diana thought it a great idea: it would clear the air for both of them. She thought it would be all right for Naomi to send postcards—it would keep Ben's spirits up. Naomi said she wouldn't call Ben before she left, and asked Diana to explain it to him. She also asked Diana to convey another message, when she felt the time was right.

"Diana, I wanted to tell him I loved him, but it didn't seem appropriate. If he should doubt it at any time, will you please tell him how I feel?"

"Of course I will." Diana assured her, and then added, "Naomi, we'll get through all this, and I look forward to a future with you in it. This may not seem appropriate either, but I'm so glad I brought you and Ben together. We'll be good friends, you and I."

It was early afternoon before Naomi was ready to head home. She and Louise had talked and talked. As she packed the car, Naomi thought of something.

"Lou, I don't suppose I should send flowers. What do you think?"

"No, sis, I'm inclined to agree. You already showed your respect by donating so much to the children's' fund Elaine was working with. It's not like you ever met her, and they won't expect it."

Naomi drove home the way she'd come out, only this time her heart was less heavy. She knew Ben would have a few hard days, but as Diana had observed, he had already spent months grieving for Elaine. He would get through this, and then they would build a new life together. The hard part for her, Naomi thought, would be not to call him before she left on her trip. But she resolved not to intrude on his grief.

The next two weeks were a whirlwind of activity for Naomi. There were so many details to plan. First, her publishers needed to sign off on her absence. Then she needed to make arrangements for Spike. Louise had offered to have him there, but she knew he'd be happier in his own surroundings. Her neighbors were a dear, elderly couple who enjoyed feeling needed. They liked Spike, and gladly agreed to care for him. Naomi knew Spike weighed less now than he would when she returned.

The itinerary for her trip had been planned in detail: She would fly into London; spend three days there, then take a train to Edinburgh. She'd rent a car in Edinburgh, and find her way to Cavenish Castle, stopping to sightsee along the way. If time allowed, she'd drive through the English Lake District and then down to the Cotswolds, ending up on the south coast. The part she wasn't telling Louise, just yet, was that once on the coast, she'd take a ferry over to France and ride the train to Sete, where Aunt Violet had settled. Naomi didn't know what she'd find there, if anything, but she was driven by curiosity.

She tried to let the trip planning keep her mind off Ben, but he was in her thoughts constantly. Now the day before she was due to leave, she ached to call him. Diana had called a week ago. They talked about the funeral and she said Ben handled it well. Afterwards, it seemed as though a weight had been lifted from his shoulders; he was very reflective. When Diana left the ranch to come home, he was talking about heading into the hills by himself for a few days.

Instead of breaking her promise to herself and calling Ben, Naomi called Diana.

"Diana, it's Naomi, I'm off tomorrow and just wanted to touch base with you before I head out."

"I'm glad you did. Have a really wonderful trip. I told Ben you're going and he's happy for you. Actually, I think he was rather relieved. This way he won't be tempted to contact you. He'll take the time he needs to work through his feelings."

"Did he get off by himself?"

"Yes, he headed into the Three Sisters Wilderness with his backpack. He said Peggy was fussing over him too much at the ranch. She's getting ready to move out now that he's home. I think she'll get a place in Bend, since that's where she's working."

"Will Ben stay out there long? The weather could change."

"Oh, don't worry about Ben, he knows that area like the back of his hand. He carries all the right gear. I expect he'll be out a week or so, then he'll crave a shower so bad, he'll be back. Shall I give him a message?"

Naomi could think of a dozen poetic things she'd like to say, but somehow Diana didn't seem like the right vehicle. She ended up saying simply, "Just tell him he will never be far from my thoughts."

Chapter 28

Trying to sleep on the train between Paris and Sete was impossible, Naomi found. Her anticipation at finding out what happened to Aunt Violet kept her adrenaline flowing. Another few hours and she'd be in the coastal town where Aunt Violet lived out her life. She had an address, supplied by her cousin Susan. If she couldn't find out anything there, she thought the cemetery would be the next step.

Her trip had so far been a lot more fun than she expected. Ben was never far from her thoughts, but she was having so many new experiences that she didn't yearn for him. While in London, she had taken time to visit Paddington Station—where Aunt Edna had worked the kiosk. The place hadn't changed much since Edna's day. Naomi took photos to share with the family. Louise's friend Pat had the address of the house in Kensington. Finding it proved easy for Naomi, who stood gazing at the façade, allowing images to leap around in her mind. The house was in an elegant Georgian terrace, with a short flight of well-scrubbed steps leading to the door. In her mind's eye, Naomi could see the inebriated Daddy lurching up them with great effort, for his first encounter with Aunt Edna. She figured the house hadn't changed one iota since Aunt Edna lived there. Louise would be tickled with the photos she took there: an infamous piece of family history, to be sure.

Cavenish Castle was wonderful. She had a number of wet days in Scotland and Northern England, but the day she found Cavenish Castle was warm and sunny. She had no illusions as to what the castle looked like, having seen a picture. Even so, the spectacle thrilled her: remnants of turreted walls, jutting up in the middle of a grassy field. Here and there she could make out what was left of the moat and embankments. It was so exciting to stand in a castle that bears your name, Naomi thought. She amused herself hunting all over to turn up clues of she knew not what. Perhaps a name carved in a wall, or a piece of tattered tartan—somehow overlooked by the hordes of tourists who had gone before. When nothing was forthcoming, she sat in the grass, her back resting on the ancient stones. She tried to imagine the Cavenish clan in residence.

Naomi was so carried away by the sheer romance of the moment; she didn't see a tourist approach.

"I say," he said in a stiffly British accent, "is everything all right?"

Naomi was embarrassed at being caught off guard. She knew she'd been sitting there with her eyes closed and a huge grin on her face. The man's wife stood a few steps back, protecting herself from who knows what. Naomi scrambled to her feet.

"I'm fine," she explained, "just doing a little dreaming. My ancestors used to own this place."

"Oh, really," he said, drawing out the last word, "how nice for you." He turned to his wife. "Come on my dear, we must get going."

Naomi tried not to laugh. They obviously thought she was a little odd. "No, honestly, my family name is Cavenish," she explained.

"But you're American!" he said incredulously.

"Born in Canada, actually. One branch of the family went over there."

"Oh, I see, I see," he was beginning to soften.

Before long, Naomi had talked them into taking her photo amid the ruins. She envisioned using it on her Christmas cards:

a sort of 'from our house to yours' or 'Naomi Cavenish at home.' The light Highland air was intoxicating; at least that's what she blamed for her moments of silliness. She found it hard to leave the castle, and vowed to return one day with Ben. Her nephews should see it too. She'd have to talk to Louise.

The best time to sit on the beach at Sete was during the dinner hour, Naomi found. Most of the tourists departed for their evening meal, and she could sit and contemplate without dodging beach balls. It was only a short walk from her hotel to the seven miles of sandy beach. The flat, wide expanse of sand reminded her more of California beaches than of Oregon's rugged coastline. This was the third day of her visit; she had two more to go. When she first arrived, she'd been mystified as to why Aunt Violet chose this place to settle. Sete was a busy fishing port and a popular tourist spot. It is an island, she noted, flanked on one side by the Mediterranean, and a large lagoon filled with oyster beds on the other. Naomi could see why Sete, with its canals, was considered the Venice of the south coast of France. She had visualized Aunt Violet living in a quiet, little village. Sete seemed so out of character for shy, delicate Aunt Violet. It had puzzled Naomi—until yesterday. Yesterday she found her answer in the cemetery.

The address Susan supplied hadn't given her any leads. Once she'd finally located the house, no one there had heard of Violet Braun. She found it hard to make herself understood. The tenants either didn't speak English or chose not to. Either way, they weren't very friendly. The staff at city hall was a little more helpful. They supplied Naomi with street directions to two cemeteries in the area. One was close in and she went there on foot. The church was all locked up. She began walking along reading gravestones. It was a large cemetery, and the futility of what she was doing finally registered with her. Perhaps city hall could put her in contact with someone who had the records, she thought. That approach made more sense than wasting more time walking along rows.

On the off chance she'd find someone at the second cemetery, she took a taxi up there. This one was close to the top of the large hill that encompassed the middle of the island. No one was around, but this cemetery was small. It appeared to be more of a family graveyard, Naomi noticed, with many graves bearing the same name. Her eyes scanned the stones: Ducharme, Bousquet, Chantel. Pouquet. What chance was there of finding Aunt Violet in a French family plot, she wondered. About to give up, she was stopped in her tracks by a name that meant something to her: Chartier. Naomi thought back to her cousin Susan rolling the name Etienne Chartier off her tongue. He had been Aunt Violet's employer, according to Susan. Could it be that he was more than her employer? No one in the family had made that connection.

A trickle of excitement ran through her as she hurried over to the Chartier family plot. They were a prolific family, she noted, as she read headstone after headstone. There were a few 'counts' with ornate headstones. She even found one Count Etienne Chartier, but the dates were all wrong for Violet's employer. Naomi began concentrating on the newer stones, and it wasn't long before she found what she was looking for: the simple grave of her aunt's employer.

Naomi plopped down on the grass beside the grave. As she read the inscription, her eyes grew wide: Etienne Chartier; born in Sete, April 1903, died October 1975. And beneath, in newer script: And his wife Violette; born in British Columbia, Canada 1918, died July 1983. Between the two names, entwined in a vine of flowers, were words she couldn't interpret—her French just wasn't good enough.

She sat there for a long time trying to take it all in. Aunt Violet had married her employer, yet she never told the family. Why? He was a good bit older than her, Naomi noticed. Her discovery posed so many new questions; she could hardly wait to tell Louise.

Now as she sat on the beach, Naomi tried to think if there was anything more she needed to do before leaving Sete. On a return visit to city hall this morning, she had tried to find out when Aunt Violet married Etienne. The language barrier got in the way. The clerk had been quite offhand. She acted like she didn't understand, but Naomi had the distinct feeling she did. Maybe Louise would have some ideas on ferreting out the information. She'd ask her when she got home.

At the thought of home, Naomi pictured a reunion with Ben. Would he be ready, she wondered or still grieving? She rested her chin on her drawn-up knees, and gazed out to sea. The day was cooling, and she spread her white, cotton skirt out to cover her legs. Her tousled hair was pulled back and clipped at the nape of her neck. She stayed this way for quite some time, dreaming about the future—her future with Ben.

She became aware of someone watching her. A man, fortyish and looking more like a local than a tourist, was standing some distance away studying her. As she made eye contact, he strode toward her.

"Forgive me," his accent was French, "you reminded me so much of someone I once knew. She used to sit on the sand just the way you are sitting."

Naomi smiled at him.

"Mon Dieu!" he exclaimed, "You even look like dear Violette."

Naomi gasped. "You mean Violet Chartier?"

"You knew her?" Now it was his turn to sound surprised.

"She was my aunt."

"Mine too."

They both laughed.

"Permit me," he held out his hand. "I am Jean Paul Chartier. Your Aunt Violette married my Uncle Etienne."

"Yes, yes, I found that out yesterday at the cemetery," Naomi explained. "I'm Naomi Cavenish. Violet was my mother's sister. What a coincidence you finding me here like this."

He looked a little embarrassed. "I must confess; it was no accident."

Naomi looked puzzled.

Jean Paul explained. "My cousin, Odette, works for the city. You asked her about Violette's marriage this morning."

"She pretended she didn't understand."

"She was suspicious; a stranger asking about her uncle. You see Uncle Etienne went to great lengths to hide his whereabouts. My cousin saw you were on foot, and had someone follow to see which hotel you went to. From there, it was easy. She called me. A school friend works the desk at your hotel. He said you'd been visiting the beach in the evenings. When you left just now, he called. It didn't take me long to find you. It's uncanny how I found you though. Violette really did sit just like that almost every evening, with her chin on her knees." He shook his head. "I cannot get over how much you look like her."

"No one's ever told me that before," Naomi said. "They say I look like my mother, but then she and Aunt Violet were alike." Naomi suddenly thought of something. "If your cousin understood me, why didn't she help me or ask who I was?"

Jean Paul looked at her intently for a moment, and then shrugged. "It's a long story, Naomi. Can we go for coffee and I'll try to explain?"

Naomi gladly took him up on the offer. This very charming man could help her fill in the puzzle.

He took her to a small café with a central courtyard. They sat in a corner, out of the breeze. Jean Paul ordered coffee and insisted she try some local pastry. Naomi hadn't the heart to tell him she was a tea drinker. Jean Paul was obviously enjoying their meeting. He was quite a handsome man, with gaunt features—not at all like the image of his uncle that Susan had conveyed. The only thing they appeared to have in common was their height. Jean Paul was rather short. He was, he told Naomi, 47 and the son of Etienne's youngest brother.

Etienne, she learned, was the oldest son in his branch of the family. The titled Chartiers in the cemetery were cousins, but all the Chartiers were well to do. They came from a long line of lawyers, and Etienne had followed the tradition. His presence in British Columbia was due to a falling out with his father. He had returned in time to make peace with the old man before he died.

"My uncle was married to a woman his father picked out—mariage de convenance, good for family connections, you understand. Poor Etienne, his heart was not in it. When he sought a divorce, his father, he, he," Jean Paul struggled for the right word, "hit the roof, I think you say. If he had lived long enough to get to know Violette, he would have approved their marriage."

"When did they marry?"

He gave her a melancholy look. "Only weeks before he died."

"But she'd lived here for years," Naomi expressed surprise.

He nodded. "They were man and wife in the eyes of God, to be sure, but officially not until he was dying."

" I wonder why they waited so long."

"We always wondered too. I had hoped to find out. Violette and I became good friends after Etienne died. She was so frail, but always so beautiful. I used to drive her around—she wouldn't drive here, you know."

"No, I didn't know. I think she had a car in Spruce Creek, but she used to ride a bicycle a lot."

"Etienne told me she was so fit when he met her. By the time they settled here, they had been on so many cruises, I don't think she ever got back on a bicycle."

"Did she ever work here?"

"No, she had no need to; Uncle Etienne inherited a large estate. At first, I thought she resisted marrying him because she didn't want it to look as though it was for his money. He was a lot older than her, you see. But that wasn't it."

"You make it sound as though he wanted to marry, but she didn't."

"Yes, that's the way it was." Jean Paul leaned closer to her. "There was a mystery about your aunt. We never quite figured it out. Maybe you can help solve it."

Naomi gave him a wry smile. "I was rather hoping you could do the same thing. We could never understand why she virtually cut off contact with the family back home. We'd get a postcard now and then, but it wouldn't say much. No one knew about Etienne."

He raised his eyebrows. "That shouldn't surprise me. They were both secretive about her background. She always acted a little afraid. In fact, they went as far as having their mail sent to a house he owned but rented out."

"You mean they didn't live in the house on Rue Theresa?"

"No. Did you go there?"

"Yes. No wonder they didn't know who I was talking about."

He shrugged. "They are new tenants, anyway. What was your aunt afraid of, do you suppose?"

Naomi shook her head. "I don't know. She'd had a terrible life with her first husband. He used to beat her. Everyone was glad to see him dead, although I probably shouldn't say that."

"Ah, so he was dead. We wondered if perhaps he was still alive and she was scared he'd find her. How did he die?"

"In a house fire. Aunt Violet was at work when it happened. They figured he was probably drunk and caused it."

"Maybe that was punishment for what he did to Violette." Jean Paul looked pleased with the thought. "Well, she wasn't afraid of him anymore. Who was she afraid of, I wonder. His family?"

"No, he had no contact with them. They were probably just as awful as he was. I'll think about it, but right now I don't have a clue."

"When must you leave?'

"I leave the day after tomorrow."

"Good. Tomorrow, how would you like to go and visit your aunt's real home – my cousins live there now? We can talk more, and maybe lay to rest some of these questions we have."

He walked her back to her hotel, and made arrangements to pick her up in the morning. Naomi knew she'd have a hard time getting to sleep. There was so much to tell Louise. It was only 5 a.m. in Oregon; she'd have to stay awake until midnight to call her sister. She flipped the TV on, tried to make sense of what she was hearing, and then flipped it off again. Sleep finally claimed her around eleven.

By the time Jean Paul collected her in the morning, she had already worked out a few things about Aunt Violet. They, Violet and Etienne, must have been having an affair before Ralph Braun died. Otherwise, there would have been no reason for her to hide the relationship from everyone. It would have been easy enough to hide; she worked for him in Powell River, away from prying eyes in Spruce Creek. No doubt, she stayed with Ralph because she was afraid of him. Why she didn't tell the family about Etienne after Ralph died, Naomi couldn't fathom. The family would have been happy for her. It was strange for her to go off without a word—not even to Gwen, her best friend.

As to what she was afraid of, Naomi hadn't a clue. What people thought of her might be upsetting for Violet, but not something to be afraid of. There had to be more to it than that. She'd run it by Louise when she got home. After finally getting a connection to her sister this morning, Louise wasn't home. Another thing she'd have to tell Louise was that she was right; Aunt Violet didn't take Gran's money or her life. Etienne had more than enough money for both of them. Naomi was happy to think it wasn't Aunt Violet but realized she'd reached a dead-end. There were no more suspects. Could her mother have been wrong? Was euthanasia a product of her imagination? Naomi didn't know anymore.

Jean Paul arrived in a red, two-seater Mercedes. The top was up, since the weather looked uncertain this morning. Naomi had visualized a house near the top of the hill, but they soon left the town behind, drove across to the mainland and headed into the countryside. As they rounded a bend and came in sight of a lovely, big, country home, Jean Paul said with flair, "Voila, Chateau Chartier."

"My goodness, it's lovely," Naomi said. How nice that Aunt Violet lived in such beautiful surroundings, she thought—a far cry from Spruce Creek. "Did Aunt Violet live here until she died?"

"No, Naomi, she became so frail, she moved to a place where she could get help. It was not far from the beach, very nice. I'd take you there, but they had a fire. It almost burned down."

The cousins were at work, Jean Paul explained, as they neared the chateau, but they had a maid who would see to their needs. The maid welcomed them, then hurried off to make coffee while they toured the house. It had been in the family for over 100 years, Jean Paul said, and of course had a ghost.

Naomi looked startled.

Jean Paul laughed. "Just kidding, tourists usually like that sort of thing. But then, you're not a tourist, you're family."

The house was showing signs of age; some of the rooms showed the faded elegance of 20s and 30s wallpaper. In what was meant to be a large, formal dining room, the current residents had created a media room, dominated by a large-screen television. Many rooms had no furniture at all. It was too expensive to keep up these old houses, Jean Paul explained. The current owners, like Etienne and Violet before them, only lived in a few rooms. Jean Paul opened the door of the conservatory.

"This was Violette's favorite room," he said.

Naomi could see why. It was warm and light, with a wonderful view of the Mediterranean in the distance. She could picture Aunt Violet sitting here drinking her tea—or maybe she'd gone native and drank coffee.

The maid arrived with their coffee. Jean Paul waited for her to leave, and then asked, " Naomi, have you been able to figure out what dear Violette was afraid of?"

She shook her head. "It doesn't make sense. She was free to marry your uncle. I cannot imagine what motivated her fear. You say he went along with it too, so it must have been something rational."

Jean Paul shrugged. "Perhaps." He gazed off at the distant shoreline, and sat deep in thought.

Naomi broke the silence. "I do have one thought, although you may not like it."

"No, please," he urged her on.

"I've nothing to base it on—I mean I've never heard anything to the effect. Could your uncle have had shady business dealings in Canada? Maybe he owed money and was afraid someone would come to collect."

He didn't seem offended. "Knowing him, it is highly unlikely. He was a man of principal, and besides, he was heir to a small fortune. Money was the least of his worries."

"I'm sure you're right, I'm just grasping at straws here."

She wanted to ask what happened to the "small fortune" but felt it would be in bad taste.

Jean Paul must have read her mind. "His fortune, by the way, has to stay in the family. Your aunt was provided for, but with no heirs, it reverts back to the family." He sensed Naomi's discomfort. "Sorry, I thought your family would want to know."

"Thank you," she said, "someone may ask."

"As far as what they were afraid of, I still think it was Violette's fear. Why wouldn't she marry him?" He answered his own question. "Because she was afraid someone would find out. You're sure her husband died in the fire?"

"Yes, positive. My mother didn't go to the funeral, she was in Oregon by then, but we heard about it. Very few people showed up, and then it was only for Violet's sake. None of his family attended." Naomi's brow wrinkled, "You know, one suspicious thing: Aunt Violet left on a cruise almost immediately. Well, maybe it's not so suspicious; she didn't have a house anymore."

"And she could hardly wait to be with my uncle, I suppose."

"Yes, I'm sure they must have been having an affair for some while. She worked for him for a number of years. It was a small office. I don't think he employed anyone else."

Jean Paul said earnestly, "They were very much in love, you know."

Naomi thought of Ben and her love for him. They, too, had hidden their love from the world at large. She understood her aunt's feelings completely.

She smiled at Jean Paul. "You don't know how happy that makes me feel. Aunt Violet deserved to know true love. I hope they cherished every day together."

"They did."

They finished their coffee, talking about other things. He told her more about his family, his law practice and Sete. Naomi gave him more details of the Cavenish family, and of her life in Oregon. He said he'd always wanted to visit America. Naomi said when she and Ben were settled he should bring his family to visit. He said he'd like that, and that she should return to Sete one day with her family.

Before they left the house, he asked, "Is there anything else you would like to do before leaving tomorrow?"

She looked out the window at the well-tended garden, and all the flowers, thriving in this mild climate. Aunt Violet loved this room. Suddenly, Naomi knew what she wanted to do.

"Jean Paul, do you think your cousins would mind if I picked flowers to take to Aunt Violet's grave? And would you mind taking me there?"

"They would be delighted, and so would I. We all loved Violette."

Thinking about the grave reminded Naomi of something she'd been wondering about.

"I need to ask you, Jean Paul: on their gravestone are some words entwined in a vine. My French is not good; what does it say?"

"Ah, ma chere, Violette arranged that those words be added when she died. Ensemble pour toujours. It means simply, together forever."

Chapter 29

Naomi had arranged for Diana to pick her up at the airport. She was tired from the long flight, and hoped the airport construction didn't hold Diana up. You couldn't go anywhere in Portland these days without passing through a construction zone. If Diana wasn't at the gate, they had agreed to meet in front of the elevator on the baggage claim level.

Her carry-on bag was rather heavy. She'd bought her nephews everything she could find with Cavenish Castle on it and packed it in her carry-on, to keep it safe in case her luggage went astray. She had French perfume in there for Louise and Diana, and liqueur for Sam. Deciding on a gift for Ben had been near impossible. A store in Sete was noted for its fine leatherwork, and she finally settled on a hand-tooled leather belt. There was one other gift in her hand luggage. On her way back from the beach in Sete, she passed a children's boutique. In the window was an adorable little dress, with a gamin look that could only be French. On an impulse, she went inside and bought it for Kevin's baby.

It was late evening already, and the crowd at the gate was not too large. Naomi scanned the faces for Diana, but couldn't see her. She was hoisting the bag on her shoulder when she saw him. Ben. He met her astonished look with a most tender smile. The bag almost hit the floor as she rushed to him. She was oblivious to the crowd around them as she fell into his arms.

"Oh, Ben, Ben," she whispered between kisses.

"I couldn't stay away," he told her, "Naomi, I love you."

A warm glow enveloped her. "And I love you, Ben, oh, I do so love you."

It felt so wonderful to be able to say it, even in the midst of the crowd. They held on to each other, reluctant to end the moment. When they were finally ready to move on, the crowd had dispersed. Ben carried her bag, and held onto her hand. Naomi had never felt happier.

At 2:45 a.m., Naomi was wide-awake. She hadn't slept at all on the plane, nervous flyer that she was. Once in bed, she'd slept soundly, but now the time change had claimed her and she was fully alert. She was so happy, she wanted the whole world to wake up and share her joy. Louise wouldn't welcome a call at this hour. She'd call her around six; they were usually up by then. She had given her sister a quick call last night to let her know she was home safely. When she said Ben had picked her up, Louise had cut the conversation short. She ordered Naomi to call her in the morning.

Last night it felt so good to be home in her little house again. Ben carried in the luggage, while she made a fuss of Spike. The cat was pleased to see her, but let her know when she'd fussed over him enough. Ben followed her into the kitchen.

"Just show me where everything is, and I'll make you some tea. You look tired out," he said.

"I am," Naomi agreed. "I wish I could sleep on planes, but I have to stay alert in case the pilot goofs."

Ben gave her an affectionate smile. "And you would do what exactly to help?"

She laughed. "Probably lead the passengers in a panic attack."

While they drank their tea, she told him about the trip. After she finished, she said, "I'm not looking forward to telling

Louise about the trip to France. She's bound to be put out about it."

"Maybe not," Ben answered, "She may be glad that you've solved another piece of the puzzle."

Naomi wanted to say there are no pieces left, but that would do for another time. Ben had news of his own. She wondered where he was in the grieving process, and was afraid he might be ahead of himself by coming to meet her. He said the time alone in the wilderness had helped him clear his head. But what really healed him was a letter he got from Elaine's sister.

"Diana must have talked to her and told her about you," he explained. "She wrote such a lovely letter. Essentially, she said what I think I felt: that I'd already grieved for Elaine for the better part of two years. She said I shouldn't hinder my relationship with you by wondering what people would say. It was time to get on with my life, she said, and wished us both the best of luck."

"How very generous of her. She sounds like a nice person."

"She is. Anyway, I think a lot of what I was feeling was guilt about you. She helped me get beyond that. With her blessing, who cares what other people think."

Naomi was relieved to hear him speak this way. Now, if only a little could rub off on her and she could lose her guilt. Time, and Ben's new attitude would help.

Naomi's expression must have given away her thoughts. Ben took her hands and looked intently into her eyes. "Naomi, this may sound very strange. I know in my heart Elaine would have given us her blessing. Under the circumstances, she'd have wanted this to happen. Believe me."

She smiled and nodded in agreement. "If she loved you as much as I love you—and I'm sure she did—she would want your happiness. But, Ben, while we're talking about this, there's something I want you to know. I never want you to think of me as Elaine's replacement, but as someone else you love. Keep your love for her in your heart. I will always understand that."

He pulled her to him. "Thank you, my love. You are truly a beautiful person."

They continued to talk, but after awhile he saw she was having trouble keeping her eyes open. "I should go," he said. She noticed a question in his announcement. He wanted to stay.

"Please stay," she said.

Ben held her gaze, and hesitated before answering.

"Well, this wasn't how I planned it, but there's something I must do if I'm to stay." They were sitting on the sofa, and he knelt before her on one knee. "Naomi," he said with great formality, "would you do me the honor of becoming my wife?"

She started to cry, and was too choked up to reply.

"Well," he said, with mock impatience.

Naomi managed to stifle her tears enough to give him an answer. "I should like nothing more than to be your wife, Ben. I just wasn't expecting it now."

"I thought I'd better catch you when you were tired," he said with a twinkle in his eye. "Catch you with your defenses down."

"Oh, Ben, are you sure you're ready?"

"Never surer," he replied.

Naomi glanced at the clock; still only 3:05 a.m. She turned over and snuggled up to Ben, cupping her body to his back. They hadn't made love last night; she was too tired. Now, he felt her closeness, turned and groggily reached out for her. She nestled into his chest and listened to his heart beating. A warm glow flushed through her body, and soon turned to passion. Ben was still sleeping. She began caressing him gently, running her hands over his torso. His body responded to her touch, and when he reached for her, she was ready.

They made love this time without the intensity of their first encounter. They explored each other's bodies tenderly, allowing the passion to build. Ben was an attentive lover, satisfying her completely. She fell asleep in his arms, exhausted, contented.

Ben left early. He was going to Diana's to get his things. It was an easy decision for him to move in. They didn't want to be separated now they were free to love each other. Until Naomi was able to sell the house, they would live here, and go to the ranch for long weekends. There were a number of small things he could help her with before the house was ready for sale. Naomi needed to talk to Louise about the wedding, but thought she'd like it to be in Redmond, preferably outdoors.

Ben was barely out of sight before Naomi dialed Louise.

"I knew it would be you," Louise said, and then with her usual candor, "Can I be a flower girl?"

Naomi laughed. "Lou, you're dreadful. I can never surprise you with anything."

"I was only kidding. Are you telling me Ben proposed?"

"Yes."

"Hallelujah! Oh, I'm so happy for you, sis. When's it to be?"

"We'll need to talk about that, Lou. I'm a bit sensitive about doing it too soon, although Ben is not. What do you think?"

They talked at length. Naomi told her about the letter Elaine's sister sent Ben. Louise said she also felt Ben had grieved for two years already.

"If he says he's ready, sis, he probably is," she emphasized. "But how about you? Are you sure?"

"Very sure, Lou. It feels so right. With Ben being a writer, I don't think I'll run into the problems I did with Kevin. Plus, I learned a few things."

Louise liked the idea of having the wedding in Central Oregon. She said she'd put on her thinking cap, and they could all discuss it the next time Naomi and Ben came over.

The discussion then turned to Naomi's trip. Louise wanted all the details of Cavenish Castle, and Naomi's other experiences in England. Finally, there was nothing more to tell, but her visit to Sete.

"Lou, I had time to spare so I went to Sete."

There was silence on the line for a moment. When Louise spoke, it was with the older sister voice. "You planned it all along, didn't you?"

"I had it in mind, but I didn't book until I was finished in England. I knew you'd be mad."

"I'm not mad, but why didn't you tell me?"

"You know you'd have tried to put me off. I'm glad I went, Lou. Wait 'til you hear what I found out."

Naomi related her experiences in Sete: the cemetery, her meeting with Jean Paul, Aunt Violet's chateau. "It's so nice not to suspect Aunt Violet anymore. I didn't want it to be her either. Jean Paul said Etienne's family all loved her. The funny thing was, he said she was always afraid of something, and they kept their whereabouts secret. I wondered if Etienne had been in some shady business dealings in B.C. Jean Paul said no. Do you think it possible?"

"Hmm, I suppose so. He was a lawyer. It's conceivable he could have stumbled on something he shouldn't. I can't think of anything else it could be. Did he practice law when he got back?"

"No, his father died soon after and he got the inheritance."

Before they ended the conversation, Louise had a question. "Well, that's all your suspects accounted for now, Naomi. Are you ready to let the euthanasia rest?"

"Yes, Lou, I think Mum must have been feeling guilty when she said it. No one else was there. Gran probably died naturally, and it was just coincidence that Mum was out that night. I'd still like to hear about the inheritance though."

"I've had an idea on that. I'll look up e-mail addresses for Cavenish in the right areas, and try sending them a message. I might strike it lucky. Maybe I'll get to it before you come over."

Naomi hung up the phone with a sense of relief. Louise hadn't been too upset. Now she, Naomi, would have to put it out of her mind. It's funny how it had haunted her, she thought. It didn't affect Louise that way. Well, now she had her answers, it was time to move on.

There was so much to do. A check of her messages revealed a publication date for her book, and the publisher's desire to set up a book tour. It would be good to get that out of the way before the wedding, she thought. But then again, that would put it too late in the year for an outdoor ceremony. She was pondering the options when the doorbell rang.

The local florist stood on the doorstep with two-dozen red roses. They were from Ben. The card read simply, "Thank you, thank you. I love you, Ben." Naomi waltzed around the room cradling them—she felt such happiness. She dropped down on the sofa, still holding the flowers, and looked around the room. She would miss her little house and the garden. It would be hard for her to sell it; the first home she'd owned. She hoped someone with a child would buy it. She'd always thought it a lovely spot to raise a child.

Her melancholy gave way to inspiration. What about Kevin? He had a child now. Maybe he would like to buy the house back. She'd put a note in with the gift when she sent it. Somehow, the idea of Kevin living in the house seemed okay.

Naomi had almost finished unpacking when Diana called. Ben's sister was thrilled at their news. She didn't think it too soon to be married. The people who matter support you, she said, and urged Naomi to stop worrying about it. Ben left to take care of some business in town, she told Naomi, adding that he was like the old Ben today. That made her heart glad. Come tonight for dinner, she ordered, and Naomi was happy to comply.

Kevin was slow in responding to her suggestion about the house. He and Star must have needed time to talk about it. She thought she saw them drive by one day. No doubt he wanted Star to see the house, before contacting Naomi. She got a note from Star, thanking her for the dress. There was no mention of the house. Perhaps Kevin felt he couldn't live there again; his memories would get in the way. Naomi began to think it was a silly idea on her part, but one night Kevin called.

He said her suggestion came as a shock, and he needed time to think about it. Was she sure she wanted to sell the house? She'd given up a lot to keep it when they divorced.

Naomi hadn't mentioned Ben in her note; she'd simply said she was ready to sell the house. Now she told Kevin she was engaged and would be moving to Sisters.

He sounded surprised. "Wow, I had no idea. Is it Mrs. Ferguson's son? What's his name?"

"Ben."

"That's right, Ben. I heard his wife died. When are you getting married?"

"Probably not 'til spring. I've got a book tour coming up and want to get that out of the way first." Naomi paused and thought for a minute. There was really no avoiding it, so she added. "Ben has moved in here, Kevin. It was easier than commuting between here and Sisters."

"I'm happy for you, Naomi." He sounded sincere. "Star feels a bit funny about the house, but I think once she meets you she will be all right. You know I've always loved the place, and it will be great for the baby."

Naomi asked about the baby.

"She's the greatest thing that ever happened, Naomi. Every day's an adventure, and she's growing so fast." He stopped short; perhaps thinking it upset her.

"What's her name?" she asked.

"Caitlin Star Marie, that was Star's choice. We'll bring her by, if you like, when we come to see the house." He caught himself. "That is if it's okay to bring Star around to see it."

"Of course it is. I don't want it to be awkward for her though, Kevin. Would you rather go through a realtor? That way Star doesn't have to meet me."

"No, not at all. She'll be all right, especially when she hears you're getting married."

They arranged to get together Tuesday evening. Naomi thought she'd like Ben to be there. After thinking about it, she decided that wouldn't be wise. There were enough complicated relationships involved already.

A few days later, Louise called.

"Okay, sis, are you ready to hear about the Cavenish lawsuit?"

"Oh, Louise, you found someone?"

"Yes, it was remarkably easy. I wish I'd thought of it before. It only took about 15 e-mails, until I hit on a right one. She's a shirttail relative, I suppose. Anyway, her name is June Cavenish, and she says she's related to the Cavenish of Cavenish Castle. Well, she must be since she knew all about the lawsuit."

"Was she married to a Cavenish?"

"No, she's an old spinster, 78 next birthday she told me. The guy who filed the lawsuit—you remember he died already—was the son of her cousin. June said he eventually won, but it took several appeals. He was determined to see it through just on principal."

"Did she explain what the lawsuit was actually about?"

"It seems it was a bit of a test case; that's why the government fought it so hard, they didn't want to set a precedent. Our lawyer—Roland Cavenish was his name—claimed the British government didn't provide just compensation to the Cavenish family when they took over the castle and estates. He set out to prove that it didn't constitute the spoils of war, since they did relocate the family. Oh, it's so detailed, sis, I didn't follow a lot of what June said."

"Okay," Naomi said excitedly, "get to the money."

"Don't get your hopes up," Louise advised. "The government got their liability reduced a lot on appeal. By the time they located all the Cavenish heirs—there were hundreds—most people got about the equivalent of 200 U.S. dollars."

"That's all?" Naomi said incredulously.

"The whole kit and caboodle," Louise said with a laugh.

The sisters enjoyed a good laugh over their naiveté. They hadn't planned on the estate being shared with so many. No wonder it wasn't a big story in the family. They surmised that Gran probably got the check when their mother was on one of the few trips she made to visit their father in Oregon. One of the other children, or even a neighbor, could have cashed it for her.

"Who knows what she did with the money. There's no way to find out now. I'd say maybe she and Mrs. Dukes, from next door, went out for a night on the town, but Gran was bedridden by then. Anyway, I hope our gran enjoyed it," Louise finished with a flourish.

"So, Mum's friend Mamie was right all along, Lou. She must have found out about it in some way and told Mum. That's what Mum meant in the torn letter. Mamie wasn't to know the estate would be shared with so many. Somehow she got the impression it would be sizeable." Naomi sighed. "Poor Mum must have waited and waited for it to arrive."

"Yes, and maybe that's why she was suspicious of Gran's death. It was probably nothing more than that, Naomi," Louise suggested.

"I think you're right. Well, so much for the family mystery, Lou, I guess we've laid it to rest."

"It was fun while it lasted. I hope it doesn't spoil your memory of Cavenish Castle."

"No way," Naomi said. "That was a wonderful experience. We are still family after all. I pictured all these ancestors in kilts striding around the place."

"What was under the kilts, sis?"

"I'm not going there, Louise," Naomi said with a laugh.

Their conversation got around to Naomi's future plans. She told Louise her thoughts about selling the house to Kevin, if he wanted it.

"What did he say?"

"I thought for awhile he wasn't going to say anything. I mailed a gift off for their baby, and put a note in with it."

"Wait a minute, you bought a gift for his baby!"

"I couldn't resist it, Louise, it was the cutest, little dress."

"You're a class act, you know, sis," Louise said with affection.

"It's easy to forgive him now that I have Ben," Naomi explained.

"I suppose so."

"Kevin finally called and they are interested. He's bringing Star over tonight to look at the house."

"That ought to make for a cozy evening," Louise said facetiously.

"I'm not looking forward to it. They're bringing the baby; that will make it easier. I decided Ben shouldn't be here when they come."

"Probably wise. Speaking of Ben, did he move in yet?"

"Almost, he's bringing a few more things over. I won't try to sell the house until after the book tour. It will likely be spring before we move to Sisters. I can hardly wait, Lou, it will be so great to be near you guys."

"How are you going to feel living in the house, Naomi? Have you thought about it?"

"Yes. You mean because Elaine built it?"

"Precisely."

"She hardly lived there, Lou, she was on the road so much. She never really established a presence, if you know what I mean. The house doesn't have her touch—it looks more like a new, unlived in home. Ben doesn't have strong memories of living there with her, so he will be okay too."

"I can't wait to see it. Try and get over soon."

Chapter 30

A month had passed since Louise found out about the Cavenish inheritance. Naomi had all but forgotten about it, busy as she was with planning the upcoming book tour. Everything in her personal life was going well. Living with Ben was wonderful. She couldn't resist reaching out and touching him when he came close. There were new things she learned about him every day.

Kevin and Star had agreed to buy the house, taking a load off Naomi's mind. It was an awkward meeting, the night they came over. But once Naomi had fawned over the baby, Caitlin, Star seemed to relax. Naomi had been prepared to find Kevin's wife a little unworldly, and was surprised when she wasn't. She chided herself for prejudging someone by her name.

The timing on the house sale worked out perfectly. Kevin had some repairs to do on his house before putting it on the market. They wouldn't be ready to move in until spring. Ben had already begun fixing up her house.

The ranch was still under the care of Ben's sister Peggy. She had agreed to stay there through the winter. Naomi hadn't taken to Peggy as she had Diana; she found her a bit neurotic, which is how Ben described her. Peggy worried constantly over her daughter, at college in Eugene. She had called them in a flap last night: Chelsea, her daughter, needed her, Peggy said. She was driving to Eugene in the morning, and would be gone a few days. Could Ben and Naomi go out to the ranch?

It was a good excuse to visit Sam and Louise, and spend a few days alone at the ranch. They said yes, willingly. Now, with the car loaded, Naomi asked Ben to stop at the post office. A package had come, too large for their mailbox. At the post office, Kevin's cousin Angela handed her the package, and for once was civil to her. Naomi saw right away it was from Marge Jenkins in Arizona. It would be photos and such from Aunt Edna's things. Good old Marge, she thought, true to her word. She and Louise would have fun looking through it when she got to Redmond.

Ben, Sam and the two boys, Craig and Brian, were out messing around in the barn. Naomi helped Louise clean up before they sat down to go through Marge's package. There were a few photos of Spruce Creek and the family. Some they had seen before. Louise hoped to find one of Edna's "Daddy" but was disappointed. Her spirits lifted when they uncovered one of Edna in the kiosk on Paddington Station.

"Wow, here's a bit of history for you. The ultimate entrepreneur," she said with a chuckle.

Naomi had begun to read a letter to Edna from one of her friends in Spruce Creek. She was surprised to find Aunt Edna maintained contact with the woman, while practically ignoring the family. It was a lot of gossipy stuff about Spruce Creek people. Then the subject turned to Gran. As Naomi read, she gasped and held her hand to her throat.

Louise, looking over at her, noticed Naomi's face had turned pale. "What's up, sis?"

"Oh, Lou," Naomi said, alarm in her voice, "you won't believe this. Oh, no, I can't believe it."

"What is it?" Louise insisted.

"A letter from Mrs. Dukes daughter, Eileen. She writes about Gran's death. Louise, she says Mum did it," Naomi choked on the last words.

Louise looked taken aback, but gathered her thoughts quickly. "Wait a minute, Naomi, don't get upset. Something doesn't jibe here. What exactly does she say?"

Naomi, hands shaking, read the passage aloud. "It says: Like you I think a lot about your mum's sorry end. You wouldn't think she could do it, after living with her all her life. It amazes me she was able to do it.'" Naomi looked at Louise with a worried expression. "That's all she says about it; she goes on to other things next."

Louise, for once, was lost for words. She sat motionless, trying to absorb what she'd just heard. Once Naomi heard her mutter, "Oh, man."

Naomi broke the silence. "Louise, I'm going up there. I have to get to the bottom of this."

Louise said in exasperation. "Let it go, Naomi."

"Let it go," Naomi almost shouted, "let it go. Louise, that's our mother she's accusing."

"The woman's probably dead by now, sis. What good would going up there do?"

"No, Lou, I remember Michael saying he ran into her daughter in Powell River recently. She told him her mum still lived in Spruce Creek."

Louise wouldn't relent. "You're not thinking straight, Naomi. The book tour starts in a couple weeks. You don't have time for this."

"If I fly up, I've got the time. I can't go on the tour with this clouding my mind, Louise. I have to resolve it."

Louise sat with rigid jaw.

"It's haunted me for years, Lou, don't you see," Naomi pleaded.

Louise locked eyes with her sister. "And if you find out things that hurt you, how will you feel then?"

"I'm already hurt to think anyone would think Mum capable of this. I think I owe it to Mum. I'm going, Lou."

Louise pondered Naomi's determination. For once, she didn't have a quick answer. The two sisters sat in an uncomfortable silence; the air was charged with friction. Naomi couldn't remember the last time they quarreled like this. She didn't like it, but was determined not to let Louise sway her on this.

Reading her thoughts, Louise said with exasperation, "Then I'm coming with you."

"You don't have to."

"I do. It's as much my responsibility as yours, but I still wish you'd change your mind."

When Naomi didn't respond, Louise went to the kitchen and didn't hurry back.

Sam and Ben came back to the house a short time later. There was still tension in the air. Both men looked perplexed. Ben gave Naomi a hug.

"Everything all right, my love?" he whispered in her ear. "You look a little pale."

She nodded, but he could tell something was amiss.

Louise had disappeared with Sam. When they returned, Sam lost no time in getting Naomi's attention. He needed advice on something in the garden. Naomi guessed it was a ploy to get her away. She watched through the window and saw Ben and Louise in deep discussion. There were no smiles, so she knew Louise was telling him about their row. Ben looked out and caught Naomi's eye. His face was etched with concern. It rankled Naomi to think Louise would drag Ben into this. No doubt she wanted him to persuade Naomi to give up the idea of going to Powell River. Louise is wasting her time; Naomi thought resolutely, I'm going to lay this thing to rest once and for all.

Ben waited until they were back at the ranch to broach the subject.

"Sweetheart, Louise told me about the letter. She's worried about you going there. Won't you change your mind?"

Naomi shook her head. "I don't know why Louise is so bent about it."

"It worries me too," he replied.

"Why?"

Her took her in his arms. "Sometimes it's better not to know the truth. It can hurt more than not knowing. Why not leave it alone?"

He saw her face change.

"Okay, okay, just a suggestion. It's your call. Just promise me you won't let emotion get the better of you. Think everything through, all right?"

She said she'd try. It was difficult though, because she loved her mother and knew she wasn't capable of doing what the letter said. Ben didn't reply to that, he just held her tightly.

It was late in the year to be traveling to British Columbia. Naomi and Louise were prepared for bad weather in Powell River. They were pleasantly surprised that, although cold, the sun made brief appearances during their stay. They got a motel on the north end of town, the cut-off to Spruce Creek being a short distance up the road to Lund.

They made their way from the motel down to Willingdon Beach, a favorite spot from childhood. The ferry from Comox was approaching. The sisters stood deep in thought, gazing out over the Strait of Georgia. Louise was still acting a little edgy, but for the most part they were getting along. After a minute or two, she turned to Naomi.

"What now? Have you given any thought to how we're going to approach this?"

"It's *all* I've been thinking about. Michael said Sharon works in a bakery on the north end of town. It won't be open this late on a Thursday. We'll go there early tomorrow and try to find Sharon."

"What if she's not there? We don't know her married name, if she is married."

"Someone there will know how to find her; Powell River's not a very big place. When we find her, I'll ask for her mother's address and we'll go from there."

Louise wrinkled her brow. "I think I really meant how are you going to get the information you want out of her mother. Are you going to come right out and ask if she knows how our gran died?"

"I'll just see how it goes, Lou. I'm hoping she'll volunteer the information without me having to pry too much." She gave her sister an imploring look. "Please help me if you can, Lou."

Louise looked contrite. "You know I will, sis, it's just that my heart's not in it."

Naomi nodded. She hugged her sister. "I know. Don't let this spoil things between us. We'll have our answer soon." She barely heard Louise's muffled response.

"That's what I'm afraid of."

They hit the bakery at nine the next morning, only to find it all locked up with a sign on the door: End of season, weekends only.

"Damn," Naomi voiced her frustration. "I didn't think of that. We'll have to come back tomorrow."

They sat in the rental car, looking down on the lumber mill, both weighing their options. Naomi finally asked, "Do you have any ideas?"

"We could take the ferry over to the island, and play around in Campbell River for the day. They've got some neat shops there," Louise suggested.

"We'd run into the same thing there; end of the season, most of the shops will be closed."

"I don't think so, most of Powell River is open. It's worth a try. What else would we do?"

Naomi gave it some thought. "Lou, I'd like to go to Spruce Creek."

Louise wrinkled her nose, but Naomi continued. "We could check at the post office there. I'll bet they could give us information. We've got to go there at some point," she added.

Louise acquiesced. "Okay, let's do it."

If Spruce Creek had changed over the years, it was barely apparent to Naomi and Louise. There had been an attempt by the logging company to spruce up some of the buildings, and the roads appeared to be in better condition. But overall, things were the same.

"I feel like I'm in a time warp," said Louise. "Look, see that old barrel under the trees there? I swear I played on it when I was six."

They found their old house, and sat out front in the car. Memories came flooding back for Louise. Naomi's memories were fewer, having been four-years-old when they moved.

"See the apple tree around the side there, with the branch hanging down," Louise said. "Before Gran was bedridden, Mum used to sit her out there in the shade. She used to watch us swinging on that branch. I had to lift you up, you couldn't reach by yourself."

"She loved us kids, didn't she?"

"We were her life then. She could barely go anywhere, because of her health. Aunt Gwen and Uncle Bill would come over sometimes with Michael and Susan. But for the most part, we were what kept her going. She doted on you, perhaps because you were the baby."

"How did Gran and Mum get along?"

"Hmm, I was only six remember, but Gran seemed to really love Mum. She was her baby after all."

"And Mum?"

Louise thought about it. "I'm sure she loved Gran, but I do remember Mum didn't smile much in those days. She was probably overwhelmed with the responsibility. And I know she missed Dad something awful."

Naomi nodded in understanding.

Afraid of making the current tenants uneasy, they moved on to the large building that housed the post office. The postmistress hadn't been there long and had trouble making out whom they were seeking. She checked her log: there were no 'Dukes' listed. Not ready to give up, she called out to someone in back, "Harry, do you know anyone name of Dukes?"

A voice called back, "They used to live on Loon Street. All gone now, to Powell River, I think."

Naomi asked the postmistress, "Does he remember the name of the last one to live there?"

The woman yelled the question back.

The reply came loud and clear. "That would be Eileen, daughter of old Mrs. Dukes."

"Did she have a married name?" Naomi yelled out the question herself.

There was a laugh from the back room. "Married? Not her. We all knew her too well."

When they were back in the car, Louise said, "I wonder what that meant."

"Let's hope we can find Sharon tomorrow and find out," Naomi responded.

Saturday morning they approached the bakery with a sense of desperation. It was a quaint little shop that had once been a house. A deck in front no doubt held table and chairs during the season, but was now empty. As Louise and Naomi approached the door, the scent of fresh-baked pastry filled the air.

"Mmm," said Louise, "we're going away from here with something, I can tell you that." She rubbed her belly.

Spying tables inside, Naomi countered, "We'll have it here."

They ordered hot-buttered currant scones and a pot of tea from the owner manning the counter. He told them Sharon was in back getting more bread and would be out in a minute.

The sisters exchanged jubilant glances.

When Sharon returned and was given the message, she eyed them with a combination of curiosity and suspicion. She sidled over to their table.

"You were asking for me?"

Naomi smiled and extended her hand. "Hi, Sharon, I'm Naomi and this my sister, Louise. Our grandmother used to live next door to yours: Mrs. Cavenish."

"Well, I never, what a small world," Sharon said, sitting down to join them. "Do you live here?"

"No, we both live in Oregon," Naomi explained. "We're just here on a visit. We are hoping to see your mother. They told us in Spruce Creek that she'd moved to Powell River."

Sharon looked surprised. "What would you want to see her for?"

Naomi decided to plunge right in. "We think she may have some information about our gran that we'd like to know. Do you think she'd talk to us?"

Sharon grimaced. "It's not whether she would, more like whether she could. She's in a care home now, you know."

"No, we didn't know. Is she in a bad way?" Louise asked.

"You could say that, but it's nothing she hasn't brought on herself."

Sharon saw the sisters exchange glances. "You moved away when you were little, didn't you? I'll bet you don't know what my mum was like."

Naomi and Louise shook their heads.

Sharon didn't pull any punches. "Well, let's put it this way: I have no idea who my father is, and neither does she. She lead my grandma on a merry old dance, she did."

"You could get DNA testing," Louise said, trying to help.

"Someone else suggested that," Sharon explained. "They could test every man in Spruce Creek and still not come up with a match. So many itinerate loggers moved through here. If they were halfway good looking and would buy her a beer, they had it made."

She saw they were starting to look uncomfortable. "Sorry, you don't need to hear this. When I get started on my mum, I don't know when to quit. I can take you to see her. Her memory's not so good; it comes and goes. If it's one of her good days, you may be lucky." She stopped and thought for a minute. "I was just thinking, I remember playing with you girls." She pointed at Naomi. "You were the baby. They used to say you were your gran's favorite." She turned to Louise, "Didn't that make you jealous?"

"I suppose it could have, but she was such a cute little rascal," Louise said, reaching over and mussing Naomi's hair.

Naomi stuck her tongue out at her sister.

"I liked your gran," Sharon said, "She was always nice to me. Your mum took care of her, didn't she?"

"Yes, until she died," Louise said.

They talked a few minutes more, before Sharon had to get back to work. She arranged to meet them at their motel around 2p.m. There would be just enough time, she said, to visit her mum before she had to pick her son up from school. Naomi said if she gave them the address, they'd be happy to go by themselves. Sharon said that wouldn't be a good idea. Knowing her mum, she might refuse to see them. That's just the way she is, she explained.

Sharon walked ahead of them into Waterview Care Center. An attendant catching sight of her immediately began lodging a complaint.

"Oh, Sharon, we've been having trouble with your mum again, she…" catching sight of Naomi and Louise she stopped mid-sentence. " Sorry, I didn't know you had company."

As they walked down the corridor, Sharon said with a long face, "That's usually the way they greet me." She stopped in front of room 19A. "Right, here we are. Let's all go in together, that way she won't have any say in the matter."

Eileen Duke was watching television. Looking at her, Naomi thought, she looks like a cast off snakeskin. Even her hair was leaving her body in great clumps. She was wizened way beyond her years; the wild living had finally caught up with her. She was nothing now, but this empty shell with a dowager's hump.

Seeing Sharon, she snapped, "I'm right in the middle of my program." When she noticed the sisters, she shouted, "Who are they?"

"Hush up, Mum," Sharon said. "They've come to see you. They're the granddaughters of Mrs. Cavenish. You remember, from next door. This is Louise and Naomi."

"Don't know them," Eileen snapped.

"They were little girls, lived with their gran. I used to play with them."

A hint of memory flitted across Eileen's face. "Next door?" she asked.

"That's right, next door," Sharon repeated.

"They were May's girls," Eileen said out of the blue.

Naomi spoke up, "That's right, Eileen, May was our mother. Do you remember when she lived there?"

Eileen's eyes bored into Naomi. "No," she blurted out, before doubling over with a bout of smoker's cough.

"Sure you do, Mum," Sharon insisted. "They lived there until Mrs. Cavenish died."

Eileen ignored her daughter and turned to Naomi. "Have you got any ciggies?"

"Sorry, no, I don't smoke," Naomi explained.

Eileen turned away and stared out the window, her jaw resolute.

Sharon winked at Naomi. "She can get you some, Mum."

Naomi caught on. "Yes, yes, what kind would you like?"

"Doesn't matter, get me forty, but hide them or those buggers will take them," she nodded to the doorway.

"We'll get them in a few minutes, won't we, Louise?" Naomi gave her sister a chance to get involved, but Louise wouldn't take it. She had been standing silent and uncomfortable. Now at Naomi's persistent stare, she mumbled, "Yes," before turning to the window, signaling the end of her involvement.

Naomi wasn't to be deterred. It looked as though they'd caught Eileen on a good day memory wise, and she was going to make the most of it, white lie or not.

"Eileen, do you remember when Mrs. Cavenish died?" she asked.

It seemed as though Eileen wasn't going to answer, but she finally muttered, "Terrible."

That got Louise's attention and she spun around with a startled look on her face. "Naomi," she said, but Naomi quieted her with a wave of her hand.

"What was terrible, Eileen?" she asked, her heart racing.

Eileen grunted, "Terrible," again, and then seemed to lose interest. She went back to watching TV.

Naomi exchanged a glance with Sharon, who mouthed, "Try again."

"Eileen, do you remember how Mrs. Cavenish died?" Naomi persisted.

"Of course I do," she snapped, eyes never leaving the screen.

"How?"

"They take my ciggies, you know," Eileen repeated.

"Okay, she'll hide them when she brings them in," Sharon lied.

"Eileen," Naomi tried again, "what happened to Mrs. Cavenish?"

The old woman turned to Naomi and sneered. "She suffocated her, with a pillow."

Naomi exchanged an agonized look with Louise, gulped, and with a shaking voice asked Eileen, "Who did it, Eileen?"

Time stood still as they waited for the answer. The old woman seemed fixed on the TV again.

Sharon finally stepped in. "Mum, you're not getting any ciggies if you don't tell her who did it."

Eileen leveled a spiteful look at her daughter, "I don't remember her name. It was the little one."

"What little one?" Sharon persisted.

Still looking at the screen, Eileen spat out, "May's little one. She was her gran's favorite."

Naomi was frozen in place. She felt as though a block of marble had fallen on her. To steady herself, she reached for the back of the old woman's chair. She caught the eye of Sharon, standing across from her, and noticed the astounded look on her face. This can't be happening, Naomi thought. Surely the old woman was lying, perhaps egging them on because of the cigarettes. She was about to challenge Eileen, but stopped in her tracks. Something akin to an electric shock was attacking her memory banks. She saw herself as plain as day, struggling to pull a pillow across Gran's bed. She was so small and the bed so high.

The pain of remembrance was more than she could bear. She turned to Louise for support. But one look at Louise, and Naomi knew; everything fell into place. Suddenly, Louise's actions through this whole thing became crystal clear.

Naomi gave a gasp, clutched her head, and just as the room was going black cried out to her sister, "You knew, you knew."

Chapter 31

Naomi

Naomi woke with a start; something in her dream was chasing her. She rolled over in bed, reaching for her mother. Her mother's space was empty, and then she remembered Mummy went out with Aunt Kath. She sat up in bed, whimpering. Louise, beside her, was sleeping heavily. After a minute or two, Naomi's whimpering subsided. She had a more urgent need now: the need to pee.

She slid off her mother's side of the bed and padded silently to the door. On the other side of the door was her gran's room, with the landing and stairway beyond. Naomi tiptoed to the side of Gran's bed, leaned over and whispered, "Gran, Gran." There was no reply. She knew Gran couldn't speak anymore, but she usually smiled at her. Gran's eyes were closed. She sometimes reached out her hand to Naomi, even when they were closed. This time she didn't. She must be sleeping, Naomi realized. She touched Gran's arm: it was cold. She tugged on the blanket to cover it. Remembering her quest for the toilet, she hurried down the stairs—there was no bathroom upstairs.

Her aunts didn't see her at first. They were all sitting at the table, drinking. There were two big bottles on the table, and one was empty. Aunt Edna and Aunt Violet had their backs to her. Naomi was about to say she had to pee, when Aunt Gwen saw her.

"Oh, Naomi, what's wrong, pet?"

"I need to go potty, Aunt Gwen."

"Come on then, my pet," she said, but her voice sounded funny. And when she got up to come and help Naomi, she stumbled into the chair. Naomi let her aunt shepherd her through the kitchen to the bathroom at the back of the house. While she was going, she heard her aunts talking.

"Do you think she heard anything?" Aunt Violet said.

"Oh, she's too young anyway," Aunt Edna replied.

Their voices sounded a bit odd, too.

When Naomi flushed the toilet, Aunt Gwen came to get her and led her back to the stairs. She would have followed Naomi upstairs, but Naomi said she could do it herself.

"Mind you go straight to bed then, and don't wake Gran up, okay, pet?"

"Okay. Gran's sleeping now," she told her aunt, then asked, "When's my mummy coming home?"

"Soon, pet. The movie will be over soon. Now off you go to bed." Her aunt clumsily returned to the others.

Naomi walked to the top of the stairs and peeked in at Gran. She was still sleeping. Rather than go back to bed by herself, she decided to wait on the stairs for Mummy. Aunt Gwen said she'd be here soon, and she wanted her mummy. She sat partway down, her head resting against the wall, and keeping very quiet so the aunts didn't hear her. She could hear them, although they were mostly talking quietly. Aunt Edna was the loudest. She was getting cross with the other two aunts.

"We agreed we'd all do it together, Violet, now pull yourself together. It's for the best," Aunt Edna was saying. "Here, have another drink."

"Don't get her too drunk, she's not used to it," Aunt Gwen scolded Aunt Edna. And then she said to Aunt Violet, "It really is for the best, Violet. It's not like we'd be killing her. She's going to die soon anyway. Think of May, it's time she had a life of her own."

Aunt Violet appeared to be crying. Naomi felt sad. Aunt Violet was so gentle; they shouldn't make her cry.

Aunt Edna spoke again. "Think of it this way, Violet; if Mum could speak, she'd be asking us to do this for her. She's not happy, just look at her; stuck in that bed for years, in pain most of the time. She wants to die, Violet. Let's help her."

Naomi wasn't sure what die was and why Gran wanted it. Mummy had said Gran would be going to God soon, and that would be a good thing because Gran was so sick.

Aunt Gwen was talking to Aunt Violet again. "If you're worried about God, Violet, he'll forgive us. Come on, pet, let's help Mum go and meet her God."

So that was it, thought Naomi, they want to help Gran go to God.

"All right, tell me again how we're going to do it," Aunt Violet was saying.

"We'll all three of us pick up the pillow together and just press it over her face. It shouldn't take long, she's so weak," Aunt Edna explained.

Aunt Violet started crying again. She didn't want to do it. The other aunts tried to calm her down.

Naomi, listening to them argue, grew tired of it and climbed the stairs. She saw Gran was still sleeping, and went through to her bed. Louise was sprawled all across the bed; there was no room for Naomi. She went back to the stairs—the aunts were still arguing. Aunt Gwen was saying again that Gran would be happy to go to God. Naomi had an idea: she could help Gran. If it would make Gran happy, she could do it. She loved her Gran.

She quietly padded back to Gran's bedside. Gran hadn't moved from before. Naomi touched Gran's arm again and it was still cold. She leaned over and whispered to her gran,

"Gran, I'll help you be happy." Aunt Edna said put a pillow on Gran's face. Naomi saw a pillow on the other side of Gran's bed, and went to get it. It was so heavy. Mummy said it was full of feathers, and she knew that was right because sometimes when they were making the bed a little feather would pop out of the cover. She dragged the pillow around the perimeter of the bed. It was difficult, because Gran's bed was so high. Gran didn't move as she pushed and pulled the pillow over her face. She tried to press it like Aunt Edna said, but she wasn't tall enough. She just held it there.

Naomi was wondering when she would see Gran go to God, when she heard a sound. The aunts were coming up the stairs. They wouldn't mind that she'd done it; after all, she was Gran's favorite. The three aunts stumbled a bit on the stairs and finally appeared in the doorway. They looked very surprised, but Naomi beamed at them.

"Oh, my God, what have you done?" Aunt Violet asked.

Naomi looked perplexed. "It's okay, Aunt Violet, I've helped Gran be happy. I've helped her go to God. Now you don't have to do it," she finished with a smile.

Aunt Violet quietly took Naomi's hand and led her back to bed. She moved Louise over to make room for Naomi, and settled Naomi down with a kiss.

"There, little one, you go back to sleep. Everything will be all right."

Chapter 32

Ben and Louise were on the ranch house front porch, leaning against the railing. Out on the wide expanse of lawn, Naomi had set up a croquet course and was attempting to teach her nephews the rudiments of the game. Their laughter was filtering back to the two watching. Louise looked on with a satisfied smile on her face. Naomi had come so far since that dreadful day in Powell River. That had been nine months ago, and poor Naomi had to leave on the book tour before she'd gotten over it. The book tour was not a great success, and she'd come home a wreck. But looking at her now, you'd never know.

"She seems so well now, Ben," she said, "How's she really doing?"

"Better than I'd anticipated. Seeing the therapist really helped. I'm glad you convinced her to go."

"I could tell she wasn't going to get over it, she was shouldering so much guilt. And I couldn't stand the rift in our relationship. We'd always been so close."

Ben nodded. "She loves you deeply, Louise, and has forgiven you. She understands now that you only withheld it from her to protect her. Once she knew the details of how Aunt Kath swore you to secrecy, she was more understanding. By the way, why did your Aunt Kath tell you?"

"In case it should ever come up in the future. Aunt Gwen had told her, because she was never sure if Aunt Edna had told anyone. Aunt Gwen wanted to be sure we had the story right."

"And your mum never knew?"

"No, they decided the night it happened not to tell her, although Mum was suspicious about the circumstances. They were afraid she'd treat Naomi differently. You see, they still thought Naomi had killed Gran."

"The therapist has convinced Naomi otherwise," Ben explained. " He told her it's 99 percent certain that she couldn't have done it. She was too little to apply the pressure needed. Anyway, he's convinced your gran was already dead of natural causes. Naomi said repeatedly Gran's arms were cold, and she didn't respond to her touch. Also, Gran would have struggled, had she been breathing."

"That's what I'd always thought—unless she was in a coma." Louise pondered that thought. "But then, the cold arms were a giveaway. Gran was a heavy lady, and she was always warm."

Ben nodded in agreement. "Did Aunt Kath tell you why the other aunts were planning to euthanize your gran in the first place?"

"It was all for Mum, and I suppose for Gran, to some degree. She was in dreadful shape, but her body just wouldn't give up. The aunts wanted Mum to be able to come to Oregon, so we could live with our dad. They'd tried convincing Mum to put Gran in a home, but she wouldn't hear of it. Poor Mum, she agonized all her life about not being there the night it happened. I think what was really eating away at her was the relief she felt at being set free. That's something she wouldn't even share with Naomi, and they were close," Louise explained. She'd been watching the game while talking, and now turned to face Ben. "You know, the first thing she asked when she came around at the care home was, did Mum know? It was such a relief to her to know Mum didn't."

"She's said that to me over and over again. That's one thing your aunts did right."

Brian called out from the lawn, "Mum, I know how to do it now, come and play with us."

Louise turned back to her brother-in-law. "And how are you doing, Ben? You've had a lot to deal with the last couple years."

"Louise, I couldn't be happier. I love being married to your sister, and that love grows every day. She's the most compassionate, wonderful woman, as you well know."

Louise agreed. "I'm sorry the wedding wasn't more memorable, but she was hardly in shape for anything more."

"It's not the wedding that counts, Lou, it's the marriage," he told her earnestly. "By the way, did Naomi tell you we got the test results back?"

"She did. So there's no reason you can't have a child?"

"Apparently not. Elaine must have had the fertility problems in my case; and with Naomi and Kevin it must not have been in the cards."

Louise hugged him. "You two deserve it. I have a feeling it won't be long." She let out a big sigh. "Thank heaven we can put the family mystery, as Naomi liked to call it, to rest. Now we can all get on with our lives." She grabbed Ben's arm. "Come on, let's go and show this bunch how to play croquet."

The end

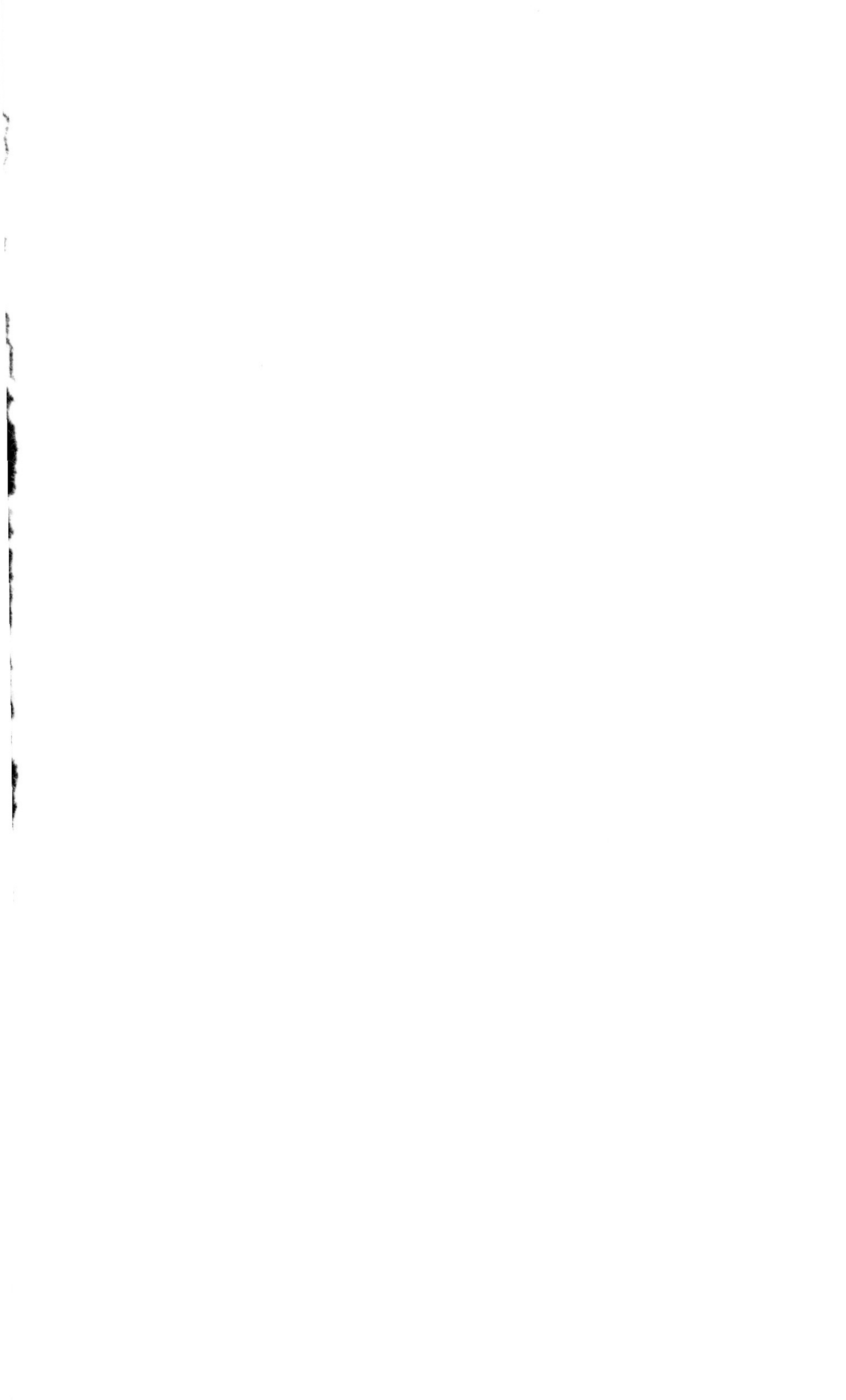

CPSIA information can be obtained at www.ICGtesting.com
232814LV00001B/20/P

9 781614 342243